DAVE HOBART

Born in 1949, Dave lived in Queensbury, Harrow. Leaving school, he secured an apprenticeship with Squires and Pegg, working on domestic plumbing. On completion of his apprenticeship, he moved to Lorne Stewart Mechanical Services in Wealdstone, Harrow, as chief design plumber (the only design plumber!). A career change came two years later, in 1972, when Dave joined the Metropolitan Police Force and realised he had found his vocation.

Moving from uniform to CID, he served on numerous crime squads, the last being murder squads in North London. In 2004, he was urgently commanded to attend Hendon Police Training School, to help set up the UK Casualty Bureau when the Boxing Day tsunami struck in the Indian Ocean.

After Dave retired from a career spanning more than forty years, he worked, for a time, as an undertaker, dealing with families at their most vulnerable. Later, he was drawn back into the police family, as a civilian investigator, working for various constabularies investigating serious crime. When retirement proper finally caught up with him, he put pen to paper, realising a long-term ambition to distil his work/life experiences into a novel about a young man wrongly accused and on the run...

BLUE EYES

Dave Hobart

BYTHEBOOK.PRESS

First published in 2024

Typeseting: ByTheBook
Print Management by Biddles Books, King's Lynn, Norfolk PE32 1SF

A CIP record for this book is available from the British Library

ISBN 978-1-917625-00-5

To my beautiful and long-suffering wife, Georgina,
whose encouragement and enthusiasm has allowed me to
dip my toe into the world of the writer.

To my gorgeous daughter, Marie, who has been an inspiration.
Her support and can-do approach finally got this book over the line.

To Grace, my delightful granddaughter, who I hope is as proud of me
for writing this book as I am so proud of her.
She always makes me happy.

To Baz, the best son-in-law any man could wish for.
His love and support for Marie and Grace, together with
our friendship and his understanding, have been amazing.

To all my friends and colleagues, for all the good times we've had.
You know who you are!

Chapter One

THE GREAT ESCAPE

The smell inside any prison is a very particular cocktail of boiled cabbage and human farts. Jack put his head under the blanket and sank his head into the single pillow. The bedclothes had been washed in the cheapest detergent but at least the sweet odour of the blankets erased the permanent stench of locked-up men.

Jack was in a cell with another occupant, a small, fat, bald-headed excuse for a human being, with a broken nose and a face like a deflated beach ball. An obnoxious little shit, he had something wrong with his mouth or had been hit in the face too many times. Only what he deserved, perhaps. He was constantly talking and dribbling, even though Jack never gave him any reply whatsoever. In fact, since Jack had been in Stamford Prison, he had not opened his mouth at all, except to confirm his name to the Admissions Officer on his transfer from London about ten months previously.

He had been sharing a cell with the gremlin for six months, and the little creature proudly and repeatedly informed him that he was serving twelve years for GBH of an elderly shopkeeper who wouldn't hand over his day's takings of £150.

'A fucking year for every time I hit him,' he slobbered. 'Daft old shit, it was his own fault. If he'd handed over the money, I wouldn't have had to hit him over the head so many times. What do you think, Jack? Eh? Eh?'

Every night after lock-up it was the same. Jack blocked out his every word. He just hunkered down and tried to ignore him and his verbal diarrhoea. The lumbering brute had told all the other prisoners on their block that Jack really was dumb.

In truth, Jack *had* been momentarily struck dumb on hearing the sentence of eighteen years when it was handed down in Courtroom 12 at the Old Bailey. The verdict and sentence were a shock. Even though he had been warned of the possible outcome by his barrister, Ms. Woodcock, it hadn't made the shock or pain any less.

Now, Jack began his nightly mind wanderings — shutting everything else out, going into his fantasy world, where everything was normal. He had made it his intention right from the start of his sentence that he wasn't going to allow the circumstances leading to his arrest, the arrest itself, the court proceedings and the sentence, to keep nagging at his brain. If he had, he thought, the torment would have screwed him up every day.

Suddenly the cell light came on and a key turned in the door, which opened loudly.

'Out of your pit, Frost, you're being moved to another prison. Get your things, the Governor wants to see you. Come on, shake a leg, we're waiting.'

Taken by surprise, Jack Frost nearly protested but, as always, he decided to do as he was told, same as he always had in the three prisons where he had been held. He pulled his day trousers over his pyjama bottoms and put on his shirt, socks and shoes.

'Come on, get a move on, the Governor's waiting.'

Chief Warder of the landing, Mr W.A.N. Kerr — first names Walter Andrew Norris — was a bullet-headed Scot who stood six-foot-three in his boots. Living with an expletive for a name demonstrated that he had been at the back of the queue when they were handing out a sense of humour.

Jack quickly gathered together all his belongings into a dirty prison shirt, especially his most prized possession of all: the small, black book which contained the phone numbers and addresses of those he could trust in the outside world.

The Chief Warder shook the hobbit in his bunk and said, 'So what's behind this move, you skanky individual? Have you two had a falling out?'

'I don't know, Mr Kerr, Sir, he's said nothing to me, Sir. He's said nothing to anybody since he's been here. Where is he going, Mr Kerr, Sir?'

'I don't know. They don't tell us anything and if I did, I wouldn't let an insignificant shit like you know.'

Jack was marched along the landing, clutching his possessions. Mr Kerr led the way down two flights of stairs. Jack caught a glimpse of the large clock which dominated the dining hall wall. Ten past eleven? You don't normally get transferred to another nick at this time of night.

Jack's mind began to race. What was happening? He hadn't made an application for a transfer. In fact, he hadn't caused any waves at all. It wasn't just in Stamford that he had been silent. He had said nothing to anyone since entering the prison system over three years ago. His previous transfers had all been automatic, usually after assessments, medical reports etc, but this move was totally unexpected.

Off the main cell block, they crossed into the prison admin

building. Through what seemed like hundreds of locked and barred doors, they arrived at the Governor's suite of offices. Mr Kerr knocked on the door, entered and announced, in a loud voice, 'Prisoner 1712124, Trevor Frost, Sir.'

Jack was ushered in. The Governor stood behind his large wooden desk with a thick blue file in front of him with Jack's name on it. There were two other men in the room. Both were suited and booted and looked for all the world like professional mourners.

'Thank you, Chief, you may leave us now.'

Chief Warder Kerr reluctantly left the office, closing the door behind him.

'Frost, this is Mr Harvey and Mr Clarke from the Home Office, and they've handed me this authorisation to release you into their custody.'

Jack found it difficult to make his voice work. He was dry and somewhat confused.

'Where am I going?' he whispered.

'You will be taken from here to another place where you will be detained in their care. Do you wish to read the authorisation?'

Jack was still finding it difficult to speak. He had so many questions that he didn't know which one to ask first. Before he could say anything, the taller of the two men, Mr Harvey, stepped forward.

'Mr Frost, we have been ordered to collect you and take you away from this prison. Everything will be explained in due course.'

Harvey looked to be a very smart, sharp-suited man of about forty-five. Well-spoken and well-groomed. His aftershave was a nice change from the stink of men that Jack had endured for the last few years.

Jack noticed that Harvey had called him Mister. What was

all this about? He was not due parole for years yet; he hadn't applied for a move, and his solicitor (who had not contacted him for months) had not informed him of any changes in his circumstances, nor of any appeals. And now he was in the custody of two gentlemen from the Home Office, calling him Mister, with the authorisation to take him away.

'Sign this form for all your personal property and you can collect it outside.' The Governor pushed some papers across the desk, together with a pen.

Jack signed on the dotted line.

'All yours, gentlemen,' the Governor said. 'Good luck, Frost.' He held out his hand to shake Jack's, but Jack ignored it.

The other man, Mr Clarke, ushered Jack to the door. Jack whispered to him, 'Can I go to the toilet first?'

'Okay, Frost, on your way.'

'Now come along, it's late,' the Governor said, and opened the office door.

Chief Warder Kerr was outside. 'See these gentlemen out, Chief,' the Governor said. 'Frost's possessions should be ready for collection; they're all signed for. Take him to the toilet before he leaves.'

'Yes, Sir,' said Kerr. 'This way, Frost.'

Jack followed Kerr and the Home Office men followed behind.

In the toilet cubicle, Jack unwrapped the dirty shirt that held his possessions and fished out his address book. He was glad it wasn't very big. Just in case his bundle was searched, he stuffed the book down the inside of his underpants.

The rest of his possessions he wrapped again in the shirt. When he rejoined the group in the reception area, a large brown paper parcel was on the desk. Jack hoped it would be the clothes he had been wearing on entering the prison system. He began to rummage through it.

'What are you after?' Mr Clarke said.

'My coat,' Jack replied. 'I might be stuck inside here, but I'm still aware that it's October out there.' His voice was sounding stronger now.

He pulled his faithful, old, zip-up jacket from the parcel and put it on. He stuffed everything else back in the paper, as best he could. Harvey and Clarke ushered him out of a side door to where a large, silver, Lexus saloon car was waiting.

Jack was even more confused. He had enough experience to know that any time a prisoner is moved from one prison to another, handcuffs were always employed, and you were always stuffed in a 'cattle wagon', or something similar.

He sat in the rear seat, accompanied by Mr Clarke. Harvey got in the front passenger seat, next to the driver. They drove out of the large prison gates into the blackness of the night.

Trevor 'Jack' Frost had been held in Category 'A' HMP Stamford, halfway up the country, many miles from London where his roots were, and where he had lived with his wife and newborn daughter, and where he had worked quite happily as a detective constable in the Metropolitan Police.

Irrespective of category, as an ex-copper, prison was not a pleasant place to be. Perhaps the authorities had heard that word had got around that Jack was an ex-copper, and were moving him quickly and quietly for his own safety.

During his trial at the Old Bailey, the overwhelmingly damning evidence presented to the judge and jury made it impossible for his barrister to defend him and it was inevitable a jury would find him guilty. The verdict was irrefutable on the evidence presented but it was the credibility of that evidence and its substance that he knew to be untrue.

Harvey looked over his shoulder. 'Mr Frost, you are no doubt confused about your current situation, but I assure you that all is correct. Read this.' He handed Jack a few sheets of paper.

Jack fumbled in his parcel to find his glasses and when he found them, he switched on the small, internal light of the car.

The pages were headed Home Office and all looked kosher. Jack read the papers carefully.

'After receiving new evidence and further investigation of the case of The Crown versus Trevor Frost, it has been decided by the Director of Public Prosecutions and the Home Office that all charges against Frost are to be dropped and that he is to be released from custody immediately, pending an application for a full pardon. It is recommended that Mr Frost be securely protected against outside bodies for his own safety. It is hereby put on record that his evidence in future prosecutions would be vital and that, as a prosecution witness, he could be under threat.'

Jack did not recognise the name of the Senior Investigating Officer. He had thought he knew most of the SIOs in the Met. Nevertheless, it had been three years, so he didn't worry about that too much.

'Can I keep these papers please? I can't read them clearly.'

'You may. We have copies,' Harvey replied.

'Where are you taking me?'

'Because of the lateness of the hour, we are taking you to a discreet hotel tonight, and tomorrow we will set you up in a safe house,' Harvey explained.

'Safe house? Safe from what? Am I not officially free?' Jack asked.

'Not quite free,' Harvey said, 'but within a few weeks all the official papers will be put in place and your pardon is guaranteed. The safe house is for your own protection.'

'From what, from whom?'

He wasn't *au fait* with the protocol regarding the release of prisoners from prison and the issue of pardons etc, but for the time being he was, at least, out of that cabbage-smelling hole and away from that farting, little slime-ball.

The clock in the car now showed 01:00, and, according to the signs, it looked like they were travelling south. The driver was avoiding any motorways and staying on the A-roads. It felt like they were making good progress.

Feeling in the pocket of his trusted zip-up jacket, Jack found a half-smoked cigarette. He pulled the dog-end out and sniffed it with fond memories.

In prison, tobacco had been a trading commodity. When his supply of cigarettes from his solicitor had dried up, Jack decided to do without them, thus avoiding getting caught up with the tobacco black market that is the mainstay of any prison economy.

Clarke watched as Jack lovingly smelled his old dog-end. 'I bet you could do with a smoke, couldn't you?' he asked.

'Not really bothered,' Jack said, quietly.

Thereafter, they travelled in silence until the driver turned into a long drive, which eventually led up to a large manor house.

'Stay there, Mr Frost, I will get you booked in. You're not really clothed for this place,' Harvey said, indicating his prison shirt and trousers. 'I won't be a minute.'

Again, this title: 'Mr' Frost; he was not being treated as a lag but as a real person.

The driver said, 'If you put the window down, you can have a fag, if you like. Here, have one of mine.'

Now, in prison, any offer like that you don't turn down, even if you smoke half of it and keep the other half for later. His first cigarette for years tasted fabulous. The rush of nicotine made him a bit giddy, but it felt good.

On seeing Harvey emerge from the front of the hotel, Jack stubbed out the cigarette and put it in his pocket. Harvey directed them round to a side entrance, where they entered and located Room 18, on the ground floor. It was nice. It had its own flush toilet, shower and a large double bed.

Harvey gave Jack some orders. 'You must not leave this room. You have all the tea- and coffee-making facilities. Your breakfast will be brought to you. We will be back in the morning with more clothes, and some cash for you. Then we will take you to a secure refuge, where you will be safe.'

'Safe from whom? Safe from what? What is all this cloak-and-dagger stuff? Please explain what this is all about. You have told me nothing. Yes, I am glad to be out of that stinking hole, but tell me what I am doing here.' Jack was beginning to get his voice back at last.

'Mr Frost, it is now a quarter past two. Clarke and I have to get to London and then get back to you. We still have a lot of work to do. Trust us. Tomorrow you will meet my boss at the safe house and he will give you a full explanation of everything. Just chill out and relax and we will see you in the morning.'

As they left, Clarke tossed Jack an open packet of cigarettes and winked. As soon as he was alone, Jack took full stock of his surroundings. He tried the window but it only opened about two inches. Even so, the smell of the cold October air was like nectar to him.

He sat on his bed, retrieved his address book from his underpants and flicked through the pages of familiar names. This little book was his bible and he would be lost without it.

He was still very shocked at the speed of what had just happened and confused at what he had learned, especially with regard to the new evidence. There had been no rumours on the prison bush telegraph, and no news from family nor friends — which was hardly a surprise because Jack had requested that they did *not* contact or visit him in prison. He had heard nothing from his solicitor, Gerry Forbes, since his last visit, over six months ago, when he had informed Jack that there was no hope of an appeal. After that, Jack had decided to just knuckle down and do his time. He knew he was innocent, but he also knew that there was no way he could prove it; going over and over it in his mind wasn't going to do him any good.

He found the packet of cigarettes that Mr Clarke had given him but then realised he didn't have a light. Perhaps the night porter would be able to help him. He went to the door and found it wouldn't open. He tried again, but it wasn't just stuck, it was actually locked.

I'm still a prisoner, he thought.

He had a brainwave and went to the phone and dialled 0 for the night porter.

'I can't get my door to open. Can you please help me?'

'You're in Room 18 on the ground floor, aren't you, Sir? I'll be along shortly,' he replied.

The old night porter arrived and unlocked the door.

'I am sorry to trouble you, but I was just going outside to have a smoke and I couldn't open the door. In fact, I don't have a key for the door to get back in, either. I was booked in by some colleagues,' Jack explained.

'No worries, Sir,' the porter replied. 'I saw the man when he booked you in. Funny sort, I thought. "Keep the door locked, no phone calls, no contact, take breakfast into bedroom 8am sharp. No other contact with the staff." Not the normal type of customer, I thought. A bit overbearing, he was. I didn't like him.'

'Is the phone cut off?' Jack asked.

'No, but all calls must come through the hotel switchboard, and I was instructed "No calls".'

'Did he say why?'

'He just told me that you were not allowed any calls, in or out, and to make sure that the door is locked at all times to stop anyone getting *in*. He never said anything about letting anyone out. Did you say you wanted a smoke?'

'Yes, that would be good. I don't suppose you'd have a light, would you?' Jack offered the porter a cigarette from the packet.

'Thanks, but we will have to go outside,' the porter said. 'No Smoking laws, you know.'

They left the bedroom and went out of the hotel by the side entrance. It was pitch dark outside, and just a bit cold, but that full cigarette tasted good. They had another.

The night porter was a chatty old boy and he rambled on about everything.

He gave Jack a box of matches. 'Here you are, lad. I know what it is like inside prison. I don't want to know what you're doing here. I just didn't like that other suited fella, that's all.'

'How did you know I'd been inside?'

The porter smiled. 'The shirt and trousers, lad. Dead giveaway. And the smell.'

They returned to the room. As the porter was about to leave, he said, 'If you want to make a phone call, come and see me. I'll dial it from the switchboard, and it won't be linked to your room.'

'Thanks for your help. What's your name?'

'Bert,' the night porter replied.

'Well, Bert, thanks again for everything and the matches.' Jack was very grateful.

'Here's a pass key in case you want another fag, but change out of those prison togs first. You stand out a mile.' Bert smiled and stepped out into the corridor. 'That bloke,' he added. 'Friend of yours?'

'Not really, no. In fact, I've never seen him before. Or the other guy.'

'Are you in trouble, lad?'

'I don't know. So far, they seem to be on my side. But this has happened so quickly, I don't really know what's going on.'

'Get your head down, lad, you look all in.' Bert shuffled off. 'Just down the corridor in reception, if you want that call.'

He thought about the last few hours and concluded that the paperwork seemed authentic, and that the Governor would not just release a prisoner if the men from the Home Office were not genuine. But surely Jack should have been told that a new enquiry had been taking place?

Who could he trust? Harvey's overbearing and officious attitude bothered Jack. He had even riled the night porter.

Lying on the bed, he thumbed through his little address book again. Jack had had a few solicitors come to see him before his trial, and when he was first in prison, one of whom was Gerry Forbes. His original solicitor, recommended by colleagues, had been pretty ineffectual — in fact, he would go so far as to say she had been useless. Gerry, though, had been sound. He always spoke the truth to Jack and told him how it was. It wasn't always good news, but it was the truth — and, right now, he trusted Gerry more than anyone.

He thought it must be about half three, but, as ever, there was no clock in the bedroom. His wife, Valerie, had hated that about the majority of hotel rooms they had stayed in. The memory brought Jack up sharp. He couldn't allow thoughts of his wife and daughter, who had been only a newborn baby when he was arrested, to linger. Emma would be coming up to five years old now. He had no idea what she was like.

Val had divorced Jack straight away after he was found guilty. He understood her revulsion. The crime was horrific — a dreadful sexual assault, which had led to the death of a young woman. But he had not committed that crime, although he had had no way of proving his innocence. Now, suddenly, he seemed to be in the clear. Or was he?

Jack decided that Gerry Forbes was his best bet and judged that he wouldn't mind being called at this time of the morning. These were, after all, unusual circumstances.

Jack slipped out of the room and went to the reception. Bert was dozing in his armchair. Jack gently woke him.

'Bert, I'd like to make a call, please.'

'Sure thing, lad. Make it from here: that way old smarty pants won't know about it.' Old Bert winked.

Jack sat in the porter's little office and called the number he had for Gerry Forbes. The phone rang for what seemed an age. When it was answered, Jack recognised Gerry's voice straight away. It was slow and sleepy, but it was definitely Gerry.

'Gerry? Gerry, this is Trevor Frost, you remember? 'Jack' Frost? You were my solicitor.'

'Jack, is that you? What are you doing at this time of night? Where are you? What do you want? God, it's four o'clock.'

'Listen, I can't say much. I was pulled out of Stamford Prison tonight, late, by two men from the Home Office who told me that there's new evidence in my case. I've been released immediately, and now I'm being kept safe, and they're going to call me as a witness for the prosecution in a new trial.'

'Jack, for Christ's sake, slow down. What do you mean you've been released? It doesn't happen like that. You're talking nonsense. Where are you calling from?' Gerry began to sound just a bit alarmed.

Jack glanced at some headed notepaper on the desk in front of him.

'These men from the Home Office have lodged me in this hotel overnight. It's called Shadwell Manor. It's in Tring, Hertfordshire. They are coming back later this morning to take me to what they are calling a safe house, give me new clothes and money and so on. Why a safe house? Safe from what?'

'Jack, the Home Office don't do things like that — are you alright?'

'Yes, I'm okay, but I can't make it add up. I'm as sceptical as you are. I don't think I trust these Home Office bods. They arranged with the hotel to keep me locked up here.'

'Hang fire a minute. Have you changed solicitors? Because I've heard nothing of this from anyone and the solicitor should have been the first to know of any change of circumstances. If they'd told me, I would have contacted you for a visiting order immediately.' Gerry sounded as panicky as Jack felt.

'No, Gerry, you are the only person I can trust. I have lost my wife, my family and all my friends. I have had no contact with anyone. I haven't changed solicitor. What do you think is going on?'

'There is definitely something not right here. Stay where you are. I'll come out. It will take me about an hour to get to Tring. Don't speak to anyone else about this, and I will see you soon.'

'Okay. Thanks, Gerry, I knew I could rely on you. This hotel is at the end of a long driveway. I will meet you at the top of that driveway, where it meets the main road.' Jack hung up the phone.

Bert was outside having a smoke.

'Thanks for that, Pop, you are a good egg,' Jack said. 'I might be leaving here very shortly. Any chance of some toast before I take off?'

'No problem, lad. Bloody silly locking someone away who has just come out of prison. I've been inside myself — a long time ago now, but you never forget. A couple of bits of toast, was it?' Bert shuffled off.

Jack returned to the room and got together his belongings, wrapped up carefully in the brown paper parcel as before. He was trying to get his thoughts together, but nothing seemed to be making sense.

Bert came in with the toast.

'You had better have your pass key back, Bert. It was good to have someone to trust. Thanks for everything.'

'I was told by my old mum years ago,' Bert said, 'don't trust anyone. Just look after number one. Good luck, lad.'

Before he left the room, Bert looked back and said, 'After you've gone, I'll lock up — then when they come to find you gone, it will make them wonder how you got out of that window. That will confuse the smart bastards.'

The toast tasted wonderful, and with a cup of tea, Jack was feeling a lot better. He made sure that everything in the room was as he found it; he didn't want to be accused of damage or theft. Then he crept along to the reception.

'Thanks, Bert, I'm off. Thanks again for everything, I —'

Bert interrupted him. 'Don't tell me anything; the less I know the better. Just look after yourself, lad. Good luck.'

Jack walked to the end of the driveway, and stood waiting. It was dark, and bloody cold with only his zip-up jacket. His clothes were loose fitting — he must have lost about two stone whilst in prison. He hid a few times from passing headlights and had a heart-stopping moment when a delivery van to the hotel picked him out in its lights whilst he was hiding, but nothing happened.

As promised, after about three quarters of an hour, Gerry turned up and Jack got in the car. Gerry sped away immediately, making towards London.

'Tell me everything, Jack.'

Jack explained in detail everything that had happened from the point Chief Warder Kerr entered his cell and woke him up.

'It doesn't make sense,' Gerry said. 'Things do not happen like that. The Home Office do not get themselves involved like this. Was the Senior Investigating Officer mentioned in the Home Office letter?'

'Yes, though I can't remember his name. I didn't recognise it. But the Governor was happy enough with the paperwork to release me. I have the documents here.'

'Good, I'll read them later. But why the hotel? Why the safe house? Why all the secrecy? I am your solicitor — they should have let me know.'

'Where are we going now? What's going to happen when the Home Office men come back later and find me gone?'

'We'll cross that bridge when we come to it. For the time being, I will take you to my sister's house. She's away at the moment. We'll still have to tread carefully, but I'll get you settled and see what comes about later today.'

They drove and talked for about another hour. It was just breaking light when they pulled into the drive of a nice, ordinary, semi-detached, three-bedroom house. Jack still didn't know where he was. He was too tired really to bother.

The house was cold, but nicely furnished, and was a poignant reminder of the lovely, family home he'd shared with his wife. He sank down onto the settee in the lounge while Gerry disappeared into the kitchen to turn the heating on and make a cup of tea. Then he went upstairs and came back down with some clothes.

'Put these on,' he said. 'They are my ex-brother-in-law's; he won't be needing them.'

Jack was warming up a bit and feeling sick with tiredness.

'Jack, listen to me, this is important. I'm going now. I have to get home and then get to work. Don't answer the phone if it rings. If I ring, you'll know it's me because I'll let it ring four times and then ring off and then phone you back. You understand? Four rings.'

'Why all the cloak-and-dagger with you, Gerry?' Jack asked.

'We can't know if those men were, in fact, from the Home Office. If, as we suspect, they were not, that makes you technically an escaped prisoner. Now, I know you are innocent of the crime, and you shouldn't have gone to prison in the first place, but, nevertheless, you *were* convicted and sentenced. I believe in you, Jack. To my mind, you have always been a good, honest sort, but there is something very fishy about this whole affair. Now, don't phone me on my mobile; they can track mobile phones. In fact, don't phone me at all. I will contact you. There is plenty of food here. Don't go out unless it is totally necessary. Don't show yourself to the neighbours. They know I am coming to keep an eye on the place, but they won't know about you.'

'Did you mean what you just said? That you believe that I am innocent? That's the first time you have said that.'

'I've been keeping a close eye on your case, ever since the end of the trial. There have been some odd movements of the prosecution witnesses: promotions, sackings and a couple have conveniently disappeared — but nothing that I could pin any hope of an appeal on for you. I have it all documented.'

'Like a jigsaw, with some pieces missing,' Jack offered.

'Yes, mate, I am sure all the pieces are there, but I cannot seem to put them all in order. Look, Jack, get your head down and keep it down. I will be back tomorrow, when I will have hopefully learned some more. They are bound to come to me and ask if you have been in contact. Until I know who is who, I am saying nothing. Just rest up and wait 'til I contact you. It's a better cell than you were in before, but for the time being you are still a prisoner.'

Jack gave him a rueful nod.

'By the way, where are those Home Office papers they gave you?'

He handed them over, and after Gerry left, curled up on the settee and put his head on the cushion. For the first time in a long while, he felt safe. He drifted off into a deep sleep. No dreams, no thoughts of anything.

Chapter Two

SEQUENCE OF EVENTS

Jack awoke feeling strange, as if he had been given an interval in all the madness to collect his thoughts. For the first time in many months, he allowed himself to think through how this whole mess started, who was involved and how it had all got so out of his control, without winding himself in tortuous knots and bitter thoughts about his losses.

He made himself a cup of tea, and found a can of beans that he warmed up. He didn't open the curtains or do anything to indicate he was there. He had a good wash in hot water, appreciating the unaccustomed luxury, and decided that if Gerry had a dossier on the whole proceedings, names and incidents etc, then perhaps he, too, should write down everything he could remember, to enable them to sort out those various pieces of the jigsaw.

He got dressed in his borrowed clothes, found some paper and a pencil, sat down at the table, and began to think.

In the old days, when he was a detective, he had found the best way of sorting out the timetable of a case was to create a sequence-of-events document, so this was what he decided to do. Some of the dates and times were blurred in his memory, but he wrote down the facts, starting with the date he joined the

Overseas and Organised Crime Squad — at least he knew that one —and his induction into what he believed was the superior detective squad in the Metropolitan Police Force.

He had been a detective for about two years when he got an invitation, from a detective superintendent that he knew quite well, to apply for a vacancy on that élite squad. It wasn't what you knew in those days, it was who you knew.

Jack allowed himself to dwell on this period of time. He had been so very happy. How lucky he had been to marry Val — God, she was terrific. His mind went back to their wedding day. He had been more than eager to recite his marriage vows in front of God and all their guests, declaring his love for this wonderful girl. He had never experienced love for another person like that. Everything was perfect. They bought their first house shortly after marrying; Val was happy in her job and Jack was over the moon with his career in the police. He was becoming a very successful detective.

Then came the brilliant news that Val was pregnant. They couldn't have been happier. Everything was going swimmingly.

Jack could hardly bear to carry on remembering. It was becoming too painful. He had trained himself in prison not to dwell on these memories, but in the back of his little notebook, he kept a small photograph of Val and the baby. Emma was beautiful, the image of her mother, and the sweetest little girl there ever was.

He got it out now, and stared at it until his tears began to well up.

This wasn't getting the sequence-of-events done. Jack pulled himself together.

The first few jobs on the new squad had been interesting and exciting and Jack had felt he fitted in quite well. He was on a team of ten officers, with a detective sergeant and a detective inspector in charge. The team was mixed, male and female and each one of them was a terrific detective. Easy to get on with and good to work with. They were all loyal, dedicated police officers. It felt good when you were all singing out of the same hymn book.

Their thorough and efficient work resulted in many convictions at Crown Court. As far as the higher-ranking officers at the Yard were concerned, they were doing very well. Jack was earning quite good money, too, with all the overtime and expenses.

Most of their jobs were intelligence-led. Jack recalled that, on this one occasion — again, the precise date escaped him — they were briefed by the DI about an international drug importation gang, bringing huge amounts of cocaine and heroin into the UK. The theory was that it was all being done via diplomatic baggage, to various embassies in London.

After their briefing, they were each given their tasks for further intelligence gathering. Jack was teamed with Rod Beckett who was an experienced detective constable, a little older than Jack, good-humoured and very streetwise. They were given two addresses — coded, for security purposes, E3 and E4 — to keep an eye on and some information about what they were looking for. E3 was a large, detached house, with its own drive-in and drive-out, in a posh suburb of north London. E4 was about half a mile away. This was also a large, detached house with its own drive, though in not quite such good condition.

They started with a recce on each address. Their observations continued for about three weeks: times of movements to and from the houses, registrations of vehicle numbers, descriptions of people seen. Sometimes they took photographs to try and ascertain the identities. After each day, Rod and Jack would compare details.

He wondered about those notes. They were handed in every night to the DS, who would then pass them to the detective inspector, or governor, as all senior officers in the Met were called. What had happened to them? He couldn't recall them being used in evidence.

Compiling a sequence-of-events was a good way to get things in order but without being able to remember dates and times, it wasn't going to be very helpful. Jack decided to try to interrogate his memories with a bit more focus: Who he had been working with? Who else was there?

The intelligence, collated from a number of sources within the Met and also MI5 and MI6, was pretty accurate, and all the persons and vehicles turned up on a regular basis. Following several debriefs with the DI, it was decided that they should concentrate all their observations on E4. After another week of observing the comings and goings, by the Friday night there seemed to be more people attending the house than usual.

Friday night. That's right! Val's mum had come to stay for a few days to help with the baby, and he had been glad to get out of the house. When was that? Jack racked his brains. It was Friday, 17th November. Emma was a week old. Jack wrote this first bit of verifiable information down. How could he have forgotten that?

He and Rod were in an unmarked police car not far from the target address with a good clear view of all the comings and goings. It must have been towards three in the morning when Rod had said, 'There must be a party going on in there. Lots more activity than usual. I think I'll take a closer look.'

He remembered remonstrating with him, telling him to get back in the car. Then Rod had disappeared.

About thirty minutes later, all hell was let loose and the road outside came alive. All of a sudden, there were numerous police vehicles, cars and vans everywhere and a vast number of uniformed police officers descended on the house and raided it. They entered the house quickly and forcefully and seemed to have the house fully in their control.

This had totally blown their observation and there was no point in staying. So where was Rod?

Suddenly, from the back of the house, came the figures of a man and a woman running. The woman was being semi-dragged by the man. They disappeared briefly and then, from the driveway of the house next door, roared a black, four-door Mercedes saloon, which sped off up the road.

He was sure he had not seen this vehicle before, and he was equally sure the occupants had come from E4. Where the devil was Rod?

In a flash, he decided to follow the Mercedes and come back later for Rod.

The Merc didn't hang about, but Jack was also a keen driver and he soon caught up with it, following — as he had been taught — at a safe and covert distance.

Before long, they were at Hyde Park Corner, heading towards Notting Hill. Jack was three cars behind the Mercedes when he saw it turn left off the Bayswater Road. After a brief stop, it drove into the gated Kensington Palace Gardens, home to several foreign embassies.

Kensington Palace Gardens are locked at night. Only permitted vehicles are allowed to enter. Who was in that car?

He couldn't follow as the gate had closed behind the Mercedes. Unable to see where it went after it entered Kensington Palace Gardens, Jack had quickly scribbled what he could remember of the registration of the vehicle onto a cigarette packet in the car. Even so, he only had a partial reg., E—NAP, dark blue or black Mercedes saloon. Then he made his way back to E4, but there was no sign of Rod. There was still a police presence, but everything seemed to have calmed down now.

Jack returned to HQ, which was located in a former warehouse that had been neatly and expertly converted into office accommodation. It had its own multi-storey parking and a high-tech complex on the top floor with every conceivable gadget: technology far beyond Jack's understanding. It had electric front doors; activated from a button in the car, they would open, swallow the car up and close automatically.

HQ even had its own petrol pumps, and the rules were to fuel up the car immediately in case it was needed at very short notice. As Jack was doing this, Rod appeared.

'Where the fuck did you get to? You just left me there with all the uniform running around me. You could have waited.'

Jack began to try and explain but Rod stopped him.

'Come downstairs now, the Guvnor's waiting for you. He isn't best pleased, and neither am I.'

In the briefing room, the mood was one of dejection. Weeks of observations and information-gathering had been blown in one quick swoop by their uniformed colleagues.

DCI Bristow got to his feet.

'Thank you for blessing us with your presence, Frost; we'll speak later. Now everyone, I don't want this pissed-off mood to last. We are a covert squad. We did not flag up our operation with anyone for security reasons, so if it gets fucked up, it's our own lookout. Not uniforms.' Now, top and tail your reports and get them submitted before you go home. Clive, Brenda, make discreet enquires at the nicks to see who was arrested tonight, what for and what is happening to them — court or bail etc. Find out what property was recovered, drugs and so on.'

'Okay, Guv, will do,' Brenda replied.

'Debrief here later tonight at 6pm. Get off home, get some kip. Frost, my office, now!' DCI shouted.

Jack entered the DCI's office with trepidation.

'Where did you disappear to? You were supposed to be on the plot with your partner, but for some reason you take it into your head to dump him and drive off. What were you thinking?'

'I can explain, Guv. There was this car that took off from next door when uniform raided the target. I thought it was odd.'

'That doesn't excuse you from abandoning Rod. No partner, no corroboration. I don't want to hear your excuses. Get out. You'll hear from me later.'

It wouldn't have happened if Rod had stayed in the car, like he should have done, instead of wanting to take a closer look around the target address.

Jack had put all his findings into his report including the registration number copied from the cigarette packet, along with details of how he had tailed the dark blue Mercedes to Kensington Palace Gardens.

Again, he wondered, whatever had happened to those reports? He'd give anything to have access to them now. He didn't have many accurate notes in his sequence-of-events, and the recollection of these operations was only producing more questions. He remained certain that the Mercedes was the key at the beginning of all this. He had saved that cigarette packet as an exhibit of an original note, but what had he done with it?

At the end of each day all the details of their observations were submitted to the squad's intelligence unit, where they were collated, and if any valuable, new intelligence was gleaned, that information would be part of the next night's briefing.

All he could remember was that, at that briefing, it was reported that target address E4 had been raided by uniformed police officers from the local nick and from the local drug squad. Eight arrests had been made (although he and Rod had counted at least forty people in that house) for drug-related offences. Discarded wraps of cocaine, heroin and cannabis and ready-made joints had been found.

No person of note was amongst those arrested, except for one well-known low-life, who had come to their attention before. He was strongly suspected of being the main supplier, but on this occasion was only in possession of a small quantity of cannabis which he insisted was for his own personal use.

Nothing in that briefing had mentioned the Mercedes, or the persons seen running out of the target address. It appeared that no work had been done on the partial registration to try and find the owner of the Mercedes or to establish the destination once it had entered Kensington Palace Gardens.

After the uniform bust on target E4, the operation went quiet, and, as a squad, they were tasked with other important investigations. But Jack hadn't forgotten what he'd seen.

A couple of days later, he had bumped into a uniformed mate of his, Roger, with whom he had worked for a few years at the same nick. Roger was now a Traffic Police Inspector, and, over a few pints, Jack told him of his nagging doubts about the occupants of the Mercedes and that partial registration number.

'Leave it to me, Jack, I'll make a few checks, and get back to you.' Again, it wasn't what you knew, but who you knew. A traffic officer making enquiries on a vehicle wouldn't draw attention, but a detective on a specialist squad would.

Roger had contacted Jack the next day. 'You've got a live

one there with that Mercedes,' he had said. 'The registration is blocked on the computer, but after more digging it has come back as belonging to an Embassy or Diplomatic Legation of some sort. It doesn't have diplomatic immunity as such, but is leased out to one of the Embassies in Kensington Palace Gardens. No specific driver or passenger is recorded, but it is believed to be based with the Russians. That's all I can tell you.'

'Can we evidence any of this information officially, Roger?' Jack had asked.

'Sorry, mate. This was all done under the table, so to speak.'

'Roger, you are a star. I'll take it from here, thanks.'

Jack had been excited and confused at the same time. How come his own squad's intelligence unit hadn't come up with this information after everything he had put in his notes that night?

At about nine-thirty, Harvey and Clarke arrived at Shadwell Manor in their government car. Accompanied by the manager, they went to Room 18, where they had left Jack the night before.

'Has he had breakfast?' enquired Harvey.

'Yes,' the manager replied. 'As per instructions, he was given his breakfast at eight. No-one has been in or out since you left.'

The manager unlocked the door with his pass key and the Home Office men entered the room.

No-one was there. They checked the bathroom. Empty.

They checked the window, but it would only open two inches and was secured.

'Where is he?' Harvey demanded. 'Who let him out? Who was on duty last night?'

'Our night porter, Bert, but he had strict instructions about your guest.' The manager was mystified.

'Get me that night porter here, right away!'

'He'll be asleep now, Sir.'

'I don't care, I want to speak to him!'

The manager scurried off and Harvey and Clarke began to search the room. Everything was in order, nothing missing. Used towels in the bathroom, uneaten breakfast on the coffee table.

'Bed's been slept in,' said Clarke. 'No other way out except the locked door.'

'That bloody night porter must have let him out!'

After about half an hour, the manager returned with Bert.

'Why did you let the guest in here get out?' Harvey began, very rudely.

'Get out, Sir? Get out? He didn't get out. He was here when I brought him his breakfast and I locked the door behind me as instructed,' old Bert replied, quite convincingly.

'When you took his meal in, did you see him?' Harvey barked.

'No, Sir, he was in the bathroom. I just left it on the table, didn't wait for a tip, called good morning and left the room. Locked the door behind me, I did, as per my instructions.' Bert was not going to be shaken by these bullying nerds.

'What time did you take the breakfast in to him?'

'Just before I went off duty at eight, Sir.'

'And did you see him or speak to him?'

'As I said, Sir, he was in the bathroom, and I didn't hear any reply when I told him his breakfast was on the table. I left the room, locking the door as per my instructions,' repeated Bert, determined that the two Government men were not going to get anything more out of him.

'Did you unlock this door at all, for any reason last night?'

'No, Sir, as per my instructions.' Bert was clearly tired of this.

'He must have slipped out as the old guy was delivering the breakfast. He can only be a couple of hours in front of us. He's got no money and no means of transport. He can't be far away,' Clarke pointed out.

Harvey stormed out of the hotel and immediately got on the phone. He wanted a full search of the area made, but his Commander at the Home Office said no; this all had to be kept under wraps. No high-level searches or any indication to the local forces that anything was amiss.

'Pay the hotel in cash and get back here ASAP,' his Commander ordered.

Harvey was still not happy. He went back to the manager.

'Did anyone come to the hotel last night, after we left?'

'No-one, Sir, except the night delivery of fresh foods for the kitchens, and he just drops the goods off at the kitchen doors.'

'Get the name and contacts for that driver and we'll question him later,' Harvey said to Clarke.

Harvey went back to the empty room but could find nothing which gave him a clue to his missing, newly freed prisoner.

In London, Gerry wearily made his way into work.

No messages (good news) and no indications that anything or anybody was looking for him or, more importantly, Trevor 'Jack' Frost. From a locked filing cabinet in the basement, he dug out two box-files of all the notes on the Frost case and placed them in a large carrier bag.

He looked through the appointments that he had for the day. Nothing urgent. He dealt with his mundane tasks until lunchtime, when he decided to escape from his office to go through the information that he had unearthed.

He told his secretary, Sharon, that he would be out for the rest of the day, as he wasn't feeling too good. He made his way to the garage where he stored his precious motorhome. The motorhome was Gerry's private escape from the real world; he could drive out into the country or to the coast where he could clear his head. He often did this when preparing a difficult case for court. No-one knew he owned it and it would be the only place that no snooping eyes would find papers etc.

He drove for about an hour, and parked up at a viewpoint overlooking the countryside. He made himself a cup of tea and sat down to go through the mountain of evidence and paperwork that the Frost case had generated.

All the evidence that had been presented to the jury by the prosecution and the defence witnesses was concrete. All avenues of truth had been established and backed up by solid forensic evidence. The jury could not help but find Jack Frost guilty on the evidence put before them. The judge had no compunction in sentencing him to eighteen years' imprisonment.

There was no leave to appeal either, and that was where Gerry found himself. He was even more baffled as to why the Home Office had now stepped in and had Jack released from prison. Why all the secrets?

He decided to speak to Jack. Ring four times. Hang up. Ring again. Jack remembered the signal and then answered the phone.

Gerry told Jack what he was doing and how so far nothing seemed to be out of order.

'I've been trying to piece together what happened,' said Jack, 'but I haven't found anything, either. Can we meet up?'

'Not yet,' Gerry said. 'You are safe there for at least another day or two until I can figure out what to do. My sister doesn't come back for a while. Get your head down and try and chill out. We have a lot of working out to do between the two of us.'

Chapter Three

THE MYSTERY DEEPENS

At the Home Office, the top men were tearing their hair out, particularly Sir William Ponsonby-Smythe, under whose remit Trevor Frost now fell. Harvey and Clarke were in deep trouble, and they knew it. Their plan to save themselves inconvenience in the late hours had gone drastically wrong.

Their problem was not a simple one.

Three years ago, Trevor Frost, a serving police officer, had been found guilty of drugs-related incidents, GBH, and the rape and murder of a female Russian national who had diplomatic immunity. The victim was never named, owing to her diplomatic status, and was referred to in court as 'Miss X'.

In the interim period, evidence had come to light to suggest that Frost was not guilty of the offences for which he had been convicted. The whole scenario had been engineered with the sole purpose of covering up a massive criminal operation involving drugs, slavery, money-laundering and sexual depravity.

It had now been decided that Frost, as the victim of a gross miscarriage of justice, should be released without delay, and that, in order to protect him from any foreign power who might want to silence him, and stop him from giving evidence, he must be kept under strict privacy conditions in a safe house.

The main worry for the Home Office was the prospect of the media discovering that foreign embassies were involved in international crime. They knew that Frost was a very astute detective, and would finally work out who was responsible for his incrimination. Just as certain foreign powers wanted him silent, so did the Home Office. If the full story were to come out, heads would roll in the Civil Service and in the highest echelons of CID, MI5 and MI6 and Government, to say nothing of the outcome for diplomatic relations with foreign embassies. It was an unthinkable disaster.

Sir Ponsonby-Smythe prowled around his large office like a trapped panther, while an underling stood near the door. Harvey and Clarke braced themselves for what was surely going to be a painful meeting.

'This is bloody disastrous. We have a wrongly convicted ex-police detective released from prison, on the authority of the Home Secretary, into the custody of two Home Office operatives who promptly lose him within hours of getting him out. Why has he gone on the run? What does he know? What is he scared of? You handled this job like a bloody amateur, Harvey. What possessed you?'

Harvey shuffled his feet and said, 'It was very late, Sir, so we thought it would be better for him to be installed in a hotel overnight, while we prepared the safe house.'

'How did he get out?' shouted Sir Ponsonby-Smythe.

'We think he got out when the night porter brought in his breakfast, Sir,' Clarke stuttered.

'What time was that?'

'Eight in the morning, Sir.'

'He must have had help.' Sir Ponsonby-Smythe glared at Clarke and Harvey. 'He must have contacted someone.'

'We've checked the phone records of the hotel, and no calls were made to or from the room, and no other persons came to or from the place during the time he was there, except a food delivery van as usual. The delivery driver has been interviewed but he saw nothing at all,' Harvey explained.

'What is Frost's family situation, friends etc?' Sir Ponsonby-Smythe was beginning to think in a lateral way.

Clarke referred to his notes. 'He has a wife and young daughter, but his wife hasn't spoken to him since the end of the trial. They are now divorced, although she remains in their marital home. He has a sister and brother-in-law living in north London but, again, we think they have not spoken to him since the trial. Not one family member or friend visited him in prison. He did receive several visits from his solicitor, a Mr Gerald Forbes, but he too has neither visited nor contacted Frost for over six months.' Clarke finished reading.

'He must have had *someone* helping him. He can't just disappear into thin air. Did he have any money?'

'He had eight pounds fifty when he was released to us, which is what his wages from prison work amounted to,' Harvey explained.

'I want his wife questioned. He may have tried to contact her. Likewise, his sister. What about his solicitor? Check him out as well.' Sir Ponsonby-Smythe gave out his orders. 'Now, get out of my sight.'

Clarke was detailed to visit Forbes, which he did without delay. He located Gerry's offices and, flashing his ID, demanded to see Mr Gerald Forbes.

The receptionist explained that Mr Forbes had called into the office that morning but, as usual when he had a difficult case to defend, he would absent himself to study the case quietly, away from distractions.

'Do you know where he's gone?' Clarke asked.

'No, I'm afraid not.'

'When Mr Forbes returns, would you ask him to ring me on either of these numbers?' Clarke gave the woman one of his visiting cards.

As he was about to leave, he turned back and said, as if it were an afterthought, 'Do you know if he has had any contact recently with Trevor Frost, the policeman he defended some years ago?'

She thought for a moment before replying. 'The one that murdered that poor girl? No, he hasn't. Not spoken to him for months.'

Looking at the card, she said, 'Home Office? Why are you interested in Trevor Frost?'

Clarke left the office.

Harvey, meanwhile, had gone to pay a visit to Trevor Frost's ex-wife, Valerie. She was now living with her nearly five-year-old daughter, Emma, in a comfortable home not far from her mother and father in a north London suburb.

Valerie was immediately wary. Who was this Home Office man and why he was asking questions about Jack?

'Has he escaped from prison and you think he is here? Please, search the place. I wouldn't have that filthy shitbag anywhere near me. He doesn't know where I live, does he?' Val felt panic rising in her chest and her throat tightened.

Harvey gave Valerie no information or reassurances. He explained that he was just trying to establish whether she had had any contact with her ex-husband recently, any phone calls or messages, but he did not inform Valerie that her husband was, after all, not guilty and had been vindicated of all the crimes of which he had been convicted. Nor did he tell her that he might be in great danger.

'He doesn't have my telephone numbers, I hope. He doesn't know where I live? We are divorced and that's the end of it. I want nothing to do with him.'

'When was the last time you spoke to him or saw him?'

'When they took him down at the Old Bailey. That's the last time I saw him. I have never spoken to him since he left for work on the day before they arrested him. He is a very nasty bastard — don't you read the papers? Anyway, you should know where he is. Tell me, has he escaped? Is he on the loose?' Desperation made Valerie's question shriller than she had intended.

Harvey replied that he was not at liberty to give any information, but assured her that she was in no danger. He said he would be in touch again, passed her his card and instructed her that if she heard from her ex-husband, she must phone him on any of the numbers or phone the police.

Harvey left satisfied that Frost had not contacted his wife.

There was a similar response from Frost's sister, Jean. She seemed very embarrassed that she was related to the infamous Trevor Frost and explained that neither she nor her husband, Peter, had spoken to him for a long time.

'Were you not close?' Harvey asked. 'No interest in his welfare?'

Peter asked the Home Office agent to leave and not to upset his wife any further. 'We have had no contact, want no contact and he is not part of our family anymore. He doesn't exist as far as we are concerned.'

Harvey and Clarke were no further forward in their efforts to trace Frost.

As far as the police and prison service were concerned, Frost was no longer a prisoner. He was not an escapee, and his details could not be circulated as such, but they had to find him to ensure that his safety was guaranteed, and that vital information he may be able to give didn't get out. As things stood, Jack Frost had no notion of the danger he was in, of how or why his life was under threat if the real story of his arrest, trial and imprisonment were to be revealed.

Gerry Forbes drove back to his garage. It was a small, unused warehouse which he rented to park his motorhome out of the weather, and safe from vandals and theft. He decided to leave all the Frost paperwork in his motorhome, and made his way back to the office.

'Strange thing,' Sharon told him. 'Had some Home Office bod in here earlier, asking whether you've been in contact with that bent copper. I said you'd not been in touch with him this year.'

'Thank you, Sharon. How odd. No, I've had no contact with Frost. Did they say why they wanted to know?'

'No,' she said. 'The man was a bit tight-lipped about it all, really. Creepy bloke, he was. He left his card for you to contact him, if you hear from Frost.'

'I don't think I will be hearing from him for a long time, or not for at least another seven years,' Gerry lied, examining the calling card carefully.

Matthew Clarke,
Senior Investigation Officer,
HM Home Office

He toyed with whether to ring Clarke or just let it ride. After some careful thought, Gerry thought it might be wise to confer with one of his office elders in the legal practice.

'Why, after all this time, should I get a visit from the Home Office asking questions about one of my old clients who was imprisoned after losing his case in court? I've not spoken to him since I saw him back in the spring to tell him there was no chance of an appeal.'

'Give the Home Office a ring, Gerry,' Mr Jackson, the senior partner, said. 'You've got nothing to lose. After all, you were this Frost's solicitor and by rights you should be informed of any changes in his circumstances unless he has changed his brief to another firm.'

The number on the card rang through to an office and the operator on the other end was very unhelpful. Nevertheless, by the end of the call, Gerry had managed to obtain Clarke's mobile number from her.

'Good afternoon, Gerry Forbes here, from Jackson and Jackson, Solicitors. You visited my offices today in relation to one of my ex-clients, a Trevor Frost.'

'Yes, Mr Forbes, thank you for calling back. I was enquiring whether you had had any recent contact with Mr Frost.'

'May I ask in what context you are making your enquiry?'

'It was just that we wanted to know if Mr Frost had contacted you in any way for any reason,' Clarke hedged.

'Well, owing to client confidentiality, I would not normally be able to reveal that, but, since you are from the Home Office, I am prepared to divulge that I've had no contact with him since the start of the year. I assume now that he has another solicitor and that I no longer act for him. May I ask why you at the Home Office are asking after him?'

'Unfortunately, Mr Forbes, I am not at liberty to say, but I assure you there is nothing to worry about. Would you please contact me again if you hear from him in any way? It's for his own good.' Clarke tried to finish the conversation.

'What do you mean, for his own good?'

'As I said, I cannot tell you anything at the moment.' Clarke again tried to stall Gerry's questions.

'Okay, I will get in contact with Mr Frost in prison to ascertain if I am still working on his behalf. Could you tell me in which prison he is currently housed?' Gerry enquired, provocatively.

'I'm afraid I cannot give you that information, Mr Forbes. Goodbye for now.' Clarke hung up.

Gerry was more intrigued than ever. He decided to go one step further, by contacting Her Majesty's Prisoner Location Service and asking them where Trevor Frost was being held. A very helpful operator answered and, after some delay, informed him that Trevor Frost was being held in HMP Stamford and his earliest parole hearing was about seven years away. Interesting!

Gerry phoned HMP Stamford and explained that he was the solicitor for Trevor Frost and wished to request a visitor's order to come to the prison to talk with him. There was a short interlude where he was kept hanging on the line, until eventually a member of the prison staff spoke.

'I am afraid that prisoner Frost has requested that he has *no* contact with anyone and would not support you having a visitor's order. I am sorry.'

His voice sounded very official and direct, and carried a certain authority, but Gerry knew he was prevaricating.

'But I am his solicitor. I have vital information for him on a delicate matter. I need to see him.'

'I am sorry, Mr Forbes, but you had better write to him personally. I cannot help you any further. Goodbye.' The conversation was ended abruptly.

So, the prison was not prepared to admit that Jack Frost

wasn't there, nor had his release been officially announced. This was very curious. Gerry noted down the time and the content of the phone calls for future reference.

Having caught up with the office tasks that had arisen while he was out, Gerry decided to go to his sister's house to pay a call on Jack. The neighbours would not think it unusual to see him arriving at the house as they knew he was keeping an eye on the place whilst his sister was away.

As he went in, Gerry could neither see nor hear Jack, and immediately began to worry.

'Jack, where are you?' He spoke in a loud whisper.

'Up here, Gerry.' Jack appeared on the landing. Not knowing who was entering the house, Jack had taken the precaution of hiding himself in the bathroom.

'Come down, I've got some interesting news for you.'

He filled Jack in about the visit from the Home Office man, Matthew Clarke, and their subsequent phone call, and the fact that Stamford had been evasive and let it be understood that he was there but wanted no contact.

'Gerry, something big must have happened. Something so big that they think I am in danger from someone, but I don't understand what.'

'For you to be released from prison on Home Office authority' — Gerry began, slowly, to work it out — 'must mean that compelling evidence has been presented that contradicts all the evidence used in court: new evidence which vindicates you and proves you are innocent, and therefore must be released immediately by law, whilst further investigations are carried out.'

'What further evidence could there be, Gerry?' Jack sounded baffled. 'I've heard nothing about this case since I was sent down.'

'I have an idea. We will leave here tonight, get some supplies, and I will take you to my motorhome, where you can stay as long as you like. No-one will know you are there. All your papers are there as well, and I'll take a few days off and we'll go through the whole case, piece by piece, witness by witness, to try and get to the bottom of this.'

'Won't taking time off be a bit obvious, Gerry?'

'No, I often take a few days off; my boss knows that. In the meantime, I will buy two Pay-As-You-Go mobiles, just for us to keep in touch with each other.'

'Gerry, I have no money. I have nothing except your ex-brother-in-law's clothes.'

'Don't worry about that now. We can sort all that out later.'

It was by now late in the evening, and dark, and they slipped out of the house into Gerry's car. They drove to a supermarket, where Gerry went in on his own and bought a mountain of stuff, including two mobile phones. They then headed to the garage where the motorhome was stored.

Jack was impressed. The motorhome was quite large and had every facility you could want. It received an electric supply from the mains and all the appliances were working.

'Right. Get yourself settled in, Jack, and make this your home for now. I will go now and then come back here soon, as I often do. I'll leave my car at the station, so if anyone starts poking around, everything will be as normal. I will tell Sharon in the office what I am doing, tomorrow.'

'Gerry, I can't thank you enough for all this — you were the only one I could turn to.'

'No problem, Jack. This is bigger than we both first thought and you are going to need some friendly help. Look, here is fifty quid in cash. You won't really need it, as I don't want you to show your face outside this garage. Unfortunately, it seems you are still a prisoner until we can verify that you are officially a free man and that this unknown 'danger' hanging over you has been eradicated.'

Gerry left and Jack closed the garage doors behind him. For the first time for a long time, Jack was able to walk around and get a bit of exercise. He made himself comfortable and cooked some dinner — no cabbage —and settled down to start reading the copious notes that Gerry had brought from his office.

The next day, Gerry phoned Jack on their new mobiles.

'I've just spoken to Dave Page, contact of mine from the CPS. Quite high up. He tells me that whatever has happened is major, involving the USA, Russia and other countries and right now it is all very hush-hush. Only senior people from the CPS are involved: no information is coming out. They have even set up a separate covert office to handle the investigation. It's big, Jack, very big, and all he could tell me is that you are the centre of it all. I didn't tell him we are in contact — just that I'd heard something on the grapevine, and am an interested party, being your solicitor.'

'What do we do now, Gerry?' Jack asked, trying to take this news in.

'Absolutely nothing. Zilch. Sit tight, don't talk to anyone. Something's going to break soon, and we shall be there to soak it all up. What these other countries have got to do with it, I don't know, but you are the innocent party.'

Chapter Four

GOING TO PRESS

Valerie was beside herself with anxiety. It had been three weeks since the Home Office official had visited her, with his sinister questions about contact with Jack.

Was Jack about to come and find her? Would he be violent towards her and Emma? What would she do if he turned up without warning? Eventually, she confided in her parents, telling them about the Home Office visit. Why would they be asking if she had had contact with Jack? Her mum and dad tried to comfort her, but Valerie was beyond consoling.

'Get in touch with your solicitor, the one who handled your divorce. He may be able to advise you in some way,' her dad said.

Valerie didn't have a great deal of confidence in the wishy-washy Mr Paul Lewis, but she agreed it was worth a try. Lewis promised her he would make a few enquiries on her behalf and get back to her. Nevertheless, it was a whole week before he contacted her.

'I have made enquiries with the Prison Service to find out in which prison Mr Frost is being kept, but they inform me that there is *no* prisoner in the UK prison system by that name with his date of birth etc. I presented all the details of his trial dates and sentence but they could not, or would not, give me any further information, so I must conclude that your ex-husband is no longer in prison and has been mysteriously released.'

Valerie was devastated. Terrified for her own and Emma's safety, she decided she would go to stay with her brother in the country for a few days. Her dad advised that before she did, she should contact the local police and demand some protection. They would and should be able to make her feel a bit safer.

A detective eventually attended the home — some forty-eight hours later — and sat down to talk the problem over with Valerie and her parents. He made a few notes and then proceeded to belittle all of Valerie's fears. He cockily informed her that without evidence of any contact with her ex-husband, the police could not do anything at all except put her fears on record for further action if needed.

'What about an alarm button to the police in case of an emergency?' Valerie desperately asked.

'Too expensive to install without concrete evidence that your ex-husband intends you harm,' the detective explained.

'I don't think you understand. He is a dangerous, vile, sexual deviant and he is bound to come after us.' Valerie was crying uncontrollably. The detective made his insincere apologies and left.

'What about contacting Jean? She might know something,' Valerie's mum suggested.

After Jack's trial, Jean had stayed in contact with Valerie and her family. Whatever her evil brother had done, it was nothing to do with her, and she absolutely adored her little niece. Calling Jean was a good idea, Val thought. Maybe she could shed some light on the mystery and make Val feel less alarmed.

Jean said that she had also had a visit from the Home Office making the same enquiries. She had given the same answers.

'Something is definitely wrong here,' Valerie said. 'My solicitor has found out that Jack is not in prison and therefore he must be out, not escaped but released. I am scared, Jean.'

'Somebody must know something, but they are not telling us anything,' Jean said to her husband, as she put the phone down.

Peter got up. 'I've got an idea. Back soon.'

He pulled on his coat and made his way to his local pub. Sure enough, his friend was sitting at the bar.

'Hywel, can I have a private word?'

Hywel Jones — who was definitely Welsh — was a regular reporter for a local paper, the *Herald and Messenger*, but sometimes covered bigger stories that had hit the public interest. He had covered the trial of Trevor Frost — 'THE DEVIANT DETECTIVE' — and produced good copy for his newspaper, accurately reporting the trial.

Peter related to Hywel all the information about Jack's mysterious disappearance from jail only three years into his prison sentence. Hywel slowed down his drinking, and began to take notes and ask questions.

'What evidence have you got for him going missing?'

Peter ran through everything they knew, concluding with the information from the Prison Locations Department that there was no Trevor Frost on any database within the UK jail system.

'This is impossible,' said Hywel. 'You can't be eligible for parole after only three years, and even if he were, his release would have been reported somewhere. Who were these Home Office men who visited Jean and Valerie?'

Peter showed Hywel the calling card that the officer had left with Jean.

'Senior Investigating Officer, Home Office. Hmm — a bit vague. What department are they from? If they are investigating

Trevor, they don't know where he is either, Hywel surmised. 'A dangerous, sexual deviant and convicted murderer disappears from the prison system and nobody knows where he is. No escape news, nothing. This could be huge, Peter. Would you leave it with me, and I will get back to you? Can we arrange a meeting with me, Valerie, Jean and yourself and I will take as much information from you all as I can? In the meantime, I will talk to my editor and get some enquires made to bottom out all your information.'

'No photographs or pictures, Hywel. I want to protect the family as much as possible,' Peter said.

'Understood. I am sure we have some library pictures of Frost anyway, but none of the family will be used, I promise.'

Two days later, Valerie and Ted arrived at Jean and Peter's, having left Emma with her grandma at a friend's house. Hywel was next to arrive and Peter made the introductions. Hywel then produced a voice recorder to record the whole interview with the families.

He began by stating that he had also made enquiries with the Prison Locations Department at the Home Office who confirmed what they had already heard. Trevor Frost was no longer held anywhere in the UK prison system.

He had called the phone numbers for the Home Office. No replies, but he had left messages for them to call him back. Hywel had also approached Trevor Frost's trial and divorce solicitor, Gerry Forbes. A helpful receptionist had informed him that Mr Forbes was away on vacation, but owing to the urgency of his enquiry, she would attempt to get a message to him.

He had also dug out the press cuttings from all the national and local newspapers.

The main Press Office for the Metropolitan Police had been

less than helpful, but agreed to register Hywel's interest and forward his contact details to the Chief Press Officer.

'So still a dead end then?' Valerie said. 'He can't have just vanished into thin air. He's not in prison, where he should be, and nobody seems to know or be willing to tell us where he is. Dad, I'm really scared.'

'You have a right to be scared,' Hywel said. 'And someone must know something. They shouldn't be hiding it from us. What I intend to do is this: I am going to prepare a story detailing the information I have received from all authorities. I'll head it 'MISSING DEVIANT DETECTIVE'. Before I present it to my editor and our legal boys for approval, I will show it to you all to get your thumbs up. The only pictures I will include will be library photos of Frost. None of your personal details will be in the article. How would that be?'

The room was silent for a moment or two as everyone looked at each other. All were stunned. Finally, Peter said, 'Will this get you into trouble, Hywel? Are we all jumping the gun here? There may be a perfectly legitimate reason for Jack to be missing.'

'Jumping the gun? Jumping the gun?' Valerie shouted. 'I am scared witless that he will come to get me and Emma. I divorced him because of his unthinkable behaviour. It will be us he comes for first.'

Hywel tried to calm the meeting down a little. 'None of us will get into trouble. The Home Office started this and if they don't know where he is, then someone does.'

'I just don't like the title 'DEVIANT DETECTIVE', that's all,' Peter commented.

'It's just an eye-catching title that sells newspapers, Pete, and it's a phrase the nationals used before.'

Ted calmly spoke up. 'I can see what Peter means. We could

be jumping the gun, there may be a legitimate reason for Jack not being in prison where he is supposed to be, but on the other hand it's the Home Office who should know where he is. I always liked Jack and I still can't believe he was found guilty of all the things they said he had done. There is something definitely mysterious here and if you can help, Hywel, then I, for one, will back you all the way.'

Jean nodded and cuddled closer to Peter but said nothing. Valerie started to pace the room.

'Where am I to go? Where can Emma and I go to feel safe until this is all published and answers are found? I am terrified he will come for us.'

Ted suggested that they went to her brother in Devon, as planned, but Valerie vetoed that. 'Jack knows his address,' she said, 'but wherever we go, he can find us. He was a detective, don't forget.'

Hywel then joined in. 'This would be a very good angle to base my news report on. Sub-headline: 'The Terror of the Immediate Family'; theme: 'Wife and child in constant fear — sexually deviant murderer on the loose and not even the Home Office know where he is.'

'That's a bit strong,' Peter said.

'I disagree,' Hywel answered. 'I'm going to call my editor immediately. Now I've got all your backing, this could be a very big story. Valerie, we have 'safe houses' where we can place people who are under the threat of violence. You and Emma could be housed where Jack could never trace you. I'm sure my editor would agree.'

Hywel went off into another room, where he could be heard talking animatedly on his mobile.

The room was very quiet for a while. Nobody spoke.

Hywel rushed back in. 'Valerie, have you got time to come with me now to our offices and meet my editor? He wants to get the whole story, and I want him to see how scared you are.'

Valerie nodded. 'Could you get back to Mum and make sure that Emma is okay, Dad? Take her home, and don't let her out of your sight.'

Whilst Valerie was talking to the editor, Hywel Jones sat down and finished writing the news story.

MISSING DEVIANT DETECTIVE

Information has been received by this newspaper that ex-Detective Constable Trevor 'Jack' Frost, who was arrested, convicted and jailed in February 2002 for the serious sexual assault, rape and murder of a young girl, together with other drug-related offences, has gone missing from custody. Frost was serving eighteen years in prison. He was not due for parole and no appeal was in process. Frost has always vehemently denied committing the atrocities.

Neither Frost's ex-wife, nor anyone from his immediate family, has had any contact with him since his conviction and incarceration.

The Home Office has declined to comment. This newspaper has confirmed that Trevor Frost is not within the UK prison system. Frost's ex-wife is terrified that this dangerous, sexual deviant is at large and that she and their young daughter could be the target of an attack by him.

If you see this man, DO NOT approach him. He is dangerous. Inform your local police immediately.

Hywel let Valerie read the report and then showed it to his editor, who agreed to run it. The copy included some old library photos of Frost. The paper's legal team also cleared the article, so Hywel took it straight to Ted, May, Jean and Peter. All of them agreed it was good.

In the meantime, Valerie and Emma were taken to a house in the suburbs where she was settled in with a new mobile phone. She felt much safer.

The next day, the *Herald and Messenger* hit the streets. The article, which was accompanied by reports from the original trial, created a lot of interest, especially from the national newspapers. The telephones at the paper's office never stopped ringing.

Everyone was now waiting to see how the authorities would handle this catastrophe.

Chapter Five

A MEETING IS CALLED

Jack was bored, alone in the motorhome. To stop himself going crazy, he had read all the papers and magazines he could find there, especially old copies of the *Reader's Digest*. It was a good way of relaxing and filling the time. He liked the section called 'Humour In Uniform'. Jack had quite a few amusing anecdotes about his own time in uniform and he began to put them down in writing. It was just a hobby for now, but he clocked that the authors of such stories were paid for having them published. Maybe one day, he thought, he would send them off.

He had just finished lunch when Gerry called on his mobile to tell him about the newspaper article. He hated the headlines, but understood the depth of the story. The thought that Valerie was scared of him upset him deeply, and he desperately wanted to put her mind at rest.

He and Gerry had a lengthy discussion about the article, which had taken them both by surprise. Gerry explained they all they could do now was to sit and wait to see what happened. He insisted that Jack was not to contact anyone, neither Valerie nor his sister. The story was bound to make waves, especially when the national newspapers took it up.

Then they went through the security set-up, to ensure that

nobody could find out where Jack was hiding.

Jack told Gerry that he had been working out what had happened on the night he was arrested and the days leading up to it. He gave him the names of the colleagues who were with him, before and at the time of his arrest. Gerry also shared some discoveries which fitted the jigsaw of the complicated story of the murder. They agreed to meet up soon to compare notes and to make a list of the diminishing supplies that needed restocking for the motorhome.

At last, things were beginning to happen.

At the Home Office, the air was still very blue. An emergency meeting had been convened. Copies of the *Herald and Messenger* article were spread around the office. All the national newspapers, television and radio were demanding information and comment.

'Before we release anything to the media, we must find out where this bloody bloke has got to,' Sir Ponsonby-Smythe said. 'What do we know at this time?'

'He seems to have vanished into thin air. We've searched all our indices, but we've drawn a blank,' Harvey replied.

'What about the police?'

'They won't tell us anything. They are in the middle of a massive investigation to discover the true facts of the murder and the misinformation that led to Frost's arrest and conviction. There will be a few heads that will roll but right now they are very reluctant to inform anyone about their progress, except to confirm that Frost is entirely innocent. Until all the diplomatic connections in the enquiry have been exhausted, everything is top secret and no information is forthcoming. Frost's immediate release from prison was authorised by the Head of the CPS.' Harvey paused and then added, 'Might I suggest, Sir, that we delegate one of our officers to be attached to the police investigation for the duration, so that we are kept informed of their progress?'

'Good idea, get me the Commissioner on the phone now.'

The local newspaper article had also caused a massive stir at New Scotland Yard and the Press Bureau was bombarded with requests from media at home and abroad, all demanding further information.

Deputy Assistant Commissioner Gordon, in charge of the Serious Crime Squads in London, called a meeting of the investigation team that had been pulled together to reopen the case that involved DC Frost.

Present in the meeting room on the sixth floor were:

Deputy Assistant Commissioner Gordon;

Det. Supt. Fordham, assistant to the DAC;

Det. Ch. Insp. Chris Rice, SIO new Cold Case investigation;

DS Eddie Cramer, DS Pereira and DS Bell, part of the new investigation team with DCI Rice;

William Ryan, representing MI5;

Det. Ch. Insp Frazer, Special Branch;

Det. Supt. Brooker and DCI Cook, from the Cambridgeshire Constabulary, called in to oversee the enquiry as an independent team;

Paul Duncan, Head of Metropolitan Police Press Bureau;

Rupert Levy, Head of CPS;

Grant Harvey and Matthew Clarke, Home Office;

Yasmin King, stenographer;

Det. Insp. Mick Kennedy from the original investigation team.

A sweep by counter-intelligence officers confirmed there were no listening devices, and Detective Superintendent Fordham reminded everyone that the meeting was top secret. All information gathered should remain with the personnel present and was not for the public domain.

The SIO, DCI Rice, presented the facts, as far as they were known, beginning on the night of the murder.

'On the night of Friday, 24th November, 2000, a party was held at 171, Bromsgrove Terrace, N1, the home of a Mr Christopher Pagent, a self-employed finance broker, and a man of considerable wealth. Attending this party were approximately forty guests, male and female, all independently wealthy and some known to police. Among the guests were two young women, close friends, who had full diplomatic immunity in their own right, their fathers being diplomatic attachés at two different embassies in this country. One of the girls was an American, the other a Russian. Mr Pagent was not present at the party.

'The address was known to police for the regular use of drugs at the frequent parties held there and was the subject of observations by the Drug Squad from Westminster Police Station.

'On the night in question, the house was not under observation. The observations had been called off. The reason for this will become clear later.

'On that same night, DC Frost and other members of the Serious and Organised Crime Group were celebrating the birth of a baby daughter to Frost and his wife Valerie. All involved had booked off at the squad office and gone into town for a meal and drinks to wet the baby's head at the Two Chairmen Public House, here in Westminster. Afterwards, all went on to the Black Cat Club, in Soho. No officer was driving; they cabbed it everywhere.

'They were joined at the Black Cat Club by others who were known to the members of Trevor Frost's squad, but not to Trevor

Frost personally. A large volume of drink was consumed by everyone, including Frost.'

There were no questions yet from the DAC, but he and his detective superintendent were making numerous notes. Rice continued.

'From the interrogation of Frost after his arrest, it was established that he remembered leaving the Black Cat Club and going with some of his colleagues to another club, which he thought was in Mount Street, although he wasn't sure. He said it was dark and noisy, and he remembered he could smell cannabis and he wanted to get out, but he was given a lot more to drink by a very attractive female who spoke with a foreign accent. He couldn't remember who was there with him and he was pretty drunk. He said he may have fallen asleep at one stage.

'The next thing that he remembered was sitting in a big armchair in a large room in a private house, with people dancing to loud music and again the smell of cannabis. He didn't know how he got there, or who took him, but he admitted that he wasn't capable of getting there on his own.

'He remembered being given a drink. He claimed he didn't want any more, but the same foreign female forced it on him and made sure that he actually drank it. He did remember that WDS Kim Brown from his squad was there. She was a friend of the foreign girls and was also having a great time and said to him something like, "Don't worry, Jack, we'll get you home." Frost said he didn't remember anything after that until he woke up in police custody in the hospital.'

Rice looked up for a moment. Everyone was still paying attention.

'Sir, I'll now go on with the story as detailed by witnesses who were interviewed and gave evidence at Frost's trial.

'Police received an emergency call via 999 at 4.50am on the morning of the incident. The caller was a female by the name of Gloria Beesmont, who was at the party. She requested police attendance urgently as there had been a murder in the house; a female had been attacked.'

'Did she request an ambulance as well?' Gordon asked.

'No, Sir, which I agree was odd,' Rice answered.

'She must have known the girl was dead then... interesting.'

'Police arrived at the scene at 5.00am. On entering the house, uniformed PC Foster was shown to an upstairs bedroom. On the bed was the lifeless body of a young female. I have photographs here, Sir.' Rice handed over an album taken by the police photographer.

'Pretty gory,' said Gordon. 'What's all this over here? Blood?' He pointed to dark marks on the wall in one of the pictures.

'Yes, Sir.'

'Who showed the uniform officers into the house?'

'A female by the name of Miss Barbara Eames, a twenty-six-year-old bonds broker, works in Canary Wharf.'

The next photograph showed the body of a female laying on her back on a bed. She was naked and surrounded by blood. She had extensive injuries to her vaginal area and there were what appeared to be viscera on the bed.

'The organs that you see, Sir, around the body, had been manually removed via the vaginal cavity, so the post-mortem results indicate.'

A further two photographs also showed the victim and her injuries.

DCI Rice continued. 'The witness statements and the attending police officers report that DC Frost was present, slumped in a chair next to the bed. He was not responsive. He was not wearing trousers, just underpants, which were bloodstained, and his shirt, which was also bloodstained. He still had his shoes on. Both his hands were bloodstained and his left wrist and arm up to his elbow was also bloodstained. The blood proved to have come from the victim. DC Frost was photographed *in situ* by a police officer on his mobile phone. That is photograph 16 in your bundle, Sir.

'Police officers tried to rouse Frost, but he was totally unconscious and an ambulance was called. He was taken to St George's Hospital, and two police officers went with him. His clothes were seized for forensic examination.

'CID officers were summoned who then took over the murder case. I shall now break down the investigation.'

DAC Gordon interrupted. 'We are all aware of the details of the investigation, conducted by Detective Inspector Mick Kennedy — is that right?'

'Yes, Sir,' answered Rice. 'Frost was discharged from hospital after having his stomach pumped. He was taken to Canon Row Police Station where he was kept under observation until he was deemed fit to make a statement. Swabs of blood were taken from his arms, legs, groin and from his mouth, with his permission. He was examined by the divisional surgeon who stated he was fit to be detained and interviewed.

'He made a statement under caution, which was taken with no solicitor present and he answered all questions put to him. He stated he knew nothing about the incident, the female victim, or where it was supposed to have happened.'

'Remind us of the full details of the victim,' Gordon said.

'The victim was the thirty-one-year-old daughter of a high-ranking Russian diplomat, resident here in London. Her name was Natasha Popova. She was resident at the Russian Embassy and received diplomatic privilege because she was also part of the diplomatic function,' Rice detailed.

'She socialised in London with a mainly female group, mostly foreign nationals, who enjoyed the high life,' he continued. 'From what we can establish, fourteen persons were present that night. All have been traced and statements taken. Not all of them gave evidence in court. It was deemed by the prosecution counsel that this was unnecessary, given the impact of the forensic evidence,' DCI Rice concluded.

'Now, bring us all up to date,' the DAC requested.

'If I can come in here, Sir?' asked Rupert Levy. 'On collating all the evidence and information supplied to us by DI Kennedy, the original SIO, it was my decision to charge DC Frost with murder and sexual assault. Queen's Counsel Ms June Woodcock presented the case for defence to the court. It was obvious from the strong forensic evidence that DC Frost would be found guilty.'

DAC Gordon asked Detective Superintendent Brooker from the Cambridgeshire Constabulary if he was happy with the original investigation as it stood.

'Sir, I have gone through all the documentation and evidence, especially the forensic evidence, and found that all protocols were adhered to and nothing was overlooked. Perhaps more could have been done by DI Kennedy to clear up certain aspects, but he may have been swayed from doing this because of the tremendous strength of the forensic evidence.'

Rice again took up the report. 'Sir, DC Frost was found guilty at the Central Criminal Court on 14th February 2002 and was sentenced by Judge Lydia Craig to eighteen years imprisonment.'

Gordon intervened. 'So, Frost serves three years of his sentence and then what happens?'

'Correct, Sir. He was serving at HMP Stamford, from where,

I understand, he was released, at the behest of two Home Office agents who are here today, under the directions of Home Office Heads and in liaison with the CPS.'

Rupert Levy came in. 'Sir, we received instructions from Scotland Yard that new evidence has come to light. On April 12th this year, an American female, by the name of Anna Smelt, contacted the FBI in Washington, USA, and confessed to committing a murder in London. She used to work at the American Embassy in London but, at the time of her confession, was back in the United States. Apparently, she had found religion, and could no longer bear the burden of guilt on her conscience.

'A copy of her statement made to the FBI is on page 171 of your bundle. It outlines the circumstances of the murder. Anna Smelt and Natasha Popova were lesbian partners and were supplying and selling drugs in the UK. They used the money from the sale of the drugs to organise sex-slave-type parties and other nefarious activities. Popova brought the drugs into the UK via the diplomatic bag from Russia, and Anna Smelt had her drugs sent in from the USA in the same manner. They had a very wide circle of mutual friends which included many wealthy people of all sexes and ages. Both girls were users or addicts of the imported drugs, and both were earning a large income from their illegal trade.

'Detective Sergeant Kim Brown, part of DC Frost's Overseas and Organised Crime Squad, was acquainted with both Natasha Popova and Anna Smelt. According to Smelt's statement, Brown knew about the drug dealing and, in fact, was complicit in enabling it to continue. She had even transported some of the drugs across London for, and on behalf of, Natasha Popova and Anna Smelt.

'It turns out that DS Brown subsequently recruited others

for the drug runs and also supplied many other colleagues in the force and on her own squad with drugs. DC Frost was not one of her recruits.

'Incidentally, Sir, the reason why many of the organised drug busts in London failed is because they were tipped off by Brown. She was also the reason why the drug squads suspended their observations on the house that night as she supplied intelligence that the party was not going to go ahead.'

After a moment's pause, Rice continued. 'If I might read you a passage from the statement, Sir: on page 212, Smelt states, "Natasha and I had been making love in the bedroom. We were both naked and drunk and we had both taken shots of heroin. It was then I noticed a man passed out in an armchair in the room. Sometimes we had audiences whilst making love, but he was out cold. We began to argue about how much money we were making from the drug sales. Natasha accused me of taking more than my fair share and the argument got heated. We fought and Natasha made my nose bleed. I was on top of her. She was screaming and I was screaming and my hands were around her throat. I squeezed her throat and screamed at her when I suddenly realised that she was no longer breathing. I continued to scream when Kim Brown came in and pulled me off Natasha. She checked Natasha and said something like 'Leave this to me.'

"Brown then put her hands into Natasha's vagina and began to tear at her flesh. She went berserk. There was blood everywhere. She undressed the man in the chair and pulled his trousers down. She left the man's shoes on."'

Rice added, 'This is significant, Sir, because these details have never been published. She says more:

"Kim pushed something into Natasha's vagina — a knife or some other implement, I am not sure what it was — and began eviscerating her. She threw bits of Natasha's body around the room and, in particular, in the direction of where the man was still sitting unconscious in a chair. Some of the bloody flesh landed in his lap and some hit the wall next to him. There was blood everywhere. I couldn't understand what was happening, and she was shouting 'Get the Yank out of here.' I didn't mean to strangle Natasha. It happened in the heat of the moment and I was drunk and drugged up. I didn't know what I was doing.

"I went home by taxi. I was very ill for about two days. I got a text message from Kim Brown on an unknown number, asking me to ring her. She told me to leave £8,000 in a bag near her home. She needed to pay some people off. She then suggested that I return to the USA as soon as possible and say nothing to anyone about the incident. The next day I booked a flight home, where I have been ever since."'

Rice paused to let the full impact of Anna Smelt's statement sink in.

'She concludes by stating that she has recently received a message from God that she must repent of all her sins. She was accompanied to the FBI by the Bishop of her local church and her parents. Anna Smelt is now in custody in Washington. A new enquiry was set up and I was placed in charge of the team,' Rice concluded.

'DCI Frazer, have you something to input?' Gordon asked.

Frazer spoke slowly and distinctly. 'We at MI5 were contacted about twelve months ago by the Home Office Prison Service with information that Frost had been threatened with violence in prison from other inmates. Although regrettable, this was not unusual, Frost being an ex-police officer, but the situation became more serious when Frost reported to the warders that he had received the 'promise' of imminent death from a Russian prisoner on his cell block. Subsequently, it transpired that the Russian diplomat, father of Natasha Popova, deranged at the murder of his daughter, had vowed to take his revenge. He had allegedly taken out a contract for Frost's death. Frost, of course, knew nothing of the specifics.

'He was duly moved to Shepton Mallet Prison, where he was again subject to threats, and he was immediately placed into solitary. When he was finally moved to Stamford Prison, the threat seemed to diminish, and, although he was initially housed in a separate section for sex offenders and other deviants, he was eventually moved back to the main section. As we understand it, however, at this moment in time, the threat from the Russians remains. Ex-DC Frost is still in danger of his life.'

Rice again took up the narrative.

'On receiving the information from the FBI, a new investigation was opened, Sir, and I was put in charge. We began to trace everyone mentioned in Anna Smelt's statement, including DS Kim Brown, DS Karen Dewhurst and other witnesses. Kim Brown resigned from the police shortly after the result of the trial on health reasons, and we have not been able to trace her.

'Mr William Ryan from MI5, DCI Frazer from Special Branch and Mr Harvey and Mr Clarke from the Home Office, went as a delegation to the Russian Embassy to inform Mr Popov of the new information.

'Popov was inconsolable. He rejected the news and flew into a rage, saying this was a cover-up, fabricated to facilitate the release of the murdering police officer. Mr Ryan made it clear that MI5 had confirmed with the FBI that Anna Smelt's statement was genuine, and that she was currently in custody in America, pending the UK's request for extradition to be granted. Mr Popov threatened to take this matter up with the most senior diplomatic officers in London and Moscow. He then asked everyone to leave.

'As a result of this information, I contacted the Crime Prosecution Service who liaised with the Home Office, and it was decided to remove Frost from prison and place him in safe custody until the threat from the Russians could be resolved.'

Matthew Harvey joined in, and recounted the events of the night of Frost's release from Stamford. 'Owing to the lateness of the hour, we lodged him in a secluded hotel,' he finished. 'When we returned the following morning, he had gone.'

'Why was he placed in a hotel overnight? Why not the safe house?' DAC Gordon enquired.

With a certain amount of embarrassment, Harvey said, 'It was quite late at night, Sir, and Clarke and I decided that we would take Frost to the safe house the next morning. It was a poor decision on our part.'

'Was Frost told why he had been released and why you considered he was under threat from the Russians and that this American girl had confessed to the murder?' Gordon asked.

'No, Sir, we told him nothing.' Harvey looked sheepish.

There was silence for a few minutes, while everyone referred to their notes.

The DAC broke the silence. 'What a bloody mess. Where do we go from here? Detective Superintendent Brooker, what are your observations?'

'Setting aside the complications of the Russian angle and the fact that you cannot locate Frost, you must concentrate on finding the main suspects of the original murder: DS Brown, her female accomplice and the other party-goers who assisted her in this crime.'

'Rice?'

'We've set up an incident room with a hand-picked group of officers from the Met and from Cambridge. In the meantime, Sir, I suggest the combined efforts of the Met, MI5 and the Home Office concentrate on finding Frost and explaining to him the situation he is in and, lastly, I suggest we put together a well-worded press release, not giving out too much information but just enough to take the heat off the investigation.'

'I agree,' Gordon replied. 'Right, Chris, you and your team get on with the new investigation, pronto! MI5 and Special Branch — get your act together with the Home Office and get the Russian angle sorted out. Tread carefully when you come to the importation of drugs. You may want to include the Foreign Office in your discussions. God, this is so complex. Chris, do you have any leads on tracing DS Brown?'

'Not yet, Sir. One of the witnesses, a woman named Lisa Carlisle, who provided a statement and who gave evidence at the previous trial, has died. I believe it was suicide. Two other witnesses have gone abroad, but we have begun efforts with Interpol to trace them,' Rice replied.

The meeting went on for a further half an hour with suggestions on the way forward from everyone.

'So, to conclude, we have a dreadful mess to sort out,' the DAC said. 'We need to get Anna Smelt extradited from the USA, and we have to find Frost before the Russians do. Mr Duncan, can you and I get together after this meeting to get out a press release? And take note, everyone — I want to be kept in touch with every aspect of this case on a daily basis. Thank you all for your time.'

Chapter Six

INJUNCTION

Valerie Frost's new mobile phone rang.

'Yes?'

'Val?' It was her mum, May. 'I think you ought to consider taking out an injunction against Jack to ensure that if he was to threaten you in any way you will be covered by the law. Dad and I will pay for the lawyer.'

She considered the idea. She and Emma were reasonably secure and happy in the safe house provided by the *Herald and Messenger*.

'I don't know, Mum, we are pretty safe now. Jack can't find us here,' she said, but her thoughts ran on: what if Jack did find them? After all, he knew a thing or two about tracking people down. Perhaps it wouldn't hurt having an extra bit of security.

'Just do it. Dad and I will come with you. Where is the nearest Family Court to where you are?'

'I don't know, Mum. Watford or Brent, maybe? I'm not sure; I'll find out.'

Later that morning, Valerie contacted the Brent Family Court, who told her to get her solicitor to book a time with the court for a hearing.

She considered her original solicitor to be a bit of a twerp, so she asked the court receptionist if she could recommend a solicitor who dealt with family matters. She was given a name and phone number and, while she still had the momentum of her intention, she contacted them. She explained the complexity of the case, the reason for total secrecy and why she needed an injunction urgently. The solicitor agreed and within twenty-four hours Valerie was given an emergency court hearing for the following day.

Ted collected her and drove her to the court. They were shown into the private office of Circuit Judge, Wilma Braithwaite, who was sitting behind a large, polished desk.

'I fully understand, Mrs Frost, the reason for your request for this private meeting and hearing. Your solicitor has explained everything to me. I have been in contact with the Senior Investigating Officer at Scotland Yard who is investigating the disappearance of Trevor Frost and he endorses the application.'

The door opened, and a smart, middle-aged lady entered.

'This is Miss James, my secretary and clerk, who will assist.'

Everyone said good morning to each other.

'I will try and keep these proceedings as short and painless as possible,' Judge Braithwaite began. 'I know the full details of the case regarding your ex-husband and his conviction. I gather he is no longer in prison and no-one knows where he is?'

Valerie outlined the visit from the Home Office gentlemen and the enquiries made with Prisoner Locations.

'If Jack is out there, then there is a high risk that he will contact Valerie. I don't believe he would hurt her or Emma, but we must make sure,' Ted stated.

'Who's Jack?' The judge asked.

'I'm sorry, Your Honour, Jack is Trevor's nickname. You know, as in Jack Frost. Sorry, Ma'am.'

'I see, so let's get on with the official proceedings. From now on, this office is an official Family Court. Miss James will record all the details and findings and decisions made by myself. All decisions are final. Let me begin and declare that,

'One: Should Trevor Frost approach his ex-wife, Valerie Frost, in any way — by personal contact, by telephone or by post — he will be guilty of contempt of court. On conviction, he will be imprisoned; a term of imprisonment to be defined.

'Two: Should Trevor Frost in any way interfere with the lives and wellbeing of his ex-wife, Valerie Frost, or his daughter, Emma Frost, he will be guilty of contempt of court. On conviction, he will be imprisoned; a term of imprisonment to be defined.

'Three: Should Trevor Frost in any way cause any harm or distress to his ex-wife, Valerie Frost, his daughter, Emma Frost, or any member of their immediate family, he will be guilty of contempt of court. On conviction, he will be imprisoned; a term of imprisonment to be defined.

'Four: Should it be proved that any agent or other person connected to Trevor Frost, has caused interference with his wife, Valerie Frost, his daughter, Emma Frost, or any other member of the immediate family, he will be guilty of contempt of court. On conviction, he will be imprisoned; a term of imprisonment to be defined.

'I believe, Mrs Frost, these rules will protect you and your family. Miss James will now circulate these orders to all police forces, with immediate effect. Do you know who your ex-husband's solicitor is?'

'No,' said Valerie. 'I have no idea. The police might know, but they are telling me nothing.'

'This is a very unsettling time for you I know, but rest assured, Mrs Frost, that as soon as your ex-husband has been traced, he will be made aware of the restrictions placed upon him by this court. Should he infringe these, he will be imprisoned immediately, and your safety and the safety of your family will be assured.'

'I will prepare your copy of this court's findings; it won't take me long,' Miss James said. 'Please wait outside.'

Valerie and Ted thanked the judge for her time and said goodbye. They sat in the corridor and, within fifteen minutes, Miss James appeared and gave Valerie her copy of the injunction in an envelope.

As they left the court, Valerie began to cry. 'That it should come to this, Dad. We were so happy and then he did those dreadful things and I just had to break from him. He will never forgive me for divorcing him, but I just had to for Emma's sake.'

Ted put a reassuring arm around Val's shoulder. 'I still can't believe that Jack has done all of this. I liked him, you know that, Val, but the evidence was conclusive and all you could do is what you considered to be the right thing for you and the baby.'

Outside the court, Ted stopped. 'Right, I'm leaving my car here, Val. Let's get a taxi,' Ted said, ushering Val along the street.

'What's the matter, Dad?' Val said. 'Why are we getting a taxi?'

Just around the corner from the court, Ted managed to hail a black cab, and they got in quickly.

'Just drive, cabby, and make sure the big black BMW that is just coming round the corner doesn't follow us,' Ted said.

'Thanks, mate, I've always wanted to do this, just like in the films. Leave it to me. He won't be able to follow me where I'm going.'

'What black car, Dad? What's happening? You're scaring me.'

'I'm not taking any chances, that's all. When we walked up

the steps into the court, I noticed two men in a black car on the other side of the road, and they were still in the same place when we came out. I don't know who they are or what they want — maybe it's just coincidence — but, just in case, I thought it best to take a precaution. Whoever they are, they are not going to get us or find out where we are living,' Ted explained.

'Dad, I'm scared.'

'Not to worry, love, I'll lose them in just a minute. They won't follow me up here,' the cab driver piped up.

Ted kept watching out of the back of the cab. The black BMW was definitely following them.

Suddenly, the cab swerved off the main road into a narrow single lane then into a short tunnel. Out the other side, the driver swung immediately left into a no-entry with two sharp right-hand bends. Ted glanced back, but there was no sign of the BMW. Looked like they had lost it.

'There you are, that's knackered them. Where to now, Guv?' The taxi driver laughed.

'Drop us off at a tube station a little farther away, please, cabby, well done,' Ted ordered. 'Don't be too worried, Val; we can't be too careful just now.'

They got to a tube station, took a short journey, and then another cab to the safe house where Val's mum was waiting with Emma. Ted told May what happened in court and what happened when they came out.

'We must tell the police straight away. I'll —'

'No point,' Ted interrupted. 'I didn't get the bloody number of the car and anyway, they won't want to know.'

'You idiot! You didn't get the number? What were you thinking of?' May scolded Ted.

Chapter Seven

THE COMMISSIONER'S STATEMENT

It had been about ten days since the first meeting at Scotland Yard. It was decided that the time was right for the Commissioner to respond to persistent media demands for more information.

The statement had been well prepared and vetted by the Press Bureau at the Yard with the agreement of all agencies involved, including the Home Office and the Foreign Office. It was to be given by the Commissioner in person at an organised broadcast from the Yard to all the media, including television, radio and the world's press. In the large conference theatre on the third floor, everyone was assembled. A uniformed Chief Superintendent addressed the audience.

'The statement will now be made by the Commissioner. A full transcript will be made available afterwards. There will not be a question-and-answer session after the statement. There are no restrictions on publishing this statement.'

All went very quiet, and within a few minutes, the fully uniformed Commissioner entered and stood behind the podium on the stage.

'Good morning. As many of you know, nearly five years ago, a young lady was viciously sexually assaulted and murdered at a party in London. Mr Trevor Frost, a Metropolitan Police detective, was arrested at the scene and charged with her murder. He was tried at the Old Bailey and found guilty on the evidence presented to the court, and subsequently sentenced to a term of eighteen years in prison.

'Sixteen weeks ago, an American girl, who also attended that party, voluntarily presented herself to the FBI in Washington and admitted to being the perpetrator of that murderous attack. Officers from the Metropolitan Police travelled to Washington, where she was subsequently interviewed. The American girl has now been brought to the UK, so that the investigation can continue.

'As a result of the new evidence, it was concluded that the conviction of Frost was a wrongful conviction. The Director of Public Prosecutions and the Home Office decided to release him from custody immediately. Because of further investigations, it has been agreed that the location of Frost be kept secret and secure, until the new investigation is complete.

'I can now say that ex-detective Trevor Frost is completely innocent of the crimes of which he was convicted and for which he was imprisoned. He is exonerated of any blame and a complete pardon is pending.

'Further progress in these investigations will be released to the press when appropriate. Thank you.'

The Commissioner gathered his notes. Suddenly there was a barrage of shouting from the audience. The Chief Superintendent stepped forward and said, 'You were all informed that there would be no questions at the end of this statement. Thank you for your attendance and please collect your copies of the statement as you leave. Thank you.'

The statement was broadcast live on television and radio news, and was front page news in the evening papers.

Jack was relaxing in the motorhome, listening to music, all Country and Western and mainly Willie Nelson, when his mobile rang.

'Jack, Jack, have you heard? Have you seen the news yet?'

'No...'

'Turn the television on. The Met Commissioner has released a statement stating you are innocent, and that was the reason you were released.' Gerry was very excited.

'What do you mean, Gerry? You're not talking sense. What statement? When was this?'

'Not half an hour ago, the Commissioner issued a statement declaring that an American woman has admitted to the murder. You have been exonerated. It's all over the news. It's official: you are free and a pardon is expected in the very near future. Stay where you are, I'm coming over.'

Within the hour, Gerry arrived.

'What's this all about, Gerry? I've heard nothing on the radio and I can't get a proper signal on the tv.'

'Listen. A woman in America has confessed to the murder of the Russian that you were convicted of. The Commissioner said there was clear evidence that it *was* the American woman who was responsible for the murder and that you have been totally exonerated. That was why you were released.'

'If that was the reason, why was I secretly removed from prison? Why all the cloak-and-dagger and high secrecy?'

'I'll get in touch with the Yard, and inform them that I am now your instructed solicitor and request more information,' Gerry proposed.

'They'll want to know where I am, perhaps re-interview me. I'm not having that. I'm not going anywhere near them.' Jack was adamant.

'No worries, Jack. Client confidentiality comes into its own here. I'll not tell them anything. I'll use my phone from the office. What I might have to do is bring someone into our confidence to help sort this out so that if I am tailed or traced contacting you, your location is not compromised.'

'Who? Who are you going to get? I trust you, Gerry, but I don't seem to be able to trust anyone else anymore.' Jack was suddenly agitated.

'Thanks for your confidence, Jack. Don't worry, Lee is a good and loyal friend of mine. We were at law school together and we were flatmates for a few years. I know I can trust him and you will be able to as well.'

'Lee who?'

'Lee Wooding. He's the same age as me and single. Works for a firm in the same building as me, actually. Come to think of it, I could get *him* to ring the Yard and see what information he can get, and I can be left out of the frame altogether.'

Jack was apprehensive. 'Okay, if you say he's alright, but I'm still not sure.'

'Tell you what, Jack, how about we go out for a meal to celebrate tonight? Get you out of this motorised cell? I know an out-of-the-way place. I could get Lee to meet us and we could talk over our next moves. He still won't know where you are located if that makes you feel a little safer?'

'That's a great idea. It would be good to get out of here. Don't think I'm being ungrateful, Gerry, but up until now I have trusted no-one, only you. After all, everyone else I trusted has shat on me from a great height. All this secret squirrel business is beginning to spook me.'

'That's understandable. Great, I'll phone Lee now. How about a slap-up Chinese meal in a lovely little restaurant I know?'

'Great,' said Jack. 'I'll get changed.'

They were just about to leave when Gerry, fiddling about with the signal on the portable television in the motorhome, found a news programme about to start.

'Jack, quick, come and see this!'

Together, they watched the broadcast which transmitted the Commissioner's statement in full.

'Bingo!' shouted Gerry. 'What did I tell you? There you are. They're making out they know where you are but *we* know that they don't. They're in a bit of a fix, I'd say.'

'It was good to hear that from the Commissioner's own mouth. He can't go back on that, can he? But why all the secrecy about my release? I wonder what's going on with this American woman, and what she has told the police. It's all bloody complicated,' Jack exclaimed.

'That's why there's a brand-new investigation, but I'll get Lee to find out more. Come on, Jack, I'm starving, let's go.'

They didn't talk much until they reached north London. Jack recognised pubs and shops as they passed.

'Too many memories around here, Gerry. It's a bit painful. Val and I went to some of those pubs in our happier days.' Jack sounded sad.

'Cheer up, Jack, delicious food will lift your spirits. Lee is meeting us there.'

They managed to park just off the Regent's Park Road and they walked, cautiously, around the corner and into a lovely, little Chinese restaurant.

Lee — slim, fairly good-looking and smartly dressed — was sitting at a table in a corner at the rear of the main restaurant, and Gerry and Jack joined him. Introductions made, they sat down and perused the menu. They ordered their food, and then Gerry said, excitedly, 'Well, what did you find out, Lee?'

'Guys, you won't believe what I have found out. It is truly amazing. It's like a spy thriller,' Lee began. 'Gerry filled me in, Jack, on the whole story, and, as he suggested, I contacted the Yard and was put in touch with a DS Cramer who is investigating the latest information regarding the murder of the Russian woman. They are desperate to contact you. When I pressed them as to why, all they would say was that they are of the opinion that you could be in danger from an outside agency, as that agency believes you are still guilty, and that your release is a smoke-screen to protect our own and distort the truth.'

'What else did this Cramer say?' asked Jack.

'He said he needed to speak to you about the people you remembered from the night of the murder. Again, I pressed him as to why and he opened up a bit, revealing that the father of the murdered woman was a Russian diplomat. The victim, and the woman they now believe to be the real murderer, also had diplomatic immunity. When he was told that the American woman had confessed to the murder, the father refused to believe it. He still blames you for what happened to his daughter. He wants to find you.'

'This is crazy,' said Jack. 'They don't need to speak to me. I've already told them everything I know. I don't know anything about Americans and Russians. I don't want to speak to anyone. I've got nothing to say.'

'No worry there, Jack, you're not speaking to anyone but us. Did this Cramer mention anyone else, Lee?' Gerry asked.

'He didn't, no, but he did say that the other detectives who gave evidence in court against you were also under investigation, and that there were further arrests to be made. I have to say, he was most insistent that he needed to speak to you, Jack. I didn't promise him, but I told him that I would see what I could do. This is big, guys, but be in no doubt, Jack, we will protect you and your anonymity throughout.'

'Thanks, Lee, you've done very well. Things are a bit clearer now.' Jack shook Lee's hand.

The first course arrived.

'Lots of time for further discussion later. Grub up, enjoy,' Gerry said.

All three enjoyed the meal, including a few beers, although Jack was careful not to drink too much.

Gerry changed the subject of conversation and talked about the antics he and Lee got up to at law school. Jack enjoyed himself. It was good to laugh at stories that had nothing to do with the situation he found himself in.

After the meal, they all went back to Lee's flat, which was not far away in Camden Town. It was a comfortable, one-bedroom flat, quite modern. Jack began to relax and, with a belly full of good food, he made himself comfortable in an armchair and began to doze. Meanwhile, Gerry and Lee discussed their next moves.

Lee had a full copy of the Commissioner's statement and they went through it, word by word, paragraph by paragraph, adding in the information that he had obtained from Cramer.

'We have to find out more, and see how far they've got with the new investigation,' Gerry said. 'But without Jack seeing or speaking to them, it's going to be hard. It's obvious that all the people who gave evidence against Jack were lying. Back in the motorhome, I have the list of called witnesses who gave evidence. If we go through each one, perhaps we can get a picture of what went on that night.'

'To put the full blame on Jack, forensic evidence must have been falsified,' Lee said.

'Next move, Lee, I think, is to prepare a reply from ex-detective Trevor Frost to be published through a Press Agency, in reply to the Commissioner's statement,' Gerry suggested.

'Not too soon though. Let them all sweat.'

'Good idea. First, I must find Jack somewhere to live and get him out of that motorhome of mine — perhaps a flat similar to this.'

'What about money, has he got any?' Lee asked.

'Jack has nothing, but if all goes to plan, he should receive a large sum in compensation. He wants nothing to do with any money from the newspapers for an exclusive, so until the compensation comes through, I can bank roll him,' Gerry said.

'I've got some spare cash as well. He's welcome to it, poor bugger. He's really been served a bad hand,' Lee added.

'What are you doing tomorrow, Lee? Jack and I have already started a sequence-of-events document about what happened that fateful night, including a list of those present, as far as he can remember. Perhaps the three of us can start piecing all this together. There's a lot more to this than meets the eye. Do you think you'll be able to continue with this? After all, I want to stay away from the police, as they know I am connected to Jack.'

'I have a couple of appointments, but could be with you by about one o'clock, if that's okay. Believe me, Gerry, I'm with you all the way. I can handle the police, don't worry.'

'We might have to take a bit of time off work to sort this out. I'm owed a few days anyway,' Gerry declared.

'Me too,' Lee said. 'I've got over two weeks' holiday owing, and Jack is going to need all the help he can get.'

'Yes, but only from the right people. People that we can trust.

With the Russians involved, who knows what can happen?'

Gerry woke Jack. 'Time to get back to the motorhome. I'm going to ask Lee to come up and join us there tomorrow — is that okay with you? We'll go through everything, and then prepare a statement from you to be issued to the media.'

'Sure.'

Gerry scribbled down directions for Lee, adding, 'I'll pick you up from the station if you ring me when you're there.'

The next day, after breakfast, Jack got out all the papers that he and Gerry had been working on, and was feeling optimistic about sorting out the mystery behind the Russian and American involvement.

Gerry and Lee arrived at about noon. Over coffee, they discussed the events of the previous day.

'The Commissioner's statement was clear that the reason you were released was because you have been exonerated. He also gave the impression that the police know where you are.' Gerry paused. 'I think we should, at this stage, reply to the Commissioner's statement with a statement of our own, Jack.'

'A very carefully worded statement — yes, I agree,' said Lee. 'However, I have some bad news, Jack. Sergeant Cramer contacted me this morning and informed me that a court injunction has been issued against you by your wife. If you contact her, or her family, in any way, you will be in contempt of court and risk immediate imprisonment.'

'Injunction? Contempt of court? Why? I wouldn't hurt Val or our daughter. I love them, for God's sake. Why is she doing this to me?' Jack was beside himself.

'Calm down, Jack, this is even more reason for you to stay hidden away from everyone. It would have been a natural move for Val to take out an injunction. She probably applied for it before the Commissioner made his statement. Nonetheless, let's stay focused. Where's that list of witnesses who gave evidence against you?' Gerry asked.

Lee started slowly, 'We now know that those witnesses lied.'

'And,' Jack jumped in, 'someone must have tampered with the forensic evidence!'

'True. They say forensic evidence doesn't lie, but, at some point, before the police collected it for submission to the labs, that evidence was *made* to lie — and that lie convicted you,' Gerry said.

'Who took you to that house, Jack? Can you remember?'

'No, I can't. At the drink-up, there was Kim Brown, who was my DS, and Karen Dewhurst, a DC, both from my squad, and a few of their friends, male and female. I do remember Karen saying she would look after me, and we got a taxi, I think, from the club to the house, but I'd had so much to drink.'

'Was there anyone else from your squad there?' Lee asked.

'No, not at the house, I don't think. There were quite a few at the pub and then at the club, but I am not sure about afterwards.'

'Who are Jennifer Wilson, Barbara Hancock, Lisa Carlisle and Patrizia Rossi?' asked Gerry. 'They all gave evidence against you.'

'I don't know any of them. Even when I saw them in court, I didn't recognise them. It was like I'd never seen them before,' Jack admitted.

'I didn't want to bring this up at this point, but did it not occur to you that these females were all batting for the other side? You know — lesbians?' Lee asked.

'I knew Kim Brown was gay, and Karen, but that made no difference to me. They were both terrific coppers and good friends of mine. I trusted them with my life. No, being gay had nothing to do with it,' Jack exclaimed.

'What do you remember about the American girl?'

'Nothing,' Jack answered.

Gerry leaned forward. 'And the Russian girl, the victim?'

'All I remember is this woman with a foreign accent gave me a drink. She was laughing and telling me to drink it up. I have no idea if she was Russian; I have no idea if she was the victim. I didn't recognise her from the police photographs I was shown,' Jack replied. Then after a pause, he whispered, 'I can't believe Valerie would even think I would hurt her.'

Chapter Eight

JACK'S STATEMENT

'How about coming back to London with me, and we shall see if we can find you a place to live permanently?' Gerry suggested.

'How can I? I haven't got a pot to piss in. I might as well be back in that shit-hole of a prison,' Jack replied, very despondent.

'Look, you two, let's concentrate on the statement we are going to release. What do you want to say, Jack?' Lee changed the topic of conversation and the mood.

'Let me say just briefly that I want to be left alone and not be bothered by anyone until everything is over,' Jack suggested.

'You've got to fill it out a bit, Jack.' Gerry grabbed a pad and pencil.

'Alright, how about this? "In response to the statement made by the Commissioner of the Metropolitan Police, I, Trevor Frost, have no wish to take part in any investigation conducted by the police, working on new information that they may have received. I have always pleaded my innocence of the crime for which I was charged, tried and convicted, and I hope that this new investigation gets to the truth of the matter. I am grateful to have been released from wrongful imprisonment and until completion of the new police investigation I will be making no further comments." Does that work?'

'Brilliant,' said Lee.

'Spot on,' said Gerry. 'We'll put this out, probably via Reuters, and then nobody can come back at us.

'I have already declared that I am working for Jack, so after this we had better not meet, and only communicate through Gerry,' Lee said. 'Okay with you, Gerry?'

'Fine. They are bound to be up your arse though, day and night, trying to find Jack.'

'When shall we put this out?' Jack asked.

'Not yet,' said Lee. 'Let them sweat. The most important thing at the moment, is to find you some more creature comforts and a permanent place to live. You are no longer a prisoner, and you should be able to live somewhere better than this.' He gestured around. 'No offence, Gerry.'

'As I've said, I haven't got a pot to piss in. I have nothing, no money, no bank account, nothing.' Jack held out his open palms.

'We've got that covered, Jack, don't worry. Let's get house hunting,' Gerry said.

Back in north London, they picked up a couple of local papers which advertised flats and houses. They bought three new Pay-As-You-Go mobile phones and then went to Lee's flat.

'I wish I could find somewhere near Val and Emma,' Jack said, wistfully, as they went through the property-for-rent pages.

'No, you don't, Jack,' Gerry insisted. 'I'm really getting pissed off with you. If you were even to be seen in the same supermarket as her, you would be nicked and sent straight back to prison. Do you want that?'

'I'm sorry, I know you're right. I'm in your hands, I won't mention Val again. Sorry, mate.'

They began again to search through potential properties, but Jack's heart wasn't really in it.

'I want to write to Valerie and put her mind at rest,' said Jack. 'Just to let her know I'm alright and that I still love her and Emma.'

'No!' Both Gerry and Lee were emphatic.

'That's exactly what you don't do. Any contact will be a reason for arrest.'

'I want to see Val and my baby girl. I haven't seen them in years,' Jack pleaded.

'You can't do that, Jack, the injunction in force will guarantee that you go straight back to prison,' Gerry said.

'But I'm innocent! The Commissioner said so publicly,' Jack protested.

'Of the murder, yes, Jack, but this is a separate case, and a separate judge has said that if you go anywhere near Val, or contact her or her family, you are guilty of Contempt of Court and they will put you away again.'

'Jack, concentrate on now. Are you happy with that statement we put together?' Lee asked.

'Yes, I'm sorry, lads, let's get to it. When shall we release it to the press?'

'I'll contact Reuters in London, and fax a copy over to them, tomorrow morning about ten o'clock. That will give them time to circulate the news to all media across the country and the world. I will fax it from my office, and I will have all calls vetted before they reach me. In fact, I will have all calls turned around; I will answer none of them,' Lee said.

'Right,' said Gerry. 'Let's get all this sorted out. First the phones. Let's make sure we are added as contacts. We only call each other with important info; no idle chit-chat. If you leave the motorhome or the flat, only go out at night, no roaming around. After tomorrow, your picture will be all over the papers again.'

'What flat?' said Jack.

'All in good time,' answered Gerry. 'Got to get you some transport, too, but before that we must create a new identity, and get some documents for you.'

'I can arrange all that,' said Lee. 'In our profession, we get to meet some very interesting and helpful characters. All I'll need is a photograph of you and a new name. What name do you fancy, Jack?'

'I don't know. Something simple. William Harris, perhaps?'

'Great,' said Gerry.

During the afternoon, they viewed four flats but none were suitable. Furnished flats were all a bit tatty: cheap furniture and appliances. The last on the list was a first-floor flat in Belsize Park. It was nice: a pleasant area and the flat was well-appointed.

Jack agreed it was exactly what he needed, and Gerry made all the arrangements, using the name William Harris. For the payment of a hefty deposit, the first month's rent, and a generous consideration for the agent in lieu of a credit check, Jack would be able to move in the next day. As soon as that was signed off, the three men went shopping for food and other provisions.

That night, they all went back to Lee's place.

'We've got you a new name and a new address. All I need now is a photograph, and I'll get the documents under way. You can stay here tonight, Jack, and move into your new home tomorrow.'

'Great, I'll get your stuff from the motorhome and bring it along. I'll pick you up in the morning and move you into the new flat,' said Gerry.

There was still a lot to sort out, but they had had enough for the day.

In the main incident room of the new enquiry, DS Cramer went into DCI Chris Rice's office.

'I've been contacted by a Mr Lee Wooding, who says he's a solicitor for Trevor Frost, and wants to know what's going on.'

'Great. At last, we have a small breakthrough — did you find out where Frost is?'

'Sorry, Sir. No.'

Rice gave a sigh but kept his temper. He had had Smelt interviewed again, and was totally satisfied that, given the details she was able to provide, she was indeed responsible for the death of Natasha Popova. There were details in her confession which had never been published. Therefore, he concluded, she had to have been there and, so, it was reasonable to assume that her assertion of her own guilt was valid.

When she realised that she had killed Natasha, Smelt said she went to pieces, and that Kim Brown had taken over and caused the other horrific injuries to the dead girl, including producing enough forensic evidence to implicate Frost.

Smelt described how Kim Brown had done this, with the help of Karen Dewhurst and two others. She only knew their Christian names as 'Jennifer' and 'Lisa': that would have been Jennifer Wilson and Lisa Carlisle. All four had given evidence at Frost's trial. Smelt declared that she had personally witnessed all this before she was taken out of the house.

Warrants had been obtained for the arrest of Kim Brown, who had since resigned from the police force, and Karen Dewhurst, who had also resigned, and was believed to be living in Australia.

Details of the other girls, Jennifer Wilson, Barbara Hancock, Lisa Carlisle and Patrizia Rossi, had all been circulated, but, so far, none had been traced.

The biggest problem for Rice was the Russian connection to the enquiry. Neither the Foreign Office, the Home Office, nor any of the senior management from the police could convince Mr

Popov that the American girl's confession was genuine and true. He continued to believe it was a conspiracy to free Trevor Frost from prison and to have his country's diplomatic advantages questioned.

'We must find Frost ASAP,' said Rice. 'God knows what the Russians will do to him if they catch him. How did you leave it with this Wooding guy?'

'He is cooperating but, citing client confidentiality, he won't tell us where Frost is. I intend to ring him on a daily basis just to keep the contact going. I also told him that Valerie Frost had taken out an injunction against her ex-husband. She must have taken it out before the Commissioner made his statement, so she wasn't aware that Frost was not responsible for the murder.'

'Bloody hell. Why didn't anyone tell her? Now, we will never find him. Give me her phone number.'

'We don't have it, Guv,' Cramer confessed, sheepishly. 'She's moved out of her home, and we can't trace her yet. Now that Frost knows there is an injunction out, I doubt if he would go anywhere near her.'

Really, Rice thought, despairingly, things could not have gone worse.

In the offices of MI5, questions were being asked about the movements of Russian agents.

They had been observed and followed to the address of Valerie Frost's parents. They had followed her father to Brent Family Court. When the Frosts left court and hailed a taxi, the Russians followed them but lost them after a few streets.

Unbelievably, this information had not been passed to the incident room or to anyone else for that matter.

In the offices of Special Branch, the same applied. They were aware of the injunction on Trevor Frost but apart from that they knew nothing.

Lee Wooding wasted no time. Having taken a picture of Jack, he contacted an old client and ordered a driving licence and a birth certificate in the name of William Harris. He was told it would take about two days. He also obtained an application form for a passport, but that would take longer. He also drew out £2,000 cash to give to Jack.

The next day, all three went to the flat that was now rented in the name of William Harris. Jack got settled in, with the help of Gerry and Lee.

'Right, I'm off now to the office to release your statement to Reuters,' Lee said, once they were all in. 'Be ready with the television and radio and wait for it to hit the news.'

'Thank you, Lee, for everything,' said Jack. 'Especially for the money, but I don't know where I'm going to spend it.'

'You'll need to grow a beard, Jack — I mean Bill — then you can go out, but even then, be careful. Buy a newspaper and some food, but no pubs or clubs,' Gerry said.

Back at his office, Lee faxed Jack's statement over to Reuters' London office and waited for the backlash. Within ten minutes he was contacted by the news desk to check the authenticity and to confirm they had permission to circulate it. An hour later, DS Cramer also contacted him to authenticate the statement and again asked for the location of Jack.

'Jack has no wish to be contacted and will not be making any further statements.'

'Can you tell us what shape he is in?'

'I wish to state categorically that I have not met Trevor Frost in person. All contact has been by phone.'

'And you are certain that the person you are dealing with is not an impersonator?'

'I am. And I can confirm that I hold a letter of confirmation from Mr Frost that I am authorised to act on his behalf.'

'Are you or Frost at all conscious of the Russian danger in this investigation?'

'I can assure you that Mr Frost is fully aware of the gravity of his situation.'

After the call, Lee phoned Gerry and, in turn, Gerry phoned Jack.

'Start watching the news from now on, Jack. The agency has put your statement out.'

In the offices of the Metropolitan Police, MI5, Special Branch, the Home Office, the Foreign Office and at the Russian Embassy, things were buzzing. Everyone wanted to speak to Jack.

Chapter Nine

LIVING A LIE

Six weeks went by with no spectacular incidents either in the new investigation or in Jack's life. Christmas and the New Year came and went without celebration.

He was lonely and bored, and cautious about going out in case he was recognised. Gerry had brought him a few more magazines, to keep him amused. Reading 'Humour in Uniform', he remembered the notes he'd made on his own experiences, back in the motorhome. Using the laptop that Lee had loaned him, he started typing them up. More ideas came to him — some true, some fictitious, some jokes that he converted into humorous stories — and he wrote them all down. He decided to send them off, using his new name, William Harris.

Lo and behold, the *Reader's Digest* sent him a cheque for £250 for four stories and, in their correspondence, asked Jack for more. In addition to this, having read articles in popular magazines, Jack found he often had a logical and reasonable comment to make about the content. He decided to put his opinion into print, and again, after submitting them, his responses were accepted.

The editors of two of the high-profile magazines wrote to Jack asking if he would like to submit a monthly article on any subject he wanted. They obviously liked his style of writing and, of course, they were willing to pay him for them.

This was good for Jack: he could get out of his system all his pent-up anger and feelings, and get paid for it. The income from these writings wasn't marvellous, but it made Jack feel better to be earning a wage. Nothing great, nothing life changing, but it helped him feel he was getting back to some sort of normality

When his time wasn't occupied by writing, he kept thinking about Val and little Emma. Little? She wouldn't be very little now, after all this time. She had turned five in November. Jack had spent the day in bed, mourning the fact that he could not send her a present or a card.

His thoughts kept returning to how things used to be, when life was normal — their house, their respective families, and the fun times he and Val used to have together. The memories upset him, and, just as he had in prison, he came to the conclusion that he should try and put thoughts of his family to the back of his mind. He was going stir crazy; he had to get out, so, making sure he was not being followed, and hoping he would not be recognised, he ventured out onto the street.

He had grown a short beard and let his hair grow, and he wore an anorak with a hood to hide his features, if necessary.

Lee had come up with the driving licence and passport in the name of William Harris. The passport Jack left at home, but he put the driving licence in the pocket of his anorak. Thoughtfully, Lee had also opened a bank account in name of William Harris and bank cards were issued. For convenience, Lee was going to have access to the account, which contained £4,000: two thousand from Gerry and two thousand from himself. Jack had no idea how he was going to repay them. The income from his articles would only go so far.

Lee had suggested that Jack buy a cheap, second-hand car,

just to potter around in. Together, they went to a car sales place in the back of Camden Town, run by a friend of Lee's, and bought — with some haggling — a little Nissan Sunny saloon with 68,000 miles on the clock. They got the price down to £800 and Jack paid with his newly obtained credit card. The salesman assured him it was a good little runner, one old lady owner from new. Bollocks, thought Jack; that little old lady must have done a few thousand miles each day! But it was clean, and it would do.

Jack posted the paperwork to DVLC and, after finding some cheap insurance, collected the car. Before he returned to the flat, he took a trip around some of the places he used to know. It was a great feeling to be mobile again, though it was sobering how many of the places and buildings had changed or been pulled down, while he had been inside. Life changes quickly, he reflected.

Shortly after getting the car, Jack took a nostalgic trip to see the house where he had happily lived with Valerie. He parked up and stared at the house. Memories were running through his head. Happy memories. Remembering the new furniture they had bought. Decorating the rooms and the laughter of family and friends at the house-warming party.

The words and music of one of Jack's favourite songs, *She is Gone* by Willie Nelson, ran through his head. He knew it off by heart. He thought he could still feel Valerie's presence in the air, just like the song. His heart ached for the love that he had lost. He thought of the line 'And now my life will never be the same again' and reflected how true that was. It was as if the song had been written for him.

A short distance from their old house was a park, where he and Valerie had often walked. Jack remembered that it was on one of those walks that Valerie had told him she was pregnant. He had been over the moon. They were both so happy. Jack couldn't wait to tell Jean and Peter that they were going to be an auntie and uncle and when, that evening, they told Valerie's mum and dad, everyone was ecstatic. They had celebrated until the early hours.

Five minutes down the road was their local pub. A proper pub, not a wine bar or bistro. This warm, friendly establishment sold real ale and Guinness, and the best of all was the good English food, cooked the proper way. Jack and Valerie had eaten there three or four times a month.

With no thought to his security, or wariness about being watched or followed, Jack sauntered into the pub and ordered a pint of Guinness from the barmaid. He didn't recognise her.

It was the first Guinness he had had in years. It tasted like nectar and he almost ordered another one.

There was no sign of the original landlord or landlady, and Jack suddenly realised he had been careless with his security. He stopped himself asking the barmaid who owned the pub now. He looked around the bar. It wasn't very crowded and none of the customers was paying him the slightest attention.

He came to his senses, and decided not to push this new-found freedom any further. He left. God, that pint had tasted good, Jack thought, but discretion was the better part of valour. He grabbed some provisions from the local store, and returned to the flat.

On the laptop, Jack jotted down all the little things that came into his head, in case he forgot them. Silly things, like his previous car's registration number, the old address of his dentist, names of his old police mates, anything that came into his head. Over a couple of nights, he went over the notes he'd made with Gerry when he first got out of prison.

Jack thought it was about time they had another 'scrum down' about the facts as they knew them. Both Gerry and Lee were keen, especially as Lee had some great news and Gerry also had some theories of his own which he wanted to share. It was planned for a Friday night and to make things a bit special they ordered an Indian take-away.

Jack had it all set out. The runners and riders of the so called 'witnesses' who gave evidence against him and all the other forensic evidence that was produced and submitted. They sifted through the information on the table.

Lee couldn't contain himself. 'I can't keep this to myself any longer. I have some great news, Jack.'

'Yes, it's about time, Lee. Spit it out,' said Gerry.

Lee began, 'I've been contacted nearly every day by the investigating team at the Yard. They still want to know where you are and urgently want to speak to you.'

'I bet they do,' said Jack.

'This is the best part. I told them that my client' — Lee pointed at Jack — 'that's you, will be seeking substantial compensation for the loss of his marriage, his job, his property, his family, his whole life as he knew it. I told them that until such time as a settlement is in place, there will be no cooperation by my client.'

'This is going to cost them quite bit. What figure shall we start with? £250,000?' Gerry said.

'Yes, for starters,' Lee said, 'but I think for the loss of someone's freedom, and his way of life it could be more.'

Jack didn't seem too enthusiastic. 'I'm not interested in the money. I just want to stop living this lie, I want to start all over again. Get my wife back, get my daughter back, get my life back.'

'Look, I understand. This is what they've told me so far,' Lee interrupted. 'DS Cramer has told me they have traced Kim Brown to Amsterdam and warrants for her arrest have been applied for. Her 'mate', Karen Dewhurst, is also living in Holland somewhere; again, warrants have been issued for her arrest. Of the other four who gave evidence against you, Jennifer Wilson has been arrested in Australia and they are waiting for extradition proceedings to bring her back to the UK. Lisa Carlisle is dead — she committed suicide about two years ago, went off Beachy Head. Barbara Hancock has changed her name and is believed to be living in Manchester; still no exact location for her. Lastly, Patrizia Rossi has been arrested and is currently in custody with no bail.'

Lee paused to let this sink in, then continued. 'Investigations are still ongoing but the theory is that the girls were importing drugs into the UK via their diplomatic baggage allowances and distributing them across London with the help of their Met friends. By the way, Jack, I was right. All of them — the victim and this Anna Smelt and their police friends — they were all lesbians,' Lee finished.

'There's nothing wrong with lesbians, there's nothing wrong with gays,' Jack reiterated. 'They are smashing people, good company. People who want to lead their own life their own way. Good luck to them.'

'Right. But what I am saying, Jack, is that it was a large, organised group of these women who stitched you up for this murder and then sat and watched while you were convicted.'

'Lee is right. Look at the scenario: victim Natasha Popova meets up with suspect Anna Smelt and they become partners. They organise the importation of drugs. No-one is going to intercept diplomatic bags. These two pass the drugs on to their contacts in London aided by two detectives from the Met who ensure that their distribution network is not interrupted or raided,' Gerry pointed out.

'And then,' Gerry continued, 'they recommended a solicitor to you, didn't they? What was her name?'

'Ms Freeman,' Jack replied.

'Ms Freeman, yes, that's right, fucking useless. She gave you no help at all. Then, when you got to Crown Court, you were represented by a female barrister, Ms Woodcock, who was about as welcome as a fart in a spacesuit. Are you seeing a pattern here? She didn't conduct any defence at all, Jack.'

'No, but she didn't have a great deal of ammunition for a defence, did she?' Jack replied. 'All the evidence was weighted against me. You can't ignore the forensics, Gerry.'

'You can, once you realise the forensics could have been planted. Yes, there was blood transference from the body to you. Yes, your DNA was found on the body. But Kim Brown took charge that night, and she made sure the forensic technicians didn't miss a thing. On top of that, she and Karen Dewhurst organised your solicitor, who in turn lined up your barrister. It wouldn't surprise me if they were not all in on it. I did say from the beginning that this was big,' Gerry finished.

'No, not Kim! She was my friend; she wouldn't have done such a thing. I knew she was very friendly with a lot of the girls, but it made no difference to me. She was a great copper, honest and trustworthy. I trusted her all the way,' Jack said.

Lee spoke quietly and slowly. 'This Smelt girl from America must have told them something in her interviews that has never been published to the media and that never came out in evidence or court. Something only someone present could have known. Otherwise, as you say, the evidence against you was overwhelming. Kim Brown and the others must have done everything to convict you to save themselves from being implicated. Can you think of anything, Jack, that you did or found out that would have scuppered their dealings in any way?'

'No. But everything I did was recorded. Everything — all the details of my observations and the investigations into those notes — was written down and handed in for intelligence.'

'What happened to those notes and reports?' Gerry asked.

'I handed them to Kim.' A chill ran down Jack's back. 'Oh my God! They had all the notes. They had all my observations and Rod's as well.'

'So, they had all your information and knew that you were getting close to adding two and two and making five.'

'Who suggested going out to wet the baby's head?' Lee asked.

Jack was silent as another level of realisation dawned. 'Kim.'

'So, before I pump Cramer for any more information, let's write down what we think happened,' Lee said.

'First, Jack, can you remember any of the notes you made regarding the observations on the last few weeks before that night and your arrest?'

Jack thought for a short while. 'We had been given about six addresses to look at by Intelligence, regarding drug dealing on a major scale. Rod and I had been given two of the addresses.'

'Rod being Rod Beckett, your partner? I don't believe he gave evidence at your trial — why was that?' Lee asked.

'He'd been off sick that last week with a chest infection. He didn't come out for the drinks,' Jack explained. 'On one of the last observations, we recorded lots of car numbers and recognised a few of the faces that attended this big party... That's right, I remember. Rod saw something or somebody and he got out of our car and made off on his own to get a closer look. Shortly after that there was a massive, uniformed police raid. I saw a girl being dragged from the target house into the garden of the house next door, and bundled into a black or dark blue Mercedes. The car drove off at speed. I followed it to Kensington Park Gardens, which is gated, of course, where it went through and disappeared. I'd got part of the numberplate, and I managed to obtain the owner details through a contact of mine. The owner was linked to the Russian Embassy.' Jack stood bolt upright. 'Bloody hell! That's possibly where the Russian connection comes in. I've been so slow.'

'Where did that information go?' Gerry asked.

'Into my fucking notes! And I got a bollocking from the Governor for leaving Rod behind. I gave those fucking notes to DS Kim fucking Brown.'

'We're getting there now, Jack, this is brilliant,' Lee piped up. 'Can you remember anything about the other addresses?'

'Not really, other than there were quite a few aborted drug raids on premises in north London, and Intelligence thought there was a leak on when the raids were going to be. That was why we had been called in to investigate. A lot of the new information came to us from the Obscene Publications Unit at the Yard.'

'So, we can say that you were getting close to those people who were responsible for the importation of large amounts of drugs into London?' Lee said.

'Not close, but certainly, with all the team, we could probably have got some good arrests. But nothing to do with diplomats or even sex parties,' Jack pointed out.

Lee was writing this information down.

'You can't give all this to Cramer. We have no proof of our suspicions,' Jack pointed out. 'We have no idea, really, that any of it is true.'

'I'm not giving our ideas to Cramer, but I am waiting to hear what other information he drip-feeds me, to see if it fits in with our thinking,' Lee said.

'When will you hit them with the £250,000 compensation figure, Lee?' asked Gerry.

'Not right away. When they're really desperate to speak to Jack, they may play ball. They already know that we are considering compensation,' Lee replied.

'So, what is taking their time? They must know half of what we've worked out — they are not that thick. It's taking ages, and what about this pardon? When is that coming? I want to stop living this lie. I don't want to be William Harris.' Jack was ranting.

'Calm down, Jack, you must be patient. The official pardon takes time to come through. It is on its way. As for the false identity, it's essential. Remember, it's not only the police that want to speak to you, but the Russians as well, and they may want to do more than just talk,' Gerry said.

'If you know, they know, and everyone who reads a paper or watches television knows, that I didn't commit the murder or do all those awful things. And Valerie must know too. Can't you arrange it, Gerry, for me to at least speak to her through you or through her solicitor?'

'No, Jack, absolutely not! Don't you see? Everyone in the world knows you didn't do it, but the bastards in the Russian Embassy don't want to believe that. You contact Valerie, and you put everyone — her, Emma, and all the family — in danger of being picked up by them, and held hostage until they get hold of you.' There was no doubt as to the anger behind Gerry's response.

'I'm sorry, Gerry, I know you're right. It's just this lying business. You can't imagine how much I want to see my daughter. God, she must be three feet tall by now. She doesn't know me.'

Lee changed the subject back to the matter in hand. 'We now have the main idea of what happened. We just have to work out how to use it to our advantage.'

'The Russians and Americans will by now have had their diplomatic privileges closely examined by the Foreign and Home Office. Bet that's causing some shit,' Gerry said.

'If their efforts are anything like those of the two twerps from the Home Office who came to get me out of Stamford, God help them. They are not going to resolve that sticky question. Diplomatic immunity means immunity,' Jack said.

'Australia, Holland, France and other countries will all come under scrutiny from now on. This is not just a murder enquiry they have got on their hands, it's an international drug investigation, with Met detectives involved. I bet there are a good number of other coppers of senior rank involved as well. Brown paper envelopes being passed covertly all over the place.'

'What bothers me, Gerry, is: if what we have worked out is true, why was I implicated in a murder? Why couldn't Kim and the others have implicated me in some other crime to get me booted out of the squad or the police? Why implicate me in a murder?'

'Opportunity, Jack, opportunity. The death of this Russian girl came at just the right moment for Kim and the others, a murder would get you put away for a long time. All she had to do was make sure everyone believed it was you who committed the atrocities. It was a perfect solution to their problem of you busting their drug deals,' Lee said.

'Kim Brown and Karen Dewhurst were the perfect combination to make sure you were convicted,' Gerry added.

'I can't believe that Kim would do this to me. We were such good friends,' Jack said, dejectedly.

'Yeah, well, it just goes to show. Anyway, I'll be off. I'll get back to you as soon as I hear anything new.' Lee stood up, as did Gerry.

'I'll be off too, Jack. Look, bear in mind what I've told you. It's better to be safe than sorry. It's better to hide behind this alias that we've created, for the time being anyway. You're not living a lie; you're living. In the meantime, I'll look into the question of you having visitation rights for Emma. I can't promise anything, but I will look into it for you.'

Jack was very happy with the outcome of their 'scrum down' and whilst it was all fresh in his mind, he committed everything they had discussed onto the laptop under the file title 'WHAT HAPPENED TO THOSE NOTES?'

Chapter Ten

MEANWHILE

In the offices of the murder investigation room, there was organised confusion.

Anna Smelt had been remanded in custody in HMP Bronzefield in Surrey, and the recordings of her interviews had been scrutinised by the team. She and her solicitor had made no application for bail and were willing to wait while the investigation took its course.

The Dutch police and Interpol were still working on trying to trace Kim Brown and Karen Dewhurst. Patrizia Rossi had been arrested and placed in custody. After three 'No Comment' interviews, she had been charged with perverting the course of justice, and had appeared before a magistrate's court where she had been remanded in custody, also in Bronzefield.

The Coroner's Inquest into the death of Lisa Carlisle had returned a verdict of 'death by suicide'. Carlisle had been twenty-two years old and her police service record was impeccable. She had been transferred to the Serious and Organised Crime Squad about twenty-four months before her death and died about twelve months after the murder trial. This was not thought to have had any bearing on her state of mind at the time, so it had not been mentioned at the inquest. Her live-in partner at the time of the murder was not interviewed, nor did she give evidence at the inquest. It is not known if she was also at the party where the murder was committed.

The fact that Lisa Carlisle's partner had not been traced or interviewed was pointed out by Detective Superintendent Brooker from the Cambridgeshire Constabulary. He wanted this oversight corrected, and officers were actioned to trace and interview her, not only about the party and the murder, but about the circumstances around the break-up of their relationship and the subsequent suicide.

The forensic evidence had been overwhelmingly against Trevor Frost. His DNA was found on the victim's body, including the vaginal area, stomach and breasts. The victim's blood was found on Frost's, hands, arms, genital area, and on most of his clothing. The fact that Frost had been in an alcoholic stupor had not been considered to be a defence.

His clothing had been seized, and when he came round, forensic samples were taken from him, including personal samples for DNA, all with his permission. Frost cooperated in every way.

He was eventually interviewed and, during questioning, he admitted to being at the house, but knew nothing of the assault and murder of the girl. The interviews were conducted in the presence of his solicitor, Ms Freeman.

Their main problem, at this stage, was the investigation into the importation of the drugs via the diplomatic bags, which Anna Smelt said had been accomplished with the assistance of Legation staff in America, and Legation staff at their Embassy in London.

Two officers from the squad had been sent out to Washington DC. They were to be assisted by Agents from the FBI. There was no cooperation at all from the Russian Embassy. Although the Russians had been shown a copy of Smelt's statement, they still would not accept it.

The Russian Embassy had now refused any more contact with police or the Foreign Office, and had said that they would carry out their own investigations, and handle the result in their own way.

Detective Superintendent Brooker was highly unimpressed with the previous murder investigation. He set two of the officers of the new Investigation team to trace the other people at the party, and to interview them, under caution if necessary. Cramer reported daily to Chris Rice, informing him as to the content of his phone calls to Lee Wooding, most recently concerning the compensation request, and the apparently delayed pardon.

Rice, in turn, informed the Home Office of the request, adding that if the pardon and compensation could be arranged quickly, then Wooding would facilitate a meeting with Frost, who, up until now, had remained silent and hidden, while the peril of his situation was daily amplified.

The Home Office, for its part, was not going to be strong-armed into making any decisions — not until further arrests had been made, and a more concrete prosecution of the suspects looked imminent.

This attitude was corroborated by the CPS head, Rupert Levy. He did, however, agree that the pardon proceedings should go ahead without delay.

There was no feedback to the Investigation team from MI5 or Special Branch, who were investigating the importation of drugs through diplomatic channels.

The SIO and his team were supplied with the details of Anna Smelt's contacts and friends in London, plus those of her father.

Either they had come up with nothing, or the information they had was too sensitive for mere police officers investigating a complicated, international murder and drugs enquiry.

DCI Chris Rice decided to get the Commissioner involved and told him that the two departments were not cooperating. There were some very tricky enquiries to make, especially involving the Russian side of the story.

The national press hadn't let up either. They were constantly on the phone for an update on the investigation and any arrests, but, as it gained the investigation nothing to have press coverage at this stage, they were being kept at bay.

Gerry Forbes was sorting through papers that related to the Trevor and Valerie Frost divorce. He had asked the advice of a colleague about applying for paternal access after a divorce.

Given the fact that Jack was living under an assumed name, was wanted by police for help in their investigations, and was possibly in danger of being abducted by the Russians, Gerry was sure this would be a non-starter from the word go.

Nevertheless, Gerry prepared an application address to put before a judge of the Family Court, although it had to be agreed in advance by Valerie in order to keep proceedings secret.

Gerry had a brainwave. Perhaps if he contacted Jack's sister, Jean, and got her to talk to Valerie to try and get some agreement from her, they would stand a chance of repealing the order. He would have to run the idea past Jack first.

There was a lot to dislike about the plan. Jack hadn't spoken to his sister since he went down and was reluctant to involve her in any way. But if there was the slightest chance of seeing his daughter again, he would have to agree. He was very anxious, not only about his location and secret identity being discovered, but also about compromising the safety of Val and Emma.

Gerry talked over the apparently intractable problems regarding the strategy for applying to the Family Court with Lee, who suggested they ask their old law school principal for advice. Professor Ian McDonald remembered Lee and Gerry from their student days. They asked what he thought would be their best move forward, describing the situation without telling him who was involved, nor mentioning any names. His advice was to seek out Judge Stephen Jenner, who sat at the Family Court in Croydon.

This judge was one of his old student pals from years ago. 'Tell him I sent you, and he owes me a pint,' the professor said, with a smile. He went on to explain that a judge can overrule any other judgment made, as long as the circumstances of the original ruling have been changed. In this case, he believed that the circumstances *had* changed drastically and the father should be granted access to his child.

He helped them prepare a new opening address to deliver to the judge sitting on the bench at the Croydon Family Court, pointing out the change of circumstances since the previous injunction had been put in place by the Family Court in Brent. He suggested waiting until the free pardon had been issued, as it would make the whole situation easier. Valerie would be approached, either through her solicitor or directly, and her cooperation requested. If she failed to cooperate, then a full court hearing would have to be called, which would compromise security, a situation that everyone would wish to avoid. Gerry and Lee would then approach His Honour Judge Jenner privately and explain the full situation.

He was really a great help, and when Gerry and Lee explained the way forward with their application for access to Emma, Jack was more hopeful. However, he still had lots of questions; most pressingly: How were they going to contact Valerie, when they didn't know her solicitor and she wasn't at home?

He was also feeling guilty because, a few times, he had phoned his old home phone number. He was surprised to discover Val hadn't changed it, and that it was still her voice on the answerphone. It was totally against everything that Gerry had advised, but he was desperate to talk to Valerie, and to explain what was going on, and that he was totally innocent. Fortunately, or unfortunately for Jack, there had been no answer. He couldn't tell Gerry that.

'Also, it could be months before I am pardoned,' Jack said. 'We know how quickly the Home Office works.'

'Let's see what this new judge says, and then we can contact Valerie. She knows you're innocent, from all the press coverage, and she may agree for the injunction to be lifted,' Gerry suggested.

'To get your official pardon, I'll have to bargain with the police, the Home Office and the judiciary, to show that you are willing to cooperate,' Lee pointed out.

'I want nothing to do with them,' Jack vehemently replied. 'They have fucked up everything, from start to finish. There must be another way. Can't you petition the Home Office direct, Lee?'

'I could do that, but I don't think they'll play ball. Let's try contacting Valerie first,' Lee suggested. 'What was your old phone number at home, Jack?'

His duplicity made him uncomfortable but, saying nothing about his previous attempts, Jack gave Lee the number.

'I'll give this Judge Jenner a ring to see what he advises. By all accounts, he's pretty switched on and approachable,' Gerry said.

'I think we're letting far too many people know who I am, where I am and what I'm doing. I think that, if this threat is real

— and the police seem pretty confident that it is — then we're putting out too much information,' Jack fretted.

'If you want to see your daughter that badly, Jack, then this is the only avenue we can take. We have to take the risk.'

Chapter Eleven

VISITING RIGHTS

Applying for a hearing at a Family Court is quite complex, but it boils down to common sense, really. Mostly, visits are arranged through solicitors. A pre-application statement for visitation rights is provided to the judge and the two solicitors representing the father and the mother. The judge, having read the statement, arranges a court hearing. Usually, the time allotted is about forty-five minutes.

Before they sent their statement off for Judge Jenner to consider, Lee rang him. His Honour said he had already spoken to their professor, was well aware of the situation, and was sympathetic to Jack's application.

He believed that the lack of the free pardon would not be an issue. However, the fact that there were other agencies apart from the police trying to trace Jack, and that they would possibly use blackmail, by involving Valerie or his daughter, could be a serious problem.

It was very important that they spoke to Valerie to get her permission to go ahead with the court hearing. However, Jack didn't want Valerie's parents involved, and had refused to allow Gerry to contact them, so it seemed there was no way to track her down.

Eventually, Lee asked Judge Jenner if he could contact the Family Court in Brent to ascertain if they had a record of the solicitor who had instigated the initial injunction hearing. He agreed, saying that it was highly unusual, but this being a special case, he would do so.

Valerie's solicitor, Mr Harry Bradshaw, was duly traced and his details passed to Gerry.

After some complex discussions around secrecy and security, Bradshaw agreed with Gerry that the way forward would be for everyone to cooperate with each other. There would have to be some severe restrictions around the parental visits: a chaperone, no physical contact with each other etc; after all, the current injunction was still in operation. Gerry agreed.

Two days later, Bradshaw contacted Gerry, and told him Valerie had reluctantly agreed, after having been advised that it would be a hearing before a judge and no-one else.

The hearing was arranged for the following week, at Croydon Family Court. The court was a modern and imposing building, about a ten-minute walk from the main Croydon train station.

Jack, Gerry and Lee were suited and booted and looking very smart. It was a jittery walk from the station for Jack, and he wanted a cigarette before entering the court building.

'Let's not hang about too long,' Gerry said. 'You don't know who's out here.'

On entering, they were searched by a security guard. Jack went immediately over to the court list, which identified which court-room the hearings would be in, and the time.

'We're not on there!' he blurted.

'We wouldn't be,' Gerry reassured him. 'Our case will be heard *in camera*, which means it's not for the public. I'll check us in with the Family Court clerk; you wait here.'

'Calm down, Jack,' said Lee. 'You're making me nervous. Everything has been sorted out and all that remains is to see which way the judge will jump when he hears from Valerie's brief.'

When Gerry came back, he led them off to a lift that went up to the second floor and then ushered them into a side room, usually reserved for vulnerable witnesses.

'Wait here, Jack, I'll be back in a minute.' Again, Gerry disappeared.

Jack was very nervous. This would be the first time he had seen Valerie since he was arrested. He had hoped that she would have been at the trial, but the courtroom was full and he hadn't been able to see her. He still loved her very much and he didn't want her hurt in any way. Dragging her through all this legal turmoil was not what he wanted for her. He desperately wanted to nip out for another cigarette, but Lee vetoed it. Gerry returned.

'Right, Jack, the judge wants us in the court first. We shall sit on one side and then Valerie will be allowed in. You must *not* speak to her at all. Leave all the talking to me.'

'This is going to be hard,' Jack said. 'When can I speak?'

'Only when you are asked directly by the judge,' Gerry said. 'Don't smile or make any facial expressions at all. Leave it all to us.'

Jack adjusted his tie and brushed down his new suit.

'Let's go,' Gerry said.

The court was quite large, the light teak wood giving it a modern feel, with the judge's bench at the back and a desk for the clerk in front of that. There were rows of red leather seats to the left, right and centre.

Jack and Gerry sat on the right side of the court, and Gerry got out all his paperwork.

Suddenly the double doors at the rear of the court, through

which they had just entered, opened, and in walked Valerie with her solicitor. Gerry nudged Jack with his elbow to remind him not to look.

There was no noise in the court. Nobody was talking.

The usher said, loudly, 'All rise.'

The Honourable Judge Stephen Jenner entered the court, and took his seat at the centre of the bench, facing them all.

'This hearing is to be held *in camera*.' The judge looked at the usher. 'Could you please make sure the doors are locked and that no person is here in court who shouldn't be.'

The usher went to the doors at the rear of the court and then checked with Valerie and her solicitor, then checked with Gerry, Lee and Jack.

'All secure, Your Honour,' the usher declared.

'Today, Your Honour, there is a petition on behalf of Mr Trevor Frost, represented by Mr Gerald Forbes, to have lawful access to his daughter, Miss Emma Frost, five-years-old. The child's mother, ex-wife of the said Mr Trevor Frost, Mrs Valerie Frost, represented by Mr Harry Bradshaw, is also in court to defend the application,' the clerk said.

'Good morning, everyone,' the judge began. 'Thank you for coming here today; it's nice to see you all. I believe you are all in possession of the application statement made by Mr Frost, requesting permission to have access to see his daughter, Emma, after several years of separation. I will detail the salient points of the application. Firstly, Mr Frost was arrested and charged with an offence that resulted in him being sentenced to a term of imprisonment, separating him from his wife and child for a period of nearly four years, following fifteen months on remand, pre-trial. I am given to understand that during that time Mr Frost was not in contact with either his wife or daughter, is that right?'

The judge looked over his *pince-nez* glasses at Gerry.

'That is correct, Your Honour,' Gerry replied.

'It has since been revealed that the conviction of Mr Frost was flawed and he has been released, subject to further investigation by the Metropolitan Police. He is no longer incarcerated and is free to continue his life. I am also given to understand that a free pardon will be issued shortly. Mr Frost now lives in a one-bedroomed flat in London. The address is recorded here in court but is not to be released. He has a car and, more importantly, has a small income from writing. All correct so far?' The judge again looked at Gerry.

Gerry confirmed that this was so.

'Now, from information I have received, I believe there is a problem both with Mr Frost's whereabouts becoming known, and similarly the location of his estranged wife and child. Can you expand on that, Mr Forbes?' the judge asked.

'Yes, Your Honour. My colleague, Mr Lee Wooding, and I have been in contact with the new police investigation team. They have apprised us of a connection between the murder case and the Russian Embassy. The Embassy is also keen to speak to Mr Frost but the police have advised us that we must conduct ourselves with extreme caution as it is not possible to guarantee Mr Frost's safety, nor that of Mrs Frost, nor that of the child. Hence the necessity for the secrecy in court today.'

'Exactly. Do you have any questions so far, Mr Bradshaw?' asked the judge.

'No, Sir, not at this stage,' replied Mr Bradshaw.

Valerie Frost sat next to her solicitor with her head lowered. It seemed she was scared to look at Jack or anyone else in court.

She was dressed very conservatively, and was gripping a handkerchief.

'The security aspect is a cause for concern,' said Judge Jenner. 'How can Mr Frost assure his ex-wife that she and her family will be safe whilst he continues to be uncooperative with the police? After all, if access to the child is granted, this could put extra pressure on the situation and the question of security for the daughter is paramount.'

Jack was about to answer but Gerry grabbed his elbow and stood up.

'Your Honour, Mr Frost was a fully trained detective before the incident of which he was wrongly accused and convicted, and he is very surveillance-conscious. He can assure the court and Mrs Frost that he will take every precaution to ensure that his location and the location of any future meeting with his daughter will be kept secret, at least until the Metropolitan Police have concluded their investigations satisfactorily.' Gerry sat down.

'Mr Bradshaw, do you have any observations?' the judge asked.

'Sir, I am instructed to state that Mrs Frost was advised to divorce her husband after his conviction and can understand the ill-feeling that Mr Frost may have towards her regarding this. She was also advised recently to take out an injunction on Mr Frost to ensure the safety of herself and her family. This concern was shown to be well-founded as, after the injunction was granted, she and her father believe they were followed by two men in a Mercedes. She and her daughter are currently living, in fear of everybody, at a safe house in a secret location. As clever as Mr Frost is, he cannot guarantee the safety of Mrs Frost and therefore any future access to his daughter should be out of the question.' Mr Bradshaw sat down.

'That is a very good observation, Mr Bradshaw. Mrs Frost and her father being followed from court has never been mentioned before. Were you aware of this, Mr Forbes?' Judge Jenner asked.

'No, Your Honour. This is the first we have heard of this incident. The police have not advised us,' Gerry answered.

'I have just been informed by my client, Your Honour, that neither Valerie Frost nor her father reported the matter to the police,' Mr Bradshaw said.

'Why did you not inform the police?' the judge asked.

'Mrs Frost doesn't trust the police. In fact, she thought it possible it may have been the police who followed her and her father, whilst they were trying to trace her husband.'

'This puts a whole new light on the matter. Have you been contacted by the police, Mrs Frost?'

This was the first time Valerie had been given a chance to speak and the first time Jack had heard her voice in over five years.

Valerie stood up and in a shaky voice said, 'No, Sir, the only time the police have spoken to me was after Jack went missing from prison and after the Home Office men had visited me. They have not contacted me since.'

'I see. Have you seen these two men in the car again?' asked the judge.

'No, I don't think so, Sir.' Valerie began to shake and her solicitor made her sit down.

'This is quite concerning,' said Judge Jenner. 'I was considering allowing the application for visitation, obviously with conditions, but this will take more thought. I will adjourn for a few minutes to consider my actions.' Judge Jenner stood up.

'All rise,' said the usher, loudly. The judge left the court.

Jack longed to go over to Valerie and console her. He hated to see her so upset, and the news of the two men following her scared him.

'Did you know about this, Lee?' Gerry asked in a low voice.

'No, I didn't,' said Lee.

'It couldn't have been the police,' Jack added, 'because they don't have Mercedes.' He leaned forward to try and get a glimpse of Valerie but her head was bent forward and she was holding the handkerchief to her face.

After about twenty minutes, the usher came back. 'All rise.'

Judge Jenner returned to his seat on the bench and addressed the court. 'I have given this matter serious consideration. Through no fault of his own, Mr Frost has been denied access to his wife and daughter for over five years. His innocence of the crimes that he was accused of is beyond doubt. In my opinion, he is no longer a threat to his wife, daughter or the immediate family. However, the threat of an outside agency who is keen to locate Mr Frost is a not inconsiderable issue. I do not intend to overrule the details of the injunction laid down by my colleague Judge Braithwaite at the Brent Family Court, so those decisions by her will stand. Mrs Frost, if I were to agree to this application from your ex-husband, the visits will take place in a safe location, in the presence of a chaperone.'

Valerie was very nearly in tears. 'She'll be so scared. Can the chaperone be someone she knows?'

'It must be someone with a CRB-check,' the judge said.

'My best friend, Bridget O'Connor — she would do it,' exclaimed Valerie. 'She is CRB-checked. She works at Emma's former nursery school.'

'Excellent,' said Judge Jenner. 'I could approve that. I propose that Mr Frost be allowed to see Emma once a fortnight for two hours each time, in the presence of the chaperone, who will be, as Mrs Frost has suggested, Ms Bridget O'Connor. Providing this is suitable to all concerned, Mr Frost will not be left alone with his daughter and he will not be allowed to see her or take her outside of that safe place in any way. You will not have to meet your ex-husband, Mrs Frost. You will drop Emma off and place her in the care of Ms O'Connor at a mutually convenient time and you, Mr Frost, will arrive thirty minutes after the specified time, so there are no accidental meetings between you and Mrs Frost. Mrs Frost, you will arrive to collect your daughter thirty minutes after the allotted two-hour visitation is over. I will give you ten minutes to discuss these proposals with your representatives.' Judge Jenner stood up.

'All rise.' The judge left the court.

Gerry grabbed Jack's hand and began to shake it hard.

'We've won, we've won, Jack!'

'No, we haven't. Look at Valerie: she's bloody crying. I didn't want all this. I hate to see her cry.'

Valerie's solicitor approached Gerry.

'We shall obviously appeal this decision, Mr Forbes, but in the meantime, here are my contact details so that we may correspond on this matter.' He handed Gerry his business card and returned to his seat.

The judge returned. 'All rise,' said the usher again.

'Have you processed my decision, Mrs Frost?' Judge Jenner spoke directly to Valerie. Valerie just tearfully nodded.

'You must understand, Mrs Frost, that the law states nobody can deny the rights of the legal and biological father from seeing his child unless there are specific court rulings against the visitations. I understand that you took out an injunction against your ex-husband, but I feel this is an extraordinary case. You did not know the full extent of the information that is now before you. However, I have not rescinded all the conditions of that injunction, just this one. If Mr Frost breaks any of the other conditions, he will certainly be arrested and brought back before a court and if found guilty of breaking the conditions laid down, he will be sent back to prison. Does everyone understand what I have just said?' Judge Jenner peered over his glasses. Everyone assented, except Jack.

'Mr Clerk of the Court, these are my directions:

'One: Mr Trevor Frost, being the legal and biological father of Miss Emma Frost, aged five years, may have access to his daughter for the duration of two hours, once every fortnight; date and time to be agreed.

'Two:. The visitation will be supervised at all times by Ms Bridget O'Connor. At no time will Mr Frost be left alone with his daughter. At no time will Mr Frost be allowed to take Emma away from the visitation venue. Mr Bradshaw, ensure a suitable location is identified and details are passed to my clerk.

'Three: The times and date of these visits are to be arranged through the solicitors for each party, and those dates and times are to be strictly adhered to by each party, except in the case of sickness on the part of the father or the daughter.

'Four: Emma should be delivered into the care of Mrs O'Connor at least half an hour before the father's allotted time for his visit, and Mr Frost should leave immediately his two-hour visitation is over. The child should be collected at least half an hour after the visitation is over.

'Five: At no time shall Mr and Mrs Frost meet, or contact each other. This will ensure, Mrs Frost, that all other conditions of your original injunction will stand, understood?' Valerie nodded.

'Six: All reports of any misconduct on either the part of Mr Frost or Mrs Frost should be directed immediately to this court for action to be taken.

'These are my directions in this case, regarding visitation rights of Mr Trevor Frost. Are there any questions?' Judge Jenner took off his glasses.

'Is Mrs Frost allowed leave to appeal your directions, Your Honour?' Bradshaw stuttered.

'Only after the first two visitations, Mr Bradshaw. If she feels that the visitations are affecting her daughter in any detrimental way or that those arrangements are not suitable, then yes, you can appeal, but let's give this a chance, shall we?' The judge was about to rise when Gerry stood up.

'Your Honour, I'm given to understand that Mrs Frost is living at a secret address, as is my client. As a matter of security and safety, my client also has a pseudonym, as well as another representative, Mr Lee Wooding.' Lee raised his hand. 'Is it agreeable to the court and to Mr Bradshaw if this were to continue, for the time being?'

'Certainly, Mr Forbes, as long as no-one else learns of these secret names and addresses, not even Ms O'Connor.' Judge Jenner looked at Valerie and Mr Bradshaw.

'Thank you, everyone.' The judge stood up to leave the court.

'All rise,' the usher declared, perhaps unnecessarily loudly.

Everyone bowed, and Judge Jenner left the court.

The usher unlocked the rear doors and Valerie left in tears.

'Come on, Jack, let's celebrate. That Judge Jenner was a good guy,' said Lee.

'Celebrate? What is there to celebrate? I've once again reduced my lovely wife to tears. There is nothing to celebrate in that. I'm going home. Thanks, Gerry, for everything you've done. I'll be in touch.' Jack quickly walked out of the court.

'Don't bump into Valerie outside, Jack,' Lee shouted.

Chapter Twelve

DIPLOMATIC DEALINGS

Aleksandr Popov had been a very successful diplomat, working with the trade delegation within the Embassy since the early 1990s. He had been very highly thought of by the ambassador, and had been promoted several times. In 1998, his daughter, Natasha, had joined him as a delegate to assist in negotiations with other countries, particularly Britain and America.

Foreign government officials working with the Embassy and on behalf of their government are immune to the laws of the country where they are resident. Diplomats cannot be arrested or prosecuted for any crime. Diplomatic bags cannot be opened or searched by UK customs, or any other persons, even if they are suspected of being used for illegal purposes, such as drug smuggling.

It is known and accepted by the British Government and authorities, that large amounts of foreign cash are often imported this way into the UK, and nothing can be done about it.

Popov sat in his office, staring at a photograph of Natasha. Since her murder, he had felt a disabling mixture of both grief and revenge. The murder had consumed him, and he was determined to avenge her death, especially now the British police were accusing her of importing drugs. The inference was abhorrent to him. He felt that it was an insult, not only to the memory of his daughter, but also to the Russian nation.

His poor daughter's body had been returned to him and he had been informed that the person responsible would go to prison for eighteen years. That wasn't enough to satisfy his anguish. He wanted the man responsible eliminated. To this end, he had recruited a hitman, but the assassin had been unsuccessful.

After the funeral in St Petersburg, Popov was sensitively offered a government job in Moscow, but he was adamant he wanted to return to London, where he loved to work, where his friends and political connections were, and where he would be able to wreak his revenge on the murderer of his daughter.

The Russian ambassador had cause to invite Mr Aleksandr Popov to his office. He had received information that a confidential report from Moscow had been intercepted. This report had been sent directly to Popov, without going through the correct diplomatic channels, from an operative in the Federal Security Service, one of the successors of the KGB.

The report detailed the progress of their agents in the UK, in their efforts to trace Trevor Frost. The orders for these special agents had come directly from Popov.

The ambassador spoke to Popov in Russian. 'Thank you for coming to see me, Aleksandr, how are you?'

'Very well, Ambassador,' replied Popov, also in Russian, sitting down.

'I am very pleased with the way you handled the fuel negotiations with the British and the French last week, and I believe you have important meetings shortly regarding the climate control restrictions,' the ambassador said.

'Thank you, Sir. The negotiations did go well for us and we are well prepared for the future meetings next week,' Popov replied.

'That is not what I wanted to speak to you about, Alex. It has been brought to my attention that you have ordered some special investigations of your own, regarding the very sad demise of your lovely daughter, Natasha. Is this so?' asked the ambassador.

Popov was silent for a short while and lowered his head into his hands.

The ambassador was sympathetic. 'Be honest with me, Aleksandr. I am not condemning your actions, but I cannot defend them against others, if I do not know the truth.'

'My poor Natasha was horribly violated, Ambassador, and I was informed this British policeman was responsible. They thought I would be satisfied if that policeman was sent to prison. I was not satisfied. Now, out of the blue, I am told it was an American girl who murdered Natasha, and that she was importing drugs through our diplomatic bags and selling them in London. This is not true. Natasha was a good girl, a brilliant assistant to me. She was well-liked by everyone here in the Embassy, well-respected by all the legations in London with whom she had a wonderful relationship. She had her whole life ahead of her.'

'I know what a wonderful girl Natasha was; you don't have to tell me. She was a great asset to the Embassy,' the ambassador declared.

Popov was on the edge of his seat. 'On top of this injustice, because of what this American girl has said, they have released this murdering bastard from prison and he is walking free. This is a conspiracy, concocted by the British and Americans, to gloss over the murder. They release the policeman, and say that Natasha got what she had coming to her. I must avenge my daughter's death, Ambassador, so I talked to old friends in

Lubyanka who guaranteed they would resolve the matter.' Popov fell silent.

'There is no problem with this, Alex. I agree that this is the right action to take. Nevertheless, someone within the Kremlin has leaked this information to me, and if they could leak it to me, they could leak it to anyone. They must be found. Also, we must investigate whether drugs were being sent to London via our diplomatic bags. I am not aware of drugs being transported via our diplomatic bags.'

'Not my Natasha, not my Natasha.' Popov was now very upset.

'Leave it to me, Aleksandr. I will get to the bottom of this, have no worry. Who is here in London working on your behalf?' the ambassador asked.

'Do you need me to name them, Sir?'

'No, not really, but make sure they are discreet and their actions do not reflect on this embassy. Have you requested a *final* solution to this problem?' the ambassador asked.

'Yes, Sir.'

'Is there anything else you wish to share with me?'

'I only wish to set the record straight regarding the untrue information that the American girl and my Natasha were lovers. This I know to be categorically not true. My Natasha was a good girl, and she was interested in a comrade working in the Kremlin.'

'This is, as you said, Alex, a complete tissue of lies, concocted by the British and the Americans. Please keep me informed of your agents' progress and I will tell you how the investigations in the Kremlin are developing. This must be kept top secret: nothing on paper. Thank you for your frankness and honesty, Alex.' The ambassador stood and offered his hand for Popov to shake.

In America, there is a constant rivalry between the FBI and the CIA which extends to the American Embassies around the world. Agents from both organisations are very intelligent and dedicated officers but are also fiercely competitive. On this occasion, it was imperative that both organisations work in tandem. Their goal was to discover who helped Anna Smelt in the USA: those who supplied the drugs and loaded the diplomatic bags. This part of the investigation was being dealt with by the FBI.

The importation of drugs, and the distribution from the American Embassy into the London underworld, would be dealt with by the CIA. There were numerous lines of enquiry but they could only be pursued with the assistance and cooperation of the London Metropolitan Police. All were well aware of the Russian connection and the relationship between Anna Smelt and Natasha Popova.

Smelt's counsel for the defence had given both the FBI and CIA permission to interview her whilst on remand in an English jail. Questions were restricted to finding out who her connections were within the Embassy in London and the contacts she had back in the USA. They were not allowed by law to question her on any of the facts regarding the reason she was extradited, or the murder itself.

She had instructed her solicitors that she would give her full cooperation to the British police, FBI and CIA. She also added that because she 'had found God', she would be 'truthful in every way' and that she 'sought only God's forgiveness.'

Progress had already been made on tracing her accomplices in the States but the CIA was having trouble finding cooperative staff within the US Embassy in London.

Anna Smelt had been scrupulously accurate and honest in her testimony regarding her connections within the US Embassy and the connections with friends and acquaintances outside her diplomatic circle, including the Russian girl, and the associates within her social group.

She was truthful regarding her sexual preferences and also honest about how much money she made from the sale of the drugs that she imported. She claimed that she did not know how or to whom the drugs were supplied, saying only that she handed the drugs to Kim Brown and other girls within her social group and that they in turn distributed them to their contacts, and the money came back to her.

She supplied all the names of her social group, as far as she could remember, to the police in the new investigation team and a major effort to trace these people was underway. She also admitted that she was an occasional user of cannabis and cocaine, but insisted that she was not an addict.

She had had an intense relationship with Natasha Popova. They had been partners for about fourteen months, but Smelt said the relationship was 'open' and they had that they were both free to enjoy the company of other girls or boys.

On the fateful night, they had both taken drugs and drunk a lot of alcohol. They had moved to the bedroom, and were both naked on the bed. The argument had initially flared because Anna did not like Natasha showing off in front of their police friends and flirting with boys at the party who were not gay. Soon the argument developed into a full-blooded fight, mainly over the money they were receiving for the drugs and who had the biggest share. Anna was enraged and, in the struggle, she climbed on top of Natasha and grabbed her round the throat. Natasha suddenly became unresponsive. Anna screamed for her to wake up which drew Kim and Karen and a handful of curious party-goers. Kim pulled Anna off Natasha, and began to shout orders to the others.

Anna described how she had watched, transfixed, as Kim Brown did unbelievably horrific things to Natasha's body. Tearing her gaze away, she noticed, but barely registered, a man sitting in an armchair next to the bed. He was unmoving and his eyes were closed.

A girl she didn't recognise grabbed her and took her into the bathroom, doused her with cold water, calmed her down and helped her get dressed. She did remember Kim Brown screaming 'Get the fuckin' Yank out of here.'

Then she was dragged out of the house and pushed into a car. It wasn't a taxi and another girl was with her, who could have been Lisa, a policewoman friend of Kim's. She was driven home and, within days, flew back to America. She never returned to the diplomatic service.

Anna Smelt confessed that Trevor Frost had nothing to do with the death of Natasha Popova. She had killed her.

DCI Chris Rice had expanded his investigating force. The enquiry had become so complex that the team had been increased to thirty hand-picked officers from other squads, CID offices and departments. These were officers whom Rice knew he could trust to carry out each action required of them, diligently and honestly. He didn't need glory hunters in his squad. They liaised closely with the CIA, with whom they got on well.

An ongoing problem between the Metropolitan Police departments and the Home Office was lack of communication. Whatever the Home Office discovered in their investigations, they kept it to themselves, choosing not to share information with the Metropolitan Police murder squads or Special Branch.

Rice had taken this problem to the Commissioner but to no avail. Rice, Cramer and the others had not dealt with diplomatic affairs before. They were finding it difficult to understand how far they could go with their investigations without treading on someone's diplomatic 'foot'. They really needed the Home Office and the Foreign Office to help out and advise, but this wasn't forthcoming.

The squad had managed to discover Barbara Hancock's alias, and had also found out that she had moved from Manchester and relocated to Liverpool. Evidently, she had got wind that the police were looking for her and she moved quickly. This suggested that there was still corruption within the police, and was a warning to everyone to be vigilant.

DS Cramer had continued to liaise with Lee Wooding in an effort to get access to the ex-detective, but Lee maintained that Trevor Frost would only speak to them after his free pardon had been issued. Chris Rice had no control over the issuing of the free pardon. This was down to the Home Office, and they were not playing ball at all.

All Rice was able to tell Cramer was that, as far as the Commissioner and the Metropolitan Police solicitors were concerned, an offer of £25,000 could be made to Trevor Frost, as an interim payment of compensation, without prejudice.

Chapter Thirteen

THE FIRST VISITATION

It had been seven weeks since the Family Court had agreed to Jack's visitation rights, and he was becoming frustrated. He couldn't understand why it was taking so long to arrange.

He had bought a children's jigsaw and a small story book to give to Emma on their first meeting, and for himself a new shirt and tie, so that he looked smart. Jack was desperate to see his daughter and secretly hoped that maybe in time he could be reunited with Valerie too, but he acknowledged this would likely be a long time coming.

'Gerry, is there any news of me seeing Emma?' Jack was ringing on their private phones as arranged.

'Hello, Jack, I was just going to ring you. No, no news just yet, but I should be talking to Valerie's solicitor this morning. I do have some other news for you though. Lee has just rung me to say that the police are willing to forward you £25,000 in part-compensation, prior to a final compensation figure and, of course, the free pardon.' Gerry sounded very upbeat.

'Not a lot for ruining someone's life, is it? But I suppose I will have to accept it. I owe you and Lee so much money; at least I will be able to pay you both back.' As usual, Jack sounded deflated. He had been hoping for news about seeing Emma.

'We'll talk about the money later, Jack. I'll get back to you after I've spoken to Valerie's brief again.' Gerry hung up.

Utterly pissed off, Jack sank into a depression. He could not believe that whoever made the decision on the amount of compensation thought that an initial £25,000 would last until the final figure was agreed. How far would that go towards him re-establishing himself into the community, and having a normal existence with his daughter?

After about three quarters of an hour, the phone rang again. It could only be Gerry or Lee.

'Yes?' Jack said, very dejectedly.

'Jack, it's me, Gerry, I have some good news. Listen carefully, got a pen and paper?'

'Yes.'

'Next Saturday, the 22nd...' Gerry paused for effect.

'Yes?'

"Next Saturday, the 22nd, at 10am... you are going to meet your daughter. Bridget O'Connor has agreed to supervise. You will have two hours with little Emma. You must leave at twelve noon exactly. You must not take her anywhere and the visit must be in the presence of Ms O'Connor the whole time.'

'This is great, Gerry! I used to know Bridget very well. Who else knows about this meeting? And where is it?'

'Only Valerie, her solicitor and Bridget O'Connor. It's all arranged,' Gerry explained. 'I've got the address in a sealed envelope for you. I'll put it through your letterbox. They're being ridiculously cautious. Even Lee and I aren't allowed to know where it is!'

'This is fantastic, Gerry, thank you. That's only ten days away. I can't wait.'

'You will *not* see Valerie or any of her family and don't try.

I have a copy of the stipulations laid down by the original judge when the injunction was taken out, along with the stipulations laid down by the judge at the Family Court giving you the visitation rights. They are both clear that if you try and make any contact with Valerie or her family you will be nicked and sent to jail. Be careful, Jack, don't fuck this up, we have come too far.' Gerry was very stern.

'I won't "fuck this up", as you put it. I will stick to the letter of the law; don't worry,' Jack replied.

This was the best news that Jack had received in months. He was going to see his little Emma for the first time since she was a baby. The meeting place had been fixed for the nursery where Bridget O'Connor worked.

The next few days seemed like a lifetime.

Jack planned everything for his forthcoming visit about forty times — what he was going to say, what they were going to do — and the Friday night before the meeting, he just could not sleep.

On the 22nd, Jack woke up early, and, as they say in the Navy, had a 'shit, a shave and a shampoo'. He got dressed in his new shirt, tie and his new suit. He felt good.

A good breakfast and Jack was ready, but it was only half past seven. What was he going to do for the next two and a half hours? He had butterflies in his stomach. He left his flat and drove around in his car for about an hour, making sure that he wasn't being followed by anyone.

He parked a street away from the nursery, and sat for a while, having a cigarette. Then he ate a whole packet of mints to take the smell away. He didn't want Emma to be put off by his smoky breath. At about five to the hour, Jack left his car and slowly walked around the corner. He made sure there was no-one outside the nursery, especially Valerie.

At ten o'clock precisely, Jack walked through the gates and across the playground to the side doors. Bridget O'Connor met him.

'Hello, Jack, it's nice to see you.' Bridget gave Jack a peck on the cheek.

'Hello, Bridget, it's lovely to see you again.' Jack realised this was the first kiss he had had in years.

'Emma is in the playroom, Jack. In you go, you'll be alright,' said Bridget, confidently.

Emma was on the floor looking at a book, dressed in a white cotton blouse and a pretty, light blue skirt, with white woolly leggings. She had beautiful blonde hair that flowed down to her shoulders.

Emma looked up at Jack.

'Emma, love, this is your daddy, say hello,' Bridget said.

There was a slight pause and then Emma said cautiously, 'Hello.'

Jack was stuck for words. His throat and mouth dried up, and then he said, quietly, 'Hello, Peanut, it's lovely to see you.'

'Why do you call me Peanut?' Emma said. Both Jack and Bridget smiled.

'What are you reading?' Jack asked.

'A book about a unicorn,' Emma said.

She sat and read the book out loud, whilst Jack listened in awe. He couldn't remember being able to read a word when he was her age — what a bright little girl she was. Valerie had done well with her.

The ice broken, Jack and Emma played happily.

They did the jigsaw that Jack had brought, and read the little book. It was about a farm and Jack was making all the noises of the animals. This made Emma laugh.

Bridget brought a big box of coloured pencils and crayons and Emma opened a large colouring book.

'Would you help me?' Emma asked Jack.

With a big smile, Jack said, 'Yes, of course,' and they spread out further on the floor together.

After about an hour, Bridget brought in some tea and biscuits and some orange juice for Emma and they all three had a small picnic. They all enjoyed that, especially Emma.

Emma asked Jack random questions — 'Do you like carrots?' 'Do you like peppers?' 'Do you like the seaside?' — to which Jack replied each time, 'I do.'

'My best friend at school is Michael. Do you have a friend?' Emma peered into Jack's eyes.

'Yes, I do,' smiled Jack. 'I have two.'

'I've got my own bed, have you?' The questions continued and Jack was happy to answer them.

She was also full of questions about why her daddy wasn't with her mummy and where had he been for such a long time. Jack fielded most of her questions satisfactorily and Bridget just watched and listened. Jack was impressed with Emma's reading. She told him that her mummy, nanny and grandad helped her as they did with her singing and dancing.

They talked the whole time until Bridget told Jack he had ten minutes left. Where had those two hours gone?

Jack told Emma that he had to go, but that he would see her again very soon.

'Going to give Daddy a kiss goodbye?' Bridget asked Emma. Emma hesitated.

'Just give me a hug,' Jack said, holding out his arms.

Emma gave him a long hug. 'Are you really my daddy? Really?'

'Yes, I am, and I always will be, because I love you very much.'

'And do you love Mummy as well?' Emma quizzed.

'Yes, I do, very much.' Jack tried to change the subject. 'Shall I see you in two weeks' time for some more fun?'

Emma nodded, gleefully.

'Thanks for everything, Bridget. You are a star. I must go.'

Jack left the playroom slowly, waving all the time at Emma. He left the nursery dead on the stroke of twelve.

He walked back to his car, but he was dying to see Valerie again, so he crept back to the corner of the road and covertly kept a watch on the gates of the nursery.

After about ten minutes, a car pulled up and out got a man who entered the gates of the nursery. Jack recognised Ted, who had come to collect Emma.

Jack went back to his car and drove home. He stayed in for the rest of the day, just thinking about everything that happened that morning. Happy memories.

When Ted went inside to collect Emma, he asked Bridget if everything was alright. Bridget told him that everything went like clockwork and that Jack had behaved immaculately.

Bridget said she would accompany Emma and Ted back to Valerie's parent's house. Ted didn't want Bridget to know the location of Valerie's safe house. The fewer people who knew where they were staying, the better.

On their arrival, Valerie took Bridget aside whilst Ted and May took Emma into another room to play.

Valerie was in an angry mood. 'Well, what did he say about me? I bet he was slagging me off to Emma about what a terrible mother I was.'

Bridget tried to calm her down. 'Jack said nothing of the sort, Valerie. He and Emma played very nicely and he told Emma what a fabulous mother you were and how much he loved you. He was great.'

'What were they talking about? Were they talking about me?' Valerie asked.

'No, Valerie, they were not talking about you. Emma asked the most innocuous questions and Jack was polite and answered in a lovely manner. He told Emma that he loved her and that he loved you very much as well. He thought you were a terrific mother and clever. Emma was very happy to hear that. She was also very happy to have a daddy, as all her classmates have a daddy and now, she has one as well. The meeting went well, and I was glad to see Jack looking well and happy, especially after what he has been through.' Bridget was quite firm. 'I have to report back to your solicitor on how the first meeting went and I will tell him that it went very well and that Emma is looking forward to the next time,' she added.

'Did he touch Emma?'

'No, he did not. There was a small hug before he left, but there was no kissing and no touching, and that was it.' Bridget got up to leave.

'Thanks for everything, Bridget, you've been marvellous. Are you okay again for a fortnight's time?' asked Valerie.

'Yes, I'll be there in two weeks.'

Bridget said goodbye and left.

Valerie pulled herself together and went to play with Emma. She didn't ask her about the meeting with her dad.

Out of the blue, Emma said to her mother, 'I'm just like Michael and Lucy at school — I've got a daddy now,' and said no more about it. Valerie smiled. Emma was happy.

Chapter Fourteen

INVITATION TO A PARTY

The meetings between Jack and Emma, in the presence of Bridget, went without a hitch for the next five visits. The two of them put together jigsaws, read loads of books and did lots of colouring.

Most important of all, Jack and Emma became closer. They laughed together, talked together, but best of all, Emma wanted more. Spontaneously, on one occasion when they were saying goodbye, Emma hugged her dad and kissed him.

Bridget smiled and made no comment. If that was what Emma wanted, that was fine. The kiss wasn't prompted by Jack and it was only a small peck on the cheek, anyway. She saw no need to report this to Valerie or to the solicitor.

Valerie warmed somewhat to the situation, once she found out from Emma that Jack was not bad-mouthing her. In fact, Emma kept asking her why Daddy was not coming home with them, why they didn't live in the same house like other families.

'Do you love Daddy? He loves you a lot, he told me,' Emma said.

Valerie had been through so much emotional turmoil over the last few years, she just didn't know how she felt, or how to answer Emma.

Seeing the happiness Jack had given to Emma by coming

back into her life, Valerie wondered whether there was anything she could do to repair their relationship. But there had been so much mistrust between them that she didn't know if the damage could ever be healed.

Jack had always maintained he was not guilty, but she didn't believe him, she didn't trust him and she had refused to see him.

'Get rid of him, Valerie, there's no smoke without fire,' many of her friends had said.

Now he was seeing their daughter on a regular basis, and he did not seem like the monster that everyone made him out to be.

Out of the blue, Valerie realised the truth. She admitted to herself that she did like him — not love, but like — and it was nice to hear from Bridget how well the visits were going. She wanted to see for herself, but because of the injunction, and because of the conditions of the visitation order, this would not be possible. If caught, Jack would go back to prison and he would never forgive her. Valerie decided to have a word with Bridget. She thought that if she hid herself in the nursery at Jack's next visit, then she could watch and see Jack and Emma together.

Bridget was not at all happy with the idea; after all, she was responsible for the safety of these meetings. If anything went wrong, she would have to answer to the Family Court. What if the solicitors found out?

Valerie and Bridget had been the best of friends since they were schoolgirls. Valerie trusted Bridget with her life, and Bridget was keeping so many secrets from everyone, even her husband. He knew that Emma came to the nursery for a couple of hours every two weeks, but not that she was meeting her father there. As caretaker, he unlocked the doors for his wife and then returned to his morning paper.

The plan was for Valerie to bring Emma to the next visit

and to hide herself, perhaps behind the doors to the playroom where Jack and Emma played, so that she could view for herself the interaction between father and daughter. Although unhappy, Bridget went along with it because of their friendship.

After Valerie said goodbye to Emma, leaving her with Bridget, she quietly went down the corridor and made herself comfortable outside the doors in the adjacent room.

Dead on ten o'clock, Jack arrived, greeting Emma, who wanted a kiss. Bridget settled at the table while Jack and Emma sat on the floor. Emma did all the chatting and Jack just sat there and smiled.

Valerie couldn't hear every word, which was frustrating, but she could sense enough to recognise how happy the two of them were together. Peering between the crack in the double doors, she thought Jack looked well. He looked like he had when she first met and fallen in love with him. He was a good-looking bugger, had lost a bit of weight, but otherwise he looked good.

She squashed the urge to enter the playroom and grab hold of Jack and hug and kiss him. It had been so long, and she realised that she did still love him. She felt so sorry he had been through the terrible trauma of being accused and convicted when he wasn't guilty. She wanted to console him and say she was sorry, but she knew she couldn't.

Oh, why can't *I* have visiting rights to see Jack? she lamented.

Jack and Emma were doing a jigsaw and when Jack placed a piece in, Emma said, 'You are clever, Daddy. This jigsaw is hard. Do you think Mummy could do it?'

'Your mummy is a very clever girl — she could do this jigsaw better than me. She is beautiful, just like you and she is wonderful, just like you. That's why I love you both,' Jack said, warmly.

Those words nearly broke Valerie's heart. She began to weep.

Bridget had made Jack a cup of tea and brought Emma a juice, with cake for them both, and then secretly took Valerie a cup of tea and saw her crying.

'Don't even think about it, Val, it would cock everything up. Just leave them to it, he's not hurting her in any way and they are happy,' Bridget whispered. She was afraid Val would burst into the playroom and break all the rules laid down to safeguard them both.

There had been some background music playing quietly in the playroom and, although Jack and Emma ignored the song, Adele's *Make You Feel My Love*, began to play. It was Valerie's favourite song, and the tears streamed down her face. The words were so true and so pertinent to her and Jack. Given the storms they had weathered, all she wanted was to make him feel her love. She truly believed she could hold him for a million years, and that all she wanted now was to make his dreams come true. There really wasn't anything she wouldn't do to right the wrongs that they had suffered.

If Valerie could, she would do anything. Oh, how true the words to that song are! She stifled her crying in a handkerchief; she *did* still love Jack, but if she did anything now, he could be sent back to prison. She realised how wrong she had been.

The two hours went quickly and, when it was time to say goodbye, Emma ran over to Jack, who was kneeling down, threw her arms around his neck and kissed him. It was pitifully clear how sad she was to see him go.

Jack walked back to his car, unaware that Valerie had been watching.

Valerie emerged from her hiding place and quietly said to Bridget, so that Emma didn't hear, 'He still loves me, Bridget, he still loves me, I heard him say it. He really meant it.'

'I know that, Val. I've known for weeks,' Bridget said. 'But please don't do anything silly. If you're going to do anything, do it legally, so that none of us ends up in the shit.'

Valerie was over the moon. She picked Emma up and danced her around the room. Emma didn't have a clue what was going on. Over the next few days, Valerie continued to be full of excitement about seeing Jack again, glad to see the difference in Emma and generally in a much better mood. Her mother noticed it first and enquired what the change in her was. Valerie couldn't keep it to herself. She told her mum about hiding at the nursery and what she had seen and heard.

May went ballistic. 'What if you were caught? You could have put Jack in jeopardy of going to prison! You are a silly girl, and what about Emma? You could have ruined everything for her.'

Valerie sat her mum and dad down to explain what had made her go to the nursery.

'Over the past few weeks, I have seen a fantastic change in Emma. She is happier and much more confident. She runs around singing "I've got a dad". She is happier at school and is a much more contented girl than she ever was. Bridget told me how good Jack is with Emma at these meetings and how he doesn't blame me for anything. He has told Bridget and — most important of all — he has told Emma how much he still loves me. Mum, I think I still love him as well.'

'Bloody right as well!' said Ted. 'I never did believe he was guilty of anything. I have always liked that boy and the thought that he might harm either you or Emma was madness, but the injunction was the right move at the time. If you really feel like this, Val, why don't you make it official? Go back to court and have everything cancelled.'

'My solicitor advised me weeks ago to wait and see how things progressed. He said that once Jack's pardon comes through, then maybe we can go back to court. I can't wait that long. Jack has got to know that I feel the same way about him as he does about me,' Val said.

Ted came in with a suggestion. 'It's your birthday soon, Val. Mum and I planned to throw you a little party. Why don't you actually speak to Jack at the next meeting and invite him to your party? We could hold it here and most of your friends will all know the news about Jack and especially the way you feel about him. Nobody else needs to know. No solicitors or anybody. After all it is your thirtieth, love.'

'I'll be twenty-eight, Dad, not thirty.'

'Shall we do it, then? Are we agreed, May?' Ted was cuddling Valerie.

The friends invited to the party were to be chosen carefully and sworn to secrecy. Everyone would be told it was a surprise party for Valerie with no mention of Jack. Secretly, both Ted and May were worried that their carefully planned arrangements would fall apart.

Valerie and her parents began to prepare. They told Bridget of the secret plan to get Jack there, and she reluctantly agreed to cooperate. She loved Valerie as an old friend and she liked Jack very much.

At the next visitation meeting, Valerie delivered Emma in good time to Bridget and they both awaited Jack's arrival. He came to the nursery on time, at ten o'clock. He and Emma began to chat and play. When they had spread pencils and a colouring book on the floor, Valerie walked into the playroom.

'Hello, Jack!' she said.

Jack immediately stood up, dumbstruck.

'Val, I didn't realise the time. I'll go immediately, I am sorry.'

'You're not out of time, Jack,' Bridget said. 'Val is here on purpose.'

'I'll get arrested. I'll go right now. I'm not going back to prison — I couldn't bear it.' Jack was very scared. He gathered up his things to leave. Emma ran to Bridget and buried her face in her lap.

'Jack, please stay, I want to talk to you. Don't be scared. No-one knows I'm here. Please stay, Jack. I need to speak to you without solicitors getting involved,' Val pleaded. 'It's so nice to see you after all this time. You look so well, you've lost weight,' she said.

'Yes, it was the prison food; it was crap. Look, Val, it's fabulous to see and speak to you as well, but this should not be happening. I'll go immediately.' Jack's face was white. Valerie approached him and they stood face-to-face. They didn't touch.

'Jack, these last three months you've been seeing Emma, she has changed for the better. She is so happy, and these meetings are doing her such a lot of good,' Val explained.

'I love her; it's not hard work. She has also done me the world of good, too. Look, Val, I am scared to be here with you. This is against all the rules of the injunction,' Jack said.

'I know, but please don't worry, Jack. Only Mum, Dad and Bridget know I am here. Please listen. We need to talk. We need to talk about the future, for Emma's sake.' Valerie tried to calm Jack down.

'I agree, and anything you want me to do, I'll do it. Whatever you want me to sign, I will — anything, as long as I can continue to see Emma. You have got your divorce, and you can see who you want, do what you want, start a new life for yourself. I won't stand in your way. I do need to pay you some support money, which I promise I will do when my compensation is paid. I will give you anything you want, but I must be able to see Emma.' Jack was babbling and repeating himself.

'I know how you feel, Jack, and I believe I feel the same way. I don't need anyone else, but we must talk. We can't talk here, not in front of Emma, at least.' Valerie paused.

Jack was shaking a little.

'Dad is throwing me a birthday party in two weeks and I want you to be there,' Val explained. 'There will only be a few of my friends — I mean our friends — there, and whilst Mum looks after Emma, we can talk, without all this legal mumbo jumbo. Will you come, please?' Val begged.

Jack wondered what friends would be at the party. He had no friends. They had all dropped him like a stone when he was convicted. What if these so-called friends reported him and had him arrested? He wasn't sure what their reaction to him would be. He trusted no-one.

'Are the two men still following you or watching you?' he asked.

'No, I've been very careful. Our house is locked up and Emma and I are in a safe house. No repeats of that episode. Please say you will come to the party... please!'

'This has all been very sudden, Val. I am not too proud to tell you I am scared, very scared especially with other people there.' Jack stepped back, away from Valerie.

He wanted so badly to talk to her, to hold her, to hug her and to kiss her and tell her how he really felt and to apologise for all the trouble he had caused her. He was silent for a couple of minutes.

'Yes, alright, I will be there, if you're sure.'

'I am sure. You will be my best ever birthday present!' Val

gave Jack a hug. No kissing, just a hug. Her hair smelled fabulous, just like he remembered, and she felt wonderful to hold.

They began to play with Emma, just like a proper family, whilst Bridget looked on, smiling. Emma, not really understanding the enormity of the situation, was just so happy being able to play with both Mummy and Daddy.

Meanwhile, progress in the incident room had not gone too well over those ten weeks. Live enquiries aren't the same as in films or on tv. The film-makers can solve everything in an hour, but in real life things are different.

Even with all his extra staff, DCI Chris Rice was struggling. What with handling a person in custody, the extradition warrants and hearings in at least two countries for suspects abroad, the FBI, the diplomatic corps, and the putting together of information for warrants and for court appearances of the other witnesses that were now being traced, he had his work cut out.

However, to some extent, the cooperation and information from Government departments had improved, and that was helping the enquiry. A delegation from the Foreign Office was attempting to speak to the Russians again, but they didn't hold out too much hope of convincing them of the situation. They had also asked for assistance in the investigation into the import of drugs via the diplomatic bags. Their efforts to build a collaborative relationship were not going to be easy or straightforward.

A small piece of good news came Rice's way: confirmation from the Home Office that the larger sum of £500,000 had been awarded to Trevor Frost (given without prejudice) and would be paid to him within days. There was also good news regarding the pardon, which was ready to be signed off the minute the first convictions for their current enquiry were in.

Rice knew that this would not be acceptable to Frost and that he would still not be able to actually speak to him until the pardon was issued, but the money should convince him that they were doing the best they could. DS Cramer was instructed to inform Frost's solicitor, Lee Wooding, of the compensation payment as soon as possible.

Chapter Fifteen

THE PARTY

It was the day of Valerie's party and Jack was nervous, apprehensive, happy and confused all at once. He didn't know how things were going to work out. He was nervous of seeing Valerie again, and also apprehensive about meeting 'so called' friends. How would they take to him?

He hadn't told Gerry or Lee that he had actually met and spoken to Valerie. They would not have been impressed, and as for attending Valerie's birthday party, they would have been livid.

He got his clothes out ready: new shirt, suit and tie. He would wear the special cologne from Trumpers in Jermyn Street; it was an expensive perfume for men that he knew Valerie liked. She used to buy it for him every Christmas. He was now satisfied that he was fully prepared for the party.

He aimed to arrive at Ted and May's house around half five. At about two o'clock, his mobile rang.

'Hello, Jack, it's Lee. I've got some brilliant news. I've just been contacted by DS Cramer from the police incident room and he informed me that a sum of £500,000 has been awarded to you in compensation, more than the promised £250,000. Without prejudice, of course.'

'Without prejudice?' Jack asked.

'That means they are not admitting any guilt in any way, but they are willing to compensate you for the position you have found yourself in, pending a final decision. I have told them that will not be enough and we shall probably be applying for a higher sum in due course. Next week, I'll pay the money into the William Harris account. Is that alright, Jack?' Lee asked.

'Yes, Lee, that's great news. Five hundred grand is a lot of money. At least I'll be able to pay you and Gerry back the money I owe.'

'Great. Don't worry about the money, Jack. What are you doing today?'

Jack nearly blurted out that he was going to a birthday party, but stopped himself just in time.

'Me? I'm just writing a few articles; perhaps watch a bit of snooker later, nothing much. Thanks for the news, Lee. Anything more about my pardon?'

'Afraid not. That will probably come later. I did remind them that you will not talk to them until the pardon comes through officially,' Lee said.

'Thanks, Lee. Never mind; I'll just have to wait.'

Jack put the phone down. Half a million pounds was a life-changing sum and he thought things were looking up for him. Now he knew he had enough money to buy Val a nice present.

As he left the house, he was even more vigilant than usual about keeping an eye out for anybody lurking about outside.

After researching on the internet, Jack had discovered that the precious stone that depicts love is a diamond, so he made his way to the jewellers and chose a nice diamond pendant on a chain. Valerie wasn't a bling person. She liked understated but precious jewellery. He also bought a little teddy bear for Emma. Finally, he thought of buying was some flowers — Valerie loved fresh flowers — then he made his way back to the car.

He parked his car the next street down from Valerie's parents' house. He had about an hour to kill.

Just a couple of minutes before five thirty, Jack went up to the front door. It was a big moment and he hesitated before ringing the doorbell. The door was opened by May, who immediately smiled, flung her arms around him and kissed him.

She must have thought the flowers were for her, because she took them from him, saying how lovely they were and that she would put them in water. Jack followed her into the kitchen. Their conversation was stilted at first until Ted came in. Straight away, he shook Jack's hand.

'Lovely to see you, lad, you're most welcome.' He called out for Valerie who burst through the door. She looked fantastic, Jack thought. She was stunning. Her hair was as golden as when they first met, and her make-up was perfect, as always.

'Happy birthday, Val,' Jack said. He didn't kiss her. Before Valerie could reply, Emma came running in and shouted 'Daddy!'

Emma wanted a kiss and jumped up for a hug from Jack.

'Lovely to see you, Jack, thanks for coming,' Valerie said, quietly. 'You're one of the first to arrive. Would you like a drink?'

'Just a Diet Coke for me, if you have it?' said Jack. May brought it over.

'Come now, Emma, Mummy and Daddy want to talk, help me pick some flowers for the table.' May held out her hand and the little girl took it happily.

Ted said, 'I'll leave you two alone,' and joined his wife and granddaughter in the garden.

'Can we talk, Jack?' Valerie asked.

'Yes, we must. There's so much to sort out,' Jack replied.

They went into the calm of the front lounge.

'This situation we are in is none of our making. I listened to bad advice from lots of people who told me to divorce you after your conviction. I am so sorry, Jack, but I was so scared and confused. I should have trusted you and I didn't,' Valerie began.

'Please, Valerie, no post-mortems. What is done is done. I don't blame you for anything. It was the right thing to do at that time. My main concern now is seeing my daughter. I love her very much, and she is caught in the middle of this mess.'

'Where do we go from here?'

'I am desperate to continue seeing Emma, if you permit it, and I promise not to stand in your way. I will comply with any of your wishes, as long as I can go on seeing her. It breaks my heart that our relationship is finished, and I can do nothing about it, but Emma deserves to have a proper dad and I really want that to be me.'

'You have nothing to worry about there. I won't stop you seeing Emma; she thinks the world of you. I don't agree that our relationship is finished, but we will have to go slowly to get things back onto an even keel,' Valerie reassured him. 'I am sorry about the injunction, Jack. Again, I took bad advice but, as it was, you were at large, you were a convicted murderer, and no-one knew where you were. The injunction was to protect me and Emma. By the time we understood why you were out of prison, it was too late. I didn't know what to do.' Valerie was getting upset.

'I wanted to see you again and, of course, Emma, but you must know, I'm not comfortable being here; I am not comfortable at all. I know why you got the injunction, but there are now two separate court rulings that could see me going back to prison. My only thoughts at the moment are for Emma, but I have to protect myself or I will be back in the nick, and I'll never see her again.'

'Look, Jack, just for today, stay and enjoy the party and

perhaps tomorrow we could all go to the Bekonscot Model Village at Beaconsfield, all three of us as a proper family. It's not far away.' She paused. 'It's really great to see you again.' She almost took hold of him for a reassuring cuddle, but held back.

'Please accept this little gift for your birthday.'

'Thank you, Jack. You just being here is my perfect gift,' she said. Again, she nearly kissed him, but he had already moved away.

Jack found Emma and the two played, talked, laughed and eventually danced together. He tried to avoid the other party guests. Mostly, they were polite, said hello, and then moved away from him, which suited Jack. A couple of them tried to chat but it was obvious they were finding it hard to avoid questions about the murder and prison, and his current situation. The conversations didn't last long.

The atmosphere improved as the evening went on. He and Emma were inseparable, leaving Valerie to socialise with her guests. Jack kept to soft drinks, and he and Emma nibbled on the party snacks together.

Later, Jack was dancing with Emma out in the back garden, weaving through a happy group of guests swaying to the music. The DJ had set his sound system up at the end of the garden with coloured lights shining onto the grass. There was a table with a mixture of drinks: wine, beers and spirits.

Valerie was dancing with a tall man of about her own age. He was smartly dressed and was twirling her around. Once or twice, he got quite close to her, and she looked happy.

Jack showed Emma how to place her feet on his shoes, and they danced to the music. She thought this was great fun and they did it again and again until she became tired, so he lifted her up and danced gently with her in his arms, both enjoying a cuddle at the same time. The DJ was playing a Cliff Richard favourite, and Jack sang the words to Emma. As he sang, he believed he truly was 'holding the dream' and whatever money was coming to him was nothing compared to this, for with his little girl in his arms, he was as rich as a king, just like the song said.

The words were perfect.

'Are you tired, Peanut? Shall I take you up to bed?'

'Yes, please, Dad, will you tell me a story?' Emma said, in a sleepy voice.

'Of course.'

'Dad, why do you call me Peanut?'

'It's because I love peanuts and I love you,' Jack smiled.

He could see that Valerie was still dancing with the tall guy. Jack thought his name was John, a colleague from the office where Val used to work. She still looked happy, dancing close to him in the slower songs.

May and Jack took Emma upstairs. May took Emma to the bathroom where she cleaned her teeth and washed her face and then changed her into pyjamas. In the bedroom, Emma got herself comfortable in bed. Jack found a nice story book. Thankfully, the music from the party was in the back garden, on the other side of the house. Not too loud, but they could still hear it.

Jack read Emma her story, and soon he heard her gentle, rhythmic breathing. When he was sure she was in a deep sleep, Jack kissed her cheek goodnight, and whispered 'I love you.'

Downstairs, Jack looked out into the garden. Val was still dancing with John. Jack found Val's father in the kitchen. 'I'll be going now, Ted. Thanks ever so much for having me.'

Ted grasped his hand. 'You're not going? It's still quite early. I'll call Val.'

'No, don't trouble her, Ted. She's having such a good time. Say goodbye to her for me. Tell her I'll see her tomorrow as planned.'

May came in and Jack said goodbye. 'I wish you wouldn't go, Jack. I haven't seen Val or Emma so happy in years,' May confessed.

'Goodbye, May, goodbye, Ted.' Jack walked down the path, through the gate and was heading down the road when he suddenly heard a voice shouting, 'Jack, Jack.' It was Valerie.

'Jack, where are you going? Why are you leaving? Stop, stop!' She grabbed his arm, and swung him round to face her. 'Why are you leaving? It's still very early, Please come back, Jack.'

'I've got a lot to do tomorrow before we go to the model village, and there is only so much fizzy you can drink.'

'Please don't go just yet. Come back, just another hour, please don't go too soon. It'll be alright,' Valerie was now pleading.

'I must be off. It has been great to see you and Emma and I had a great time, thanks.' Jack put his arm around Val's shoulders.

'I wish you wouldn't go, but I guarantee that it will all work out okay.'

'See you tomorrow,' Jack said. He looked into her eyes. 'May I kiss you?' he whispered. Valerie gazed into his eyes, smiled and nodded. As their lips met, it seemed like a bolt of electricity went through Jack's body. The kiss was wonderful. He hadn't kissed her for such a long time.

Jack didn't want the kiss to end but when they did part, Valerie said softly and lovingly, 'It will all be alright Jack, I promise.' Jack smiled and broke away.

He hadn't been so happy in years. His car was in the next street. As he reached the corner, he turned and waved at Valerie, and she waved back.

Jack allowed himself one 'Yes!' before driving away.

Chapter Sixteen

BLUE EYES CRYING IN THE RAIN

The day after the party, Jack woke up full of the joys of spring. His head was full of happy memories of the night before, not only of his fun with Emma but his renewed connection with Val. He could still smell her perfume and the warmth of her body close to his when they kissed goodnight.

He skipped breakfast because he needed to get a child safety seat fitted into his car, ready for their day out. Jack was at the door of the Halfords store near his home even before they opened. A suitable seat was chosen and fitted, and he was just about to pull away when his phone rang. It was Gerry.

'Morning, Jack, how are you?'

'I'm fine, Gerry,' Jack replied.

'Good news from Lee yesterday about the compensation. It's not the final figure, but we are getting there. Did you watch the snooker last night? Lee said you might.'

'No, I did some writing and went to bed early.' He couldn't tell him the truth.

'So, what's happening with you today, anything special?'

'Not a lot, Gerry, I might do some more writing and get it sent off to the magazines and then perhaps go out for a walk.'

'Be careful out there, Jack. It might have gone quiet from the police point of view, but we still can't trust those Russians.'

'I'm always careful. I was trained to be careful. Don't worry about me. By the way, when Lee gets that money, tell him to take out what I owe the pair of you, then pay it in. I can't thank you two enough for your help.'

'Don't worry about all that. Shall I pop round for a drink or something? Would you like some company?' Gerry suggested.

'No! No, thanks, Gerry, I'm alright. Need some peace and quiet to get down on paper some thoughts for my next articles.' Jack had to think on his feet. 'I need a clear head with no distractions; hope you understand.'

'Okay, mate, I'll catch up with you in a couple of days. Speak soon.' Gerry hung up.

Jack was very excited about going out with Val and Emma. He knew his way to Bekonscot Model Village. It was about an hour away and perhaps, he thought, they could have a spot of dinner on the way back. Just the three of them.

That morning Bridget had brought Emma to the nursery because Valerie said she had something to do first thing and would come later. Spot on ten, Jack burst through the door and there was Emma. She squealed with pleasure and ran up to greet Jack with a big kiss.

'Hello, my little Peanut,' Jack said, and picked her up for a kiss and a cuddle. 'Where's your mummy?'

'Valerie won't be long, Jack. She said she had something important to do this morning and she would be as quick as she can,' Bridget said. 'Did you enjoy yourself last night?'

'Yes, it was grand. Emma and I danced and laughed. It was a great evening and it was nice to see Val so happy,' Jack remarked. 'Where were you? Why weren't you at your best friend's party?'

'My Frank had already booked us a night out. We went to the theatre and then we had a meal. Frank had booked it as a surprise and Ted didn't know. I was gutted when he asked me,' Bridget said.

'Daddy and I danced. I danced on his feet,' Emma said laughing.

'What shall we do today, Peanut? Would you like to go somewhere with me and mummy?' Jack asked.

'And Auntie Bridget as well?' Emma asked.

'No, just you, me and Mummy. How would that be? With something to eat on the way home.'

'What, peanuts?' Emma blurted.

Jack laughed and said 'No, no peanuts. It could be chicken nuggets, or a burger, or something else?'

'I like pizza,' Emma suggested.

'Pizza it shall be then,' said Jack.

'Where are we going, Daddy?'

'That will be our surprise to you, but I know you'll love it,' Jack said.

Bridget looked up at the sky. It was dull and overcast. 'I do hope the rain stays off. It looks a bit gloomy up there.'

'We'll be alright,' said Jack. 'The rain can't ruin our day.'

'Where did you go last night? You said you would see me in the morning but you weren't there,' Emma said.

'Well, this is the morning, and I am seeing you,' Jack said.

'We had cake and sweets, Auntie Bridget, and sausage rolls and me and Mummy got presents.' Emma was full of it. 'I thought you would be there when I woke up to have breakfast with you, Daddy. But Uncle John was there instead and mummy made me kiss him goodbye. I don't like him — he's creepy,' Emma said.

'What do you mean, Emma? What was Uncle John doing

there in the morning?' Jack was puzzled. Emma stared at him.

'Where did he sleep?' Jack was even more puzzled. He knew there were only three bedrooms in the house: Ted and May's, Valerie's, and Emma's.

'I don't know. He was just there this morning and Mummy made me kiss him goodbye. I didn't want to. He smelled funny,' Emma added.

Jack looked at Bridget, but she just shrugged her shoulders as if to say 'I don't know'.

'He wasn't there when I picked up Emma,' she said.

Jack was really perturbed.

'Is Valerie seeing this John, Bridget?' he asked, when Emma had run off to play with the dolls' house. He was distraught at what the answer would be.

'I don't think so, Jack, she hasn't told me anything. I'm sure she isn't. She used to work with him years ago and I think they just remained friends.'

'Valerie kissed me last night, Bridget, and she told me everything was going to be alright. I thought she meant it but now I don't know.'

'If she kissed you, Jack, it must mean something good, and I am sure she was right when she said that everything was going to be alright. It's about time you both got back together,' Bridget said.

'It would be great for us to be a family again and put these last few years behind us. Did Val say where she was going this morning?' Jack asked.

'No' Bridget answered. 'She only said it was important and she would be here as soon as she could.'

Emma was playing on the floor and Jack knelt down beside her.

'It made me jump when the police banged on the front door. They woke me up,' Emma blurted out.

'This morning?' Jack asked.

'No, in the night. It was dark and the banging scared me and there was a lot of shouting. I heard Grandad talking to them. I was on the landing and saw the men standing outside.' Emma's eyes were wide.

'Tell me, Peanut, what did the police do?' Jack didn't want to frighten Emma, but he needed to know why the police had come to the house.

'Well, the police came in and went out to the back garden. Grandad was talking to them. Mummy was a bit upset. I got out of bed and saw them from upstairs but Nanny came up and took me back to bed,' Emma explained.

'What about the police, Emma, what did they do?'

'They just looked around the garden and then I heard them go out of the front door. Grandad was talking to them.' Emma sat up.

'Did they come upstairs? Did the police come upstairs?' Jack was speaking very sharply.

'I don't know, Daddy. Nanny put me back to bed,' Emma whispered.

Jack stood up and turned to Bridget. 'Why were the police there? What did they want?'

Without waiting for an answer, he strode to the corner of the playroom and stood shaking his head. Suddenly, he let out a loud scream that made Bridget jump and Emma burst into tears.

'How could she do this to me? How could she do it? She said everything was going to be okay. It's all becoming clear now.' Jack was shaking, talking to himself. 'It's so simple. Why did I not see this coming?'

'Calm down, Jack. What did you not see coming?'

Jack was beside himself with anger and very near to tears. 'Don't you see it, Bridget? It's now all clear to me.' He paused and gathered himself. 'She had been seeing this long streak of piss, John, for years. When I was arrested, this was her golden chance to get rid of me for good. How lucky was she? She divorced me and then was free to do what she wanted.'

Again, Jack paused and this time tears were pouring down his face.

'But I was released from prison, which really must have cocked things up for her.' Jack paused again and Bridget could see blood on his lower lip where he had bitten it.

'She pretended to be friends with me again for Emma's sake. "It's all going to be alright," she said. And I believed her. I believed her!' Jack was repeating himself. "Come to my party," she said. "It's all going to be alright." She was dancing all night with her John while I was with Emma. I didn't get a look-in. But I scuppered her plans by leaving the party early. She didn't want me to leave. "Stay a bit longer," she said. "It's going to be alright," she said. Even Ted and May begged me not to leave — they were in on it as well. But I left the party early, *too* early, because the police hadn't arrived yet. They would have found me and arrested me and I would have been out of her hair again. Why? Why?' Jack began pacing the floor.

'I'm sure Val wouldn't have done that, Jack. She's not like that.' Bridget tried to comfort him.

'It all fits now. It's like a jigsaw. I was blind with love for Emma and Val, and I didn't see what she was doing.' Jack was silent while he was thinking, making all the pieces fit.

'Where is Val now?' he eventually asked.

'I really don't know. She asked me to be here with Emma

this morning because she had something important to do before coming over here,' Bridget replied.

'I've got to go,' Jack said, in a panic. 'She's probably gone to the police, because her little plan to have me nicked last night went wrong because I left early, and she's bringing the police here this morning. I've got to go.' He headed for the door.

'No, Jack, don't. I'm sure Val has done no such thing and she'll be here really soon,' Bridget pleaded.

'Yes, she'll bring the police with her, I bet. Don't you help her, Bridget, I know you're close friends. I've got to go. Thanks for everything you've done.' Jack was still pacing the floor and Emma watched him, bewildered and upset.

Bridget picked Emma up and followed Jack out into the playground, where a fine rain was falling. Jack took Emma from Bridget and kissed her. Tears were falling down his cheeks.

'Peanut, listen to Daddy, this is very important. I have to go away. I won't be able to see you anymore.'

Emma glared at him. 'What? Never again? Why?'

Jack couldn't look at his daughter. 'No, Emma, never again. I'm sorry.'

'What have I done, Daddy?' She began to cry.

'You've done nothing wrong at all, my lovely girl, just remember that I love you very, very much and I always will. Please remember that. It's important that you do.' Jack was cuddling Emma very closely and kissing the top of her head.

'Bridget, promise me you will look after Emma. I'll be no trouble to anyone anymore.'

He handed a crying Emma back to Bridget. 'Goodbye, my lovely Peanut, be a good girl. Remember, I love you.'

Jack made his way to the gate, turned and took one last look at Emma and waved weakly.

Jack walked briskly away. Suddenly, he stopped and went down on one knee. He was crying uncontrollably. This was the last time he was ever going to see her.

He collapsed into the car and cried uncontrollably. He knew what he had to do to end the misery he was living in. No-one would be troubled by him any longer. He could only think of Emma crying, which upset him even more. He turned the ignition on, and Willie Nelson's *Blue Eyes Crying in the Rain* began to play on the radio. It was so apt; every line broke his heart afresh. He drove away sobbing, knowing that he had only his memories, and the last of them was little Emma's huge blue eyes crying, as he kissed her goodbye. They would never meet again.

Chapter Seventeen

VAL'S DILEMMA

Three quarters of an hour after Jack had left the nursery, Valerie finally arrived. She found Bridget in the playroom, holding Emma, who was still crying uncontrollably. Alarm ricocheted through her. She wanted to know why Emma was so upset. She took Emma from Bridget, and tried to console her.

'What happened? Why is Emma crying? Why is she so upset? Where's Jack?'

'Jack has gone, and for once I don't blame him,' Bridget declared.

'What? What do you mean? What do you mean "Jack's gone"?' Val asked. 'He's meeting me here, and we're going out!'

Bridget was furious. 'I'm disgusted with you, Val! What you've done is terrible. Jack's gone. He's guessed your game. He knows what you've been up to.'

'What do you mean, Bridget? What game? What have I been up to?' Val could not make sense of what was happening.

'Jack has discovered your horrid little game, found out that you're having a sordid affair with your old boss. You were dancing with him all evening, and he stayed the night. I hate to think where he slept! You invited Jack to your party, called the police, and tried to stop him from leaving because the police hadn't arrived yet.' Bridget stopped to draw breath.

'I never called for the police. This is rubbish! What on earth did Jack do to Emma? Why is she crying like this?' Val was hugging Emma closely.

'Jack didn't do anything to Emma! All he did was say goodbye to her. She thought you were all going out somewhere, but then when he realised what you were up to, he became distraught and left. Emma thinks she's done something wrong.'

'I don't understand, Bridget. What was I up to?'

'When the police didn't get Jack last night, you knew he would be here today, so you arranged for them to pick him up here this morning. Jack is not stupid, Val.' Bridget picked up her coat and bag.

'Please, Bridget, I've not understood anything you've said. I'm not seeing John. He's just an old workmate and friend. He was there for me when Jack was arrested. He helped me. Besides, he's gay. Yes, I did dance with him last night. He was so pissed that he slept on the couch. Jack thinks there's something between me and John?'

'I think Jack has worked it out totally,' said Bridget. 'With him out of the way, you could do what you wanted when he went to prison. You divorced him, so there was nothing to stop you, but you didn't bank on him being found not guilty and then released. What you've done is devious, Val, and I can't forgive you. Jack doesn't deserve all this. I'm leaving you to sort out your own mess. Don't involve me. But I will tell you this for nothing: you will never ever see Jack alive again. You have completely crushed that man and I think it is despicable.' Bridget started to leave.

'Wait a minute, please, Bridget, what do you mean I'll never see Jack alive? Why do you say that?'

'When Jack left here this morning he was totally destroyed.

When he realised what was happening, he couldn't believe you would do this to him. He was finished — he said so — and he said that no-one would be bothered by him again. He collapsed on the way to his car. I want nothing more to do with you.'

'Bridget, please, this is all nonsense. None of what you said is true.'

Bridge turned on Val. 'Well, where you this morning? Weren't you arranging for the police to come here to nick Jack?'

'No, that's not true,' Val shouted, which made Emma throw her arms around Val's neck and squeeze hard. 'I asked you to stay here with Emma and Jack because I went to an emergency session of the Family Court this morning, and made a statement to have the injunction revoked and the conditions lifted.'

'Oh!' Bridget exclaimed.

'I want us to get back together; that's why the injunction had to be lifted. I still love him, Bridget, I've realised that for the last two months. Where is Jack now? Did he say where he was going?'

'No, Val. He said goodbye to Emma and left. He thought you were bringing the police to arrest him,' Bridget replied.

'Oh, Bridget! You don't think Jack would do anything silly, do you?'

'He was dreadfully upset. I don't know what he may do.'

'Oh, my God, I've got to find him.' Val kissed Emma and wiped away her tears. 'I'll find Daddy, I promise,' she said to Emma.

'Bridget, please, just this one more time, please look after Emma. Take her to Mum and Dad's, tell them what's happened. I must try and find him.'

'He did say you told him that everything would be alright and he believed you. But he thought you were plotting with the police for him to be put away again. Val, he's got it all so wrong and so did I. I'm so sorry,' Bridget apologised.

'Emma, darling, I must go and find Daddy. Stay with Auntie Bridget.' Val kissed Emma.

'Can't I come too?'

'No, my lovely. Mummy must rush. You go to Nanny and Grandad. I'll be back as soon as I can. Tell Mum I'll be in touch,' Val said. As she left the playroom, she turned to Bridget. 'How long has Jack been gone?'

Bridget, who was now comforting Emma, said, 'About an hour. Hurry.'

Valerie had no idea where she was going to find Jack. She didn't know where he was living; she had no idea where to start. She began to cry. What must he be thinking of her? This was all her fault.

Their first house was the place where they were happiest. That might be somewhere he would head for. She accelerated onto the A41.

Turning into their old street, she noticed a car with two men in the front, parked half-on and half-off the kerb outside a large house, four doors down from their old home. Were they the police or the Russians? She drove past them, glancing away as she drew level. She made sure in her rear-view mirror that she wasn't being followed and, as their car didn't move, was pretty sure they had not recognised her.

Perhaps Jack would have gone to see Jean and Peter. It was the only other address Valerie knew he was connected to. Now cautious and well-trained and instructed by Jack, she left her car further up the street away from Jean and Peter's house and walked back. No-one followed her. However, there was no sign of Jack's car, which wasn't good.

She rang the doorbell, and eventually Jean opened the door.

'What are you doing here?' It was an unexpectedly hostile greeting.

'Hello, Jean, I'm desperate to find Jack. There's been a terrible misunderstanding,' said Valerie. 'Have you spoken to him today?'

Jean had been crying. Her eyes were puffy and red.

'I need to speak to him,' Val pleaded.

Jean was sharp. 'He's gone. Why don't you leave him alone? Hasn't he had enough?'

'So, you've seen him, then? Please, Jean, you've got me all wrong and so has Jack. Please let me explain.'

Peter appeared at the door and moved Jean aside. He was angry. 'Don't you think you've done enough? You've destroyed Jack's life and now you want to rub his nose in it. You've succeeded in breaking him — you don't need to do any more. We thought better of you than this and you've involved poor little Emma in your scheming plans. Jack has said his goodbyes. We won't see him again. So, thank you, Valerie, and now, please, leave us alone.'

'Peter, Jean, please let me explain. Jack has got it all wrong. I must speak to him — please help me find him.'

Jean began to cry again and Peter closed the door in Valerie's face.

Shocked, Valerie made her way back to her car. The only consolation she could muster was that she truly believed that Jean and Peter would never have let Jack disappear if they thought he would do harm to himself. She sat with her head in her hands and started to cry. She was being accused of something she hadn't done and the only man she had ever loved had mistakenly blamed her for ruining his life. She had no way of being able to tell him the truth.

And the only people who had been in touch with Jack didn't believe her either.

She made her way slowly back to her mum and dad's house. What was she going to tell Emma? Bridget had obviously told May and Ted what had happened. Emma was upstairs with May.

Ted put his arms round his daughter. 'Dad, I don't know what to do, I can't find Jack to tell him the truth.'

'This is a fine, bloody mess, but I can see why and how Jack came to the conclusions he did. You danced with John all night, when you had invited Jack to your party specifically to talk with him,' Ted said.

'But Jack was there for Emma and I didn't want to spoil it for her,' Val explained.

'Nonetheless, I can see what he was thinking, Val, and what with the police turning up just after he left, he jumped to the wrong conclusion. Who the bloody hell complained to the police about our party being noisy?'

'Dad, Bridget said that Jack was going away and none of us would see him again. His own sister and brother-in-law said the same thing. You don't think he'll do something…?'

'No more talk like that please, Val, Jack is a sensible lad, he wouldn't do anything silly, besides he thinks the world of Emma and he wouldn't do anything to upset her,' Ted said.

'He's already said his goodbyes to Emma. That's *why* she is so upset,' Val wailed.

'Did you get the injunction turned around?'

'I went to the court this morning. I had to explain why I wanted the injunction cancelled and my statement will be submitted to the judge at the next court hearings in a couple of weeks. They wanted to make sure that I was not being put under pressure to cancel it, especially from Jack. They asked me if I had seen Jack, but I was careful not to let them know, just that I was now convinced that Jack was not guilty and that he wasn't a threat to me. Oh, this is such a mess, Dad.'

'Could you trace Jack through his solicitor? How about giving him a ring? Have you got his number?'

'No, I only have my solicitor's number. We're not supposed to have any contact with each other, remember? How can I ask Bradshaw to make it possible for Jack to contact me when he is officially banned from doing so? I will never be able trace him now. Nobody knows where he's gone.'

Val fished out her address book and phoned a few of Jack's old friends, but none of them had spoken to him since his conviction or, if they had, they were not telling her.

She had nowhere to turn. Jack had disappeared into the ether.

When Jack left Emma at the nursery, he could barely drive for crying. He had to stop a couple of times to pull himself together. As far as he was concerned, this was the end for him.

Finally, he decided on a course of action, one that he didn't like, but he had no choice. He was a wanted man, except by his wife. Russian agents wanted him; his ex-wife just wanted him out of the way so she could continue her relationship with streak-of-piss-John. The only one that he knew loved him was his five-year-old daughter. The thought of her blue eyes crying in the rain would haunt him now until the end.

He had tried to explain his position to Jean and Peter, who had been very sympathetic and assured Jack they would stand by him in any decision he made for his future.

Jack said there was only one solution to his situation, but didn't explain further. In the silence that followed, Peter looked at Jack's red-rimmed and haunted eyes and understood what Jack was trying to say. He gripped Jack's shoulders and pleaded with him to think again.

When Jean realised this was to be a final goodbye, she burst into tears.

'No crying, Jean. I've cried enough for everybody. It's the only way. Keep a look out for Emma for me. When she is old enough, tell her about me. Only the good things mind.' Jack smiled. 'Get rid of any of my stuff which I have left here, I won't want it. Cheers, Peter, you're a great bloke and a wonderful husband to my little sister. Thanks.' Jack left by the front door. A short wave, and he was gone.

He went back to his flat and sat for an hour or so, thinking. No more tears, just deep thought.

The previous night, he had acquired a photograph of Emma and Valerie together. He had asked Ted if he could have it, but Ted hadn't replied, so Jack had just taken it out of its frame and put it in his pocket.

He retrieved it from his jacket and sat staring at it.

He still couldn't believe that Valerie hated him that much; that she could be so vindictive, and that she would involve her mum and dad. Poor little Emma. He still loved Val, and always would, but in her eyes, he had obviously done something dreadfully wrong. There was only one answer.

Not having decided where he was going to go to end the nightmare, or how he was going to do it, he thought he had better ring Gerry to say that he would be uncontactable for a few weeks because he was going to Scotland, or Wales, or somewhere remote, and that he would be in touch when he got back.

There was no reply from Gerry, so he phoned Lee.

Lee said, 'That's no problem, mate. You need a few days to yourself anyway, to recharge your writing cells. By the way that money is in your bank account, the William Harris account, as agreed.'

'Have you taken out what I owe you and Gerry, Lee?' Jack asked.

'No, you can sort that out later. Plenty of time for that. There should be a lot more coming when I've finished with them,' Lee said, gleefully.

'Would you let Gerry know that I will be out of contact for a short while?'

'No problem, Jack, keep in touch, just in case anything major happens, but otherwise have a peaceful time. Bye for now.' Lee rang off. A peaceful time was quite possibly exactly what Jack was going to have.

He slowly packed a few things into a holdall, which included the laptop. Anything not needed, he left behind.

While rummaging through his things, Jack found his faithful little address book. Thumbing through the pages brought back memories of much happier times. He couldn't say goodbye to all of them even if they did still rate as friends of his. After all, it had been his decision to cut off all communications.

Jack stopped at one page in the book. On it were the names of Lily and Dotty Grayling. Jack's father had been a very close friend of Lily's father. Lily was his godmother and Dotty was Jean's godmother. He had known them all his life. They were travelling showmen, members of the Showman's Guild. In fact, Lily was the chairperson of that Guild.

Jack had always been very close to Lily, and he had asked her to be Emma's godmother. She had agreed with pleasure, but he had been arrested before Emma could be christened. He could not say goodbye without taking his leave of Lily, and explaining things to her. He closed up his flat and wrote a short note to the landlord, enclosing another month's rent to cover his early departure, which he dropped off at the letting agents, together with the keys.

Lily and Dotty lived in a large Winnebago in north London. This was located on four acres of land, purchased many years ago to store the rides and sideshows of the family fairground during the winter and where they also maintained the machinery.

At the gates, Jack was met, as usual, by two large, vicious-looking Alsatians who were barking and baring their teeth.

'Hello, Kim, hello, Meg. Sit down, you two, behave now. I won't bite you,' he said, with a laugh. As soon as the dogs heard Jack's voice, they stopped barking and stood quietly. Jack called out, 'Ronny? Ronny?'

Ronny was Lily's trusted foreman, more family than employee. A wiry, grey-haired man stepped out of his caravan, and greeted Jack with a firm handshake.

'Hello, Ronny, how are you doing?'

'Jack, it's wonderful to see you, come on in. You've been through some shit, mate. Are you okay? Lily and Dotty will be pleased to see you.'

As they approached the steps to Lily's home, the top of the stable door swung open, and her lovely, familiar, smiling face appeared. 'Ahoy, my lovely boy! Jack, it's wonderful to see you. Come here and give me a kiss, you lovely boy. What do you say?'

'Ahoy, lovely Lily,' Jack replied, using the old Romany language for hello.

Lily welcomed Jack into the caravan with a big kiss and a cuddle.

'Dotty, come see who's here,' Lily shouted for her sister.

Jack instantly felt at home. He relaxed into one of the big, deep-cushioned seats and the pain and tension began to drain from him.

Chapter Eighteen

LILY TO THE RESCUE

Lily and Dotty Grayling were the two matriarchs of the fairground: strong personalities, as befitted their roles. They had taken over the fairground stalls, machinery and rides from their father, who had been one of the biggest showman travellers in the country. The Grayling family was spread all over the UK, all of them successful fairground operators, and all members of the Showman's Guild.

Lily was fifty-eight and Dotty was two years younger. Lily was a warm, kindly woman to her family, but when setting up a fairground, she was formidable. Nobody could, or would, argue with her, and each fair was successful, no matter what the weather was.

When Jack's mother had died, the year he turned eleven, Jack was devastated. Lily persuaded his father to let both Jack and Jean visit as often as possible, and they were always very close. Both Lily and Dotty smothered Jack and Jean with love, and that never changed throughout their growing up. At one time, Jack was going to work on the fairgrounds, as his father had once done, but his burning ambition was to be a detective, and Lily had always encouraged him in every way.

Dotty made some tea, and Lily sat down with Jack.

'Come on, my love, tell us everything. We want to know. We tried to visit you in prison but we were told that you weren't agreeing to any visitors and would see nobody. I did write to you but you never answered my letters.' Her reprimand was gentle but serious. 'You were a bad lad, Jack. At least you could've replied.'

Jack told them everything, from his getting drunk at the wetting the baby's head party, through to the conviction and his existence in prison.'

'Why wouldn't you see me?' Lily asked.

'I just wanted to cut everyone out of my life. I was innocent but nobody I knew could help me, not after the evidence that was put before the court. The jury would've found the Pope guilty on that evidence.' Jack smiled weakly.

Dotty winked at Jack. 'No blaspheming now, there's no need for that.'

He went on to describe what happened when he was released from prison and the problems he had encountered when he tried to get permission to see Emma. He told them how he was under the threat of arrest after Valerie had taken out the injunction. He told them of the false identity that had been created for him and about how wonderful it had been to see his daughter.

Dotty served up more tea and cake. By now, Jack was feeling emotionally drained. He finished the whole sordid tale about how Valerie had called the police on him and his lucky escape.

Lily was disgusted. 'I can't believe Valerie could do that to you. You don't do that to family. What are you going to do now, my love?'

It was at this point that Jack broke down. Tears poured down his cheeks. He told them he had come to the conclusion that everyone would be happier if he was out of the way permanently. Lily and Dotty were horrified.

'You mean take your own life? You'll put those thoughts out of your mind, Jack, my boy. You have to pull yourself together. You're tired and very emotional. Go and have a lie down on my bed and we'll have a good chat about it later when you're refreshed and we've eaten one of Dotty's roast dinners. Now, stop crying.'

Lily gave him another hug, and gently pushed him towards her bedroom at the back of the caravan.

Jack was mentally drained. His mood swings during the day had taken a toll on him, and as soon as he lay on the bed, he went out like a light.

He slept for about two hours, and when he awoke, the comforting smell of roasting beef was wafting into the bedroom. He washed in the tiny wash-room, and felt refreshed after his sleep. As they sat down to enjoy the roast dinner, lovingly prepared by Dotty, Jack said, 'There are a few things that I haven't explained, about the murder, Lil.'

'We don't want all the gory details, Jack, especially over dinner. We heard them all at the trial. Now, eat up.'

'No, Lily, what you don't know is that the victim was a diplomat in the Russian Embassy. The Russians don't believe that the American girl, who has now admitted to the murder, has been telling the truth. They think this is all a set-up. Russian agents have been sent to find me to do — well, whatever they do to people like me — so, not only are the police after me, but the bloody Russians are too. The police will get me if I break any of the rules of the injunction that Val took out on me. In some ways, I think I prefer the police getting hold of me. There's no knowing what would happen to me if the Ruskies get to me first.'

'So, the Russians don't believe you; the police do believe you; you said that Valerie believed you; but now you don't believe that she does. No wonder you're confused, Jack,' Dotty said.

'Was all this the reason for you using a false name? And you tell me that Valerie and Emma are in a safe house, is that right?' asked Lily.

'Yes, either could be threatened by the Russians; they could kidnap one of them to get to me. The false name was also a way of avoiding anyone getting to me,' Jack said.

'Right, Jack, you listen to me, and you listen good. You can get all those silly ideas out of your head. You wanted to become a detective, and you did that. You were a bloody good detective, but that is all behind you now, through no fault of your own. Now you can become a showman with us, like I always wanted. As my godson, you will work for me. When this free pardon comes through, you will be able to do whatever you want. Isn't that right, Dotty?'

Dotty agreed wholeheartedly.

'Where does everyone think you are now?' Lil asked.

'Nobody knows where I am, I've just walked away.'

'What about these solicitor chaps, Gerry and Lee? What did you say their names were?'

'Gerry Forbes and Lee Wooding. They are as sound as a pound. I trust them, but I haven't even told them where I am or what I was going to do.'

'Good. Now keep it that way. Don't tell anyone, especially Valerie. From now on, you don't exist. You're part of our showmen family, and we are as close as a snake's belly. We won't tell anybody anything. Right, Dot?' Dotty nodded, enthusiastically.

'Where is your car?'

'Up the road, but it's registered in my false name,' Jack said.

'No worries, we'll get rid of that, no problem. When they find it burnt out, they'll be able to think what they like. Now, about money. I will pay you the normal rate — no more, no less — and you will work as a showman on the fair, the same as the others. You've got to start somewhere, Jack.' Lily was now in her organising role, using skills that hadn't let her down in years.

'From now on, you'll speak to no-one, only us, on the fairgrounds. Not Valerie, not your solicitors, not to poor Jean, no-one. I will take care of Jean in good time.' Lil was really getting into her motherly, protective role.

'I'm not in trouble for money, Lil. They paid me out an interim sum of £25,000 compensation and I still have a little job writing articles for magazines, which brings in a few quid,' Jack explained.

'Right, from now on you *don't* spend a penny of that money. It's not what you've got, it's the way you spend it. They would be able to trace you through the movement of the money in your bank. No, you don't use that money. Leave it where it is, and don't touch it. You write no more articles for anybody, understand?' Lily was quite strict.

Jack explained that the articles were written in his false name, William Harris. The magazines had no idea who he really was.

'Nonetheless, Jack, from now on, you have effectively been wiped off the face of the earth. Do you understand?' Lily looked at Jack with a stern but friendly face.

'Now, get your things from your car and leave it totally empty. Ronny will take care of that. If you need any money for anything, you come and see me. We've got more cash than enough, haven't we, Dotty?'

Dotty laughed. 'Yes, Lil, more than we know what to do with.'

'I should have adopted you years ago, Jack, when I had the chance. You are *family*, and we are going to take care of you from now on. Understand?'

Jack was feeling humble but was glad he actually had someone he trusted to talk to. He collected everything from his car. His few clothes and all his paperwork were in a suitcase; his laptop and a few other items were in a holdall. He checked the car for any other identifying items. On returning, he gave Lily his keys.

She went to the stable door of her caravan and shouted, 'Ronny!'

Ronny came running.

'Get a bed set up in the caravan in the corner of the yard,' Lily ordered. 'Fresh linen, mind, and make sure the heater is on. I bet it's freezing in there. When you've done that, come back here. I have a little job for you.'

'Now, Jack, how do you feel? You've got a new family who are going to take care of you, a new job and a new beginning.'

'I don't know what to say, Lily. Why are you doing this for me?' Jack said, meekly.

'Because we love you and it seems that the whole world has shat on you from a great height, and no-one shits on my godson. Right, Dotty?'

'Yes, dead right, Lil,' Dotty answered.

'Shall we have a drink to celebrate?'

'Not for me, Lil. I don't drink alcohol much anymore,' Jack said.

'No, you're right, Jack. I understand that. How about a Diet Coke or something?'

After their big dinner, they sat down comfortably and talked about the old times and then Jack's new job and what would be expected from him.

Dotty produced an album of photographs showing the history of the fairs and the showmen over the years. There were also photographs of Jack's mum and dad on their wedding day, and his own wedding to Valerie. Jack lingered over those.

'She was so beautiful, wasn't she? I vowed and promised that day, Lil, before God and all those witnesses, that I would love and cherish her all the days of my life, and I have done that. I have never even looked at another girl since that day. I still love her, even after what's happened.' Jack felt very despondent.

'I know, Jack, we were all there, but for the time being you no longer exist on this earth, until this horrible mess has been sorted out, once and for all,' Lily commanded.

Jack showed them the photograph of Valerie and Emma he had taken from Ted's house.

'Emma looks so beautiful. I know this is hurting you, Jack, but, until it's all over, you must forget them.'

Ronny knocked on the door about an hour later. 'All done, Mrs G.'

'Thanks, Ronny. The next little job I have for you will have to be done later, when it's dark. There is a small, silver Nissan Sunny parked just up the road. Reg NHW 54J. Take it and burn it somewhere. Perhaps up near Runnymede Farm, in Barnet, close to the didicoy camp. The police will blame it on them. Fuck 'em, they are the bane of our lives. They're not Romanies, not showmen, not even real genuine gypsies, just illiterate dross. Here are the keys. Make sure there is nothing in the car to connect us with it. Jack has already cleared it out, but just make sure for me. Take Charlie with you. He can bring you back in my car.'

'All understood, Mrs G, leave it to me.'

'By the way, Ronny, Jack is one of us from now on. Understand? He is my godson and he's staying with us.'

'Fully understood, Mrs G.' Ronny tipped his flat cap and disappeared.

Lil and Dot enjoyed mothering Jack for the rest of the evening. Dot went off to check Jack's sleeping arrangements in the spare caravan and to make sure it was warm, and brought back the hot water bottle to fill.

Before he said goodnight, Jack turned to them. 'I don't know how to thank you two for everything you are doing. Earlier today the bottom dropped out of my world, but I know now how good it feels to have someone I can trust at last.'

Lil pulled him into her arms and said, 'Jack, have a good night's kip tonight. Get those daft ideas out of your head once and for all, and tomorrow we'll begin to make you a showman.'

Dotty came over and kissed him goodnight and Jack took up residence in the spare caravan in the yard. He knew he was safe because no-one could get past those dogs. He was warm, well fed and relaxed. He pulled out the photograph of Val and Emma, kissed them both good night and placed the picture next to his bed.

His mobile rang. It was Gerry. Jack ignored it and turned the phone off as per Lil's instructions. As he lay in bed, he wondered how this new life would work out. He admitted to himself that it was quite exciting. He would no longer have to live a lie or blot out everything he knew and loved. He was going to be a new man. This was the only way forward now.

He fell into a deep, comfortable, safe sleep.

When Ronny returned from his late-night task, he informed Lil that the car was completely burnt out and no problems. 'Went off a treat, it did.'

'Good.' Then she asked him to bring everyone on site to her caravan. There were ten people, male and female, and they gathered outside Lily's caravan.

Lily and Dotty stood at the top of the stairs.

'Thanks for coming out. I'm sorry it's so late, but I want you all to know — and this is from me — my godson, Jack, has come to join us. Now, you all know about Jack and what he was accused of. You also know that he was *not* guilty of those acts. There are some dangerous people out there who want to get hold of him. That is *not* going to happen while he is in my care. As of tomorrow, he is going to be a showman, working alongside us. He is going to be part of our family and that means he will be afforded all our protection. Is that understood by you all?'

Lily looked around. Everyone said together, 'Understood, Lily. We'll look after him.'

Dotty turned to go in and Lil smiled 'Thanks, everyone, goodnight, and God bless.'

Chapter Nineteen

NARROWBOAT NARROW ESCAPE

After a wonderful Dotty-type breakfast, Jack was awaiting his first work orders from Lily. As the start of their winter season was coming up in a few weeks' time, some of the sideshows needed a bit of tarting up: painting and general maintenance.

'Charlie will show you what to do. Ask him to try and find you some old overalls.'

Charlie was another trusted worker who had been with the fair for many years. Not as bright as Ronny, but a cheerful chap. He and Jack went off to the workshop and set to painting some of the wooden sideshows.

By lunchtime, Jack was already painting his second panel, when Charlie told him to slow down a bit. 'We only do two panels a day, Jack. It's not a race.'

Jack sauntered back to Lily's caravan where Dotty had made another lovely lunch for them. In the afternoon, Jack painted two more panels, and Charlie said the same thing.

After a few days of this, Jack was already feeling part of the team, and was glad he'd turned to Lily for help.

Lily called Ronny to her caravan.

'Ronny, there are too many people coming and going on site.

I think Jack needs to be hidden from everybody for a few weeks, or at least until the season starts for us. Is the barge ready to go?'

'Yes, Mrs G. It's in Apsley Marina,' Ronny replied.

'Okay, lovely. Take my car, go and have a look. Fill it up with fuel and water, and check everything is suitable for few weeks' stay. Jack can stay on there until we can get him settled in his own permanent caravan or motorhome. Get some supplies in for him: milk, sugar, bread and the like. Also get some meat and eggs. I don't need to tell you what to get — just stock it up for him. No beers or spirits, Ronny. Jack don't drink much. Here's my credit card, you know the number.'

'Okay, Mrs G, leave it to me. Want me to go now?'

'Yes, please, Ronny, and if that bloke Ben still runs the Marina, give him this £20, tell him I've loaned the boat out to a friend and then wink. He will probably think I've pulled myself a toy boy.' They both laughed.

At lunch, Lily began to explain her idea for Jack's future.

'If anyone wants to hide from the world for a short while, they take to the rivers or canals. I am going to send you down to the Grand Union Canal, where we have a narrowboat called Ingrid, named after my mother. You need to get away and have a bit of down time.'

Another period alone, Jack thought. This time it was going to be a floating cell.

'The canal is ideal. No-one will bother you there and, in the meantime, I am going to organise the show on the beach at Weston. When we are all set up, you can join us. You will then learn how we operate, and how everything is packed away at the end of our short season down there. Are you up for that?'

'Yes, sure, but —'

'There are no "buts", Jack. This is what you are going to do, trust me. Now where is your mobile?'

'It's here. I only speak to Gerry or Lee on it, though. No- one else.'

'Right, make one more call to Gerry or Lee on that phone, then we shall dispose of it just like the car. If you have the phone on you, they will be able to trace where you are,' Lily explained. 'Tell him you are okay and you have lost your phone charger and that you will contact him later. Keep it short. We'll then throw it away.' She had it all figured out.

'Okay, Lily. From now on I'm in your hands,' Jack said.

'Phone him now and I'll get Ronny to get rid of it. It's the only thing that connects you to them.'

This was like getting rid of the only link he had with the outside world but Jack was totally happy. He dialled Gerry's number.

'Hello, Gerry. Any news?'

'Jack, great to hear from you. Yes, lots of news. They are finally bringing those supposed 'friends' of yours, Kim Brown and Karen Dewhurst, back to the UK. As soon as they are back, there is enough evidence to begin court proceedings. They still want to speak to you as you are now considered to be a very important witness. That's still not going to happen until the pardon is on the table, of course.'

There was a pause. No reaction from Jack at all.

'Are you alright, Jack? Lee told me that you sounded a bit down when he last spoke to you.'

'I'm going away for a few days, Gerry, but I've lost my phone charger. I'll contact you again when I can. Do I need to do anything else?' Jack asked.

'No, mate, just keep your head down. We still don't know what way the Russians are going, and the police are still badgering Lee for your location because, and this was news to both of us, the police need it for the Sexual Offences Register.' Jack was shocked.

'Fucking Sexual Offences Register? I am NOT GUILTY of any sexual offences. They know that. I don't need this, Gerry.' Jack was angry now, pacing up and down.

'Don't worry, Jack, Lee is handling that. How are the visits with little Emma going?'

'They are going alright,' Jack lied. 'Gotta go.'

Jack hung up, not waiting for any further comment.

'Did you hear that, Lily? They've put me on the Sexual Offences Register. I've not committed any sexual offences!' Jack was indignant.

'Give me that phone. I've told you, Jack, you now have nothing to do with any of them. Let them sort this shit out without you.' Lily took the phone and Jack went back to the workshop and hardly spoke for the rest of the day.

That evening, Jack sat watching the television. Apart from the bad news from Gerry, it had been a good day. He was very content to be mothered by Lil and Dot and he felt safe.

Lil said, 'Tomorrow, Jack, get your stuff together, and Ronny will take you to our narrowboat on the Grand Union. He's set it up for you. You'll love it. It's what we do when we want to get away from all the noise of the fairground and the crowds. You've got food and drink and you're fuelled up, Ronny did that for you today, so take it where you want. Have you driven a narrowboat before?'

'Yes, a couple of times. It's not too difficult.'

'There's a book on board that tells you where you can go, all the locks and marinas. It shows all the pubs on the canal. Not that that will bother you, but they do serve good food, if you don't want to cook.'

'You trust Ronny a lot, don't you?'

'Ronny is my most trusted man. He has been with me and Dot for years. He is like a brother to me, really. If you are ever in trouble and I'm not here, get hold of Ronny, and he will sort you out.'

'How will I keep in contact with you?'

'You've got my personal phone number. Just ring me when you want. There's a phone in the boat. I think you should call me at least twice a week, to let me know how you are getting on. Otherwise, don't contact anyone,' Lily ruled.

On settling down in bed that night, Jack began to think about what the near future was going to bring him. A canal boat break could be nice, except that he would be alone again. The sex offender tag bothered him but as he was leaving all 'that' life behind him, he decided to throw himself into this new role as a showman and start afresh. He kissed the photograph of Valerie and Emma and went to sleep.

The next day, Jack gathered all his clothes and personal stuff, and loaded everything into Lily's car. This did include the laptop and although Lily had instructed him *not* to send off any more articles to anyone, he thought he could still write them and send them off, albeit one day in the future.

Lily and Dotty kissed him goodbye.

'I've made a pie for you in there' — Dotty handed him a bag — 'in case you get hungry.'

'Don't forget, Jack. Keep your head down,' Lil said.

Jack and Ronny talked all the way to Hertfordshire. It was evident that Ronny was a man to be trusted. He told Jack how close he was to Lily and Dotty.

'You know all about the trouble I'm in, Ronny?' Jack enquired.

'Don't worry about all that. You're one of us now, and we'll make sure you're kept safe.'

'Thanks, Ronny,' said Jack, watching the landscape whiz by.

Ingrid was a 65-foot narrowboat and could sleep four people. She had a white hull, with a royal blue cabin line. She also had a wood-burning Aga cooker in the galley. With a double bed at the rear, and a lovely, compact bathroom with a shower and a toilet, there was everything he could need.

The fridge and larder were stocked with food and drink. The Aga he would have to get to grips with, and the stock of wooden logs was stored in a locker in the bow. There were several simple daily maintenance tasks, which were all carefully explained by Ronny.

He also showed Jack where the mobile phone was. 'It's all charged up, Jack, but remember what Lily said. Only phone her, and no-one else.'

Ronny lit the Aga and, after a short while, they both sat down to a nice cup of tea and a flick through the map book. Jack had already decided to travel north.

Ronny said, 'Don't tell me where you're going. The less I know the better and the less I will be able to tell to any other nosey parker. That's our showman's way.'

When Ronny was satisfied that Jack knew his way around the boat, he said goodbye.

'By the way, Jack, Lily told me to give you this, just before I left.' Ronny gave Jack a white envelope. 'See you soon. Good luck.'

When Ronny had gone, Jack opened the envelope. It contained £300 in cash with a little note, saying *Good luck, my love, Lil.*

He looked over the boat once again, and made sure he knew where everything was, then placed the photograph of Valerie and Emma in a prominent position next to his bed. He banked up the Aga and successfully cooked himself a bit of dinner.

The Ingrid was moored alongside other narrowboats, all of which appeared to be vacant. It was very quiet, no sounds at all: peaceful and relaxing.

Jack went out on to the rear deck, where he sat and watched the sun glitter over the canal. He referred to the guidebook, and decided where his next destination was going to be. Travelling at a maximum of four miles an hour on the canal, he wouldn't get too far, but seven or eight hours should get him up as far as White Friar's Mill.

He went back into the cabin and decided to compose an article on his laptop for one of his magazines: a scathing put-down of the Government's handling of a decision they had recently made. Free speech is wonderful, Jack thought.

He had a really comfortable sleep in a nice-smelling bed, and was amazed how much heat the Aga gave out.

Jack woke up refreshed, and made himself a nice breakfast with all the ingredients kindly supplied by Ronny. At around nine, he gave the boat one last check over, inside and out, fired up the diesel engine, untied the mooring ropes and off he went.

Travelling nice and slowly, he made his way up the Grand Union Canal. He handled the narrowboat well and enjoyed waving to the other boaters, and the people on the towpath, walking their dogs. Apart from working the locks on his own, which he found challenging, Jack was enjoying the expedition immensely. The countryside was magnificent, and he made good progress.

In accordance with the guidelines set out by the Inland

Waterways Board, travelling on the canals usually stops at about 4pm. He hadn't quite made White Friar's Mill, but that was going to be his aim the next day. He found himself a lovely, quiet spot to moor up for the night. After mastering the art of tying up the boat securely, he felt well satisfied.

That afternoon and night were incident-free and Jack fell asleep looking forward to the next day's boating.

By mid-afternoon that next day, Jack had reached White Friar's Mill. It was an old mill that had been converted into a pub, and had a good write-up for its food. That will do for me, he thought.

After tying up on the towpath, behind four other boats, Jack had a shower and felt good. While he was sitting out on the rear deck, he waved to the owner of the boat next to his, a very friendly West Indian guy, with long dreadlocks, who introduced himself as Winston. 'Although everyone calls me Winnie. My mum named me after Winston Churchill, who, incidentally, was the last white man to be called Winston before the 2000s.' They both laughed.

They swapped niceties and talked about everything in general, including the weather, their boats and the food in the pub. Winnie invited Jack onto his boat and they smoked and chatted about music, tv, books and, all-in-all, enjoyed each other's company. Jack told him nothing about his past.

'I'm going for a meal at White Friar's Mill. Do you want to come along?' Jack offered.

'No, you're alright, my allowance money hasn't come through yet.'

'Not to worry. This will be my treat.'

Winnie still didn't want to go, but Jack was very insistent. After all, he could do with the company, someone good to talk to, and certainly not about his troubles. So, they both walked the short distance along the towpath, over a small bridge and directly into the pub car park, where there was a row of Hells Angels-type motorbikes, all lined up next to each other.

'Busy place,' Jack observed.

'Yeah, it's live music night in here tonight. They always get a decent crowd in. They're not proper Hells Angels, just a group of local bikers. I don't normally come in here when it's like this, but the grub is amazing,' Winnie said.

They ordered drinks. No alcohol for Jack. He told Winnie that he was on tablets, which was a good enough excuse for Winnie. It was never mentioned again. The food was, indeed, very good, and after the meal they left the restaurant and went into the bar. The music had just started up and it sounded pretty good.

After three more drinks, one of the bikers came into the bar where Jack and Winnie were sitting.

'Didn't know they allowed you blacks this far north in our Hertfordshire.' The biker nudged Winnie.

'Cool it, man, just cool it.' Winnie turned towards the biker.

'Who you telling to cool it? This is our manor. What are you doing here?' This time, the biker pushed Winnie.

'No trouble in here, lads, take it outside,' the barman said.

'We don't have blacks drinking in our manor, do we, lads?' The biker was talking a bit louder and a couple of his mates from the back bar joined him. Suddenly, the first biker threw a punch at Winnie's head. Jack stood up. The other bikers were heading towards Winnie, fists raised.

'Leave him alone!' Jack shouted.

The first biker grabbed a bottle from the bar and smashed it on Winnie's hand, which was resting on the bar. One of the other bikers threw a punch at Winnie. Jack punched this second biker on the chin, then, without warning, slammed a good right-hand punch into one of the other bikers, which knocked this leather-clad poser to the ground, taking a table of drinks with him.

One of the customers who had been sitting at the table, minding his own business, stood up and punched one of the other bikers who, at that moment, came in from the back bar.

The fight was in full swing now.

Winnie was hurt. The bottle had broken his hand, and the first biker was still punching him. Jack set to and caught the biker squarely in the face. As he grimaced and recoiled, Jack gave him a strong, right-hand fist to his belly. The biker went down on the floor. The barman came and joined in the fight. It all happened quite quickly. Girlfriends of the bikers came from the back bar and began to join in, screaming and punching. Jack caught a couple of whacks to the head and one of the girls slapped him as well. All hell let loose, and, yes, the band was still playing. Someone called out, 'Phone the police!'

Other customers were now involved and people were hurt on both sides. The fighting only came to an end when the bikers' girlfriends screamed at them to stop.

Hearing the word 'police', Jack grabbed Winnie and helped him out of the pub. They crossed the bridge and went back down the towpath towards the boats.

'Are you alright?'

'No, they fucked my hand, man. Bastards,' Winnie replied, holding his right hand.

'Bastards,' Jack agreed. 'Have you got any long, strong rope?'

'Yeah, it's in the cupboard at the front.'

'Right, Winnie, I'm going to put a stop to their shitty behaviour. I've had enough of people shitting on me and my friends. Start your engine up.'

'What are you going to do?'

'You'll see,' Jack replied.

Jack untied Winnie's boat and manoeuvred it alongside Ingrid. He then tied the two boats together.

'I won't be long. Just be ready when I shout,' he said, taking the heavy coil of rope back along the towpath and over the bridge into the pub car park. On reaching the line of motorbikes, he dropped the rope and tied a large piece of 4x4 wooden gate post to one end of it.

Silently, he threaded the rest of the rope through the wheels of the bikes: some front wheels, some back wheels. When he had threaded the rope through eight of the bikes, he called to Winnie. 'Grab the end of this rope.'

He threw the rest of the coil of rope over the canal towards Winnie's boat, where it landed perfectly. He then tied the loose end of the rope to a metal cleat on the side of Winnie's boat.

Jack started Ingrid up and untied the mooring ropes.

'When I say "Now",' he shouted to Winnie, 'just gun your boat's engine and we'll get out of here. We'll teach the bastards.'

'Now!'

The boats moved off together at full throttle, with Jack steering both from his helm. Suddenly, the rope went taut and they heard the grinding sound of eight, lovely, shiny, very expensive motorbikes being dragged across the concrete car park and down the embankment towards and into the canal.

Jack nodded and laughed at Winnie, and Winnie untied his end of the rope from the cleat.

'That will teach those prats not to muck around with Ebony and Ivory,' Winnie said, laughing.

Chapter Twenty

WINNIE AND MILLIE

Fleeing the destruction, at four miles per hour, in the dark, on two narrowboats, wasn't the ideal getaway, but nevertheless they had a good head start on their pursuers. The lights on the front of the boats were good, but the canal had many bends and hazards so they had to take it carefully. It was a good job Winnie knew this stretch well, so they had no real problems. He had taken a couple of painkillers for his hand, and was able to steer his boat.

After about thirty minutes of navigating the canal, Winnie informed Jack that very shortly, coming up on the opposite bank, was a disused lock and to cut their speed. On their right appeared an opening in the canal and they both turned slowly into the gap. There were two open lock gates that looked like they hadn't been used in years. They entered the disused lock and Jack untied their boats and moored them separately, one behind the other.

Winnie offered Jack a drag of his spliff, but Jack declined and had a regular cigarette of his own.

'Thanks for your help back there, mate. You were awesome. You sure know how to handle yourself,' Winnie said. 'It only takes a few brainless pricks and their slaggy girlfriends to ruin someone's night,' he added.

'I can't stand bigoted bullies with their pack instinct who

think they can do and say what they want,' Jack said.

'You moved pretty quick back there, Jack, when someone shouted out "Police". You got something to hide?' Winnie asked, laughing. 'You can tell me. After all we are co-offenders in a crime.'

Jack went quiet for a few minutes, and then got up and went to his bedroom at the back of Ingrid. When he returned, he handed the photograph of Valerie and Emma to Winnie.

'This is my wife and lovely daughter. I'm divorced now, but Val and I were once very happily married. God, I miss them,' Jack explained.

'How long have you been divorced?' Winnie asked.

'About four years, too bloody long for my liking. How's your hand?'

'Easing up a bit. I've had a couple of painkillers, but I'm sure this vodka and milk will kick in soon.'

'Vodka and milk? Where did you get that combination from?' Jack enquired.

Winnie grinned and poured himself another large vodka, topping it up with cold milk.

'It's a drink that a lot of West Indians drink. The milk is for the ulcers and the vodka is for my liver. I want to keep my liver, so I decided to pickle it.' Winnie gave a loud laugh, then deftly returned to his line of questioning.

'So, why are you hiding on the canals?'

Jack told Winnie that he had been a detective, which surprised Winnie, who discreetly palmed the spliff. Jack smiled, and dismissed Winnie's efforts to get rid of the drugged cigarette.

He told him the whole story.

Winnie was quite surprised. 'You're a copper, then, are you?'

'Ex-copper! They saw to that. No, I'm not a copper any longer, and now they've made it impossible for me to see my daughter.'

Winnie didn't really like policemen; he'd had many run-ins with law enforcement officers, and he hadn't always come out on top, but Jack was so descriptive of life in the prison as an ex-copper, that Winnie became very sympathetic.

The explanation of his release from prison was a little complicated because Jack didn't really understand it himself. He showed Winnie the copy of the Police Commissioner's statement, that detailed how an American girl had confessed to the murder and how Jack was totally vindicated. He didn't mention the Russians.

'This is amazing, Jack. You've been through it — but if you are not guilty, why are you hiding on the canals? Is it the Child Support Agency?' Winnie asked.

'No. I'd been given visitation rights to see Emma and things were going quite well until...' Jack went silent and got quite emotional for a few minutes.

'Want a drink, mate?'

'No, thanks,' said Jack, patting Winnie on the shoulder. Quickly, he ran through the events of the last few days.

'That's it, Winnie, that's me, but when that stupid shit picked on you tonight, that was enough, I just had to step in.'

'I'm glad you did, man, thanks. So, I guess this makes us good friends,' Winnie said, and poured himself another drink.

'My story is not as bad as yours,' he said. 'I was busted for using, not selling, drugs. Just puff, you know? But I lost my job and just a bit of my self-esteem, so I thought fuck 'em. I sold my flat and my car, and I bought my boat and, as you said, now I slip along under everyone's radar.'

'What was your job?' asked Jack.

'I was an aero-engineer. Top dog as well, in charge of my own team, but I got busted at a festival for smoking puff. The firm didn't want a 'druggy' working on their aeroplanes: end of.'

'What are you hiding from?' Jack asked.

'From the CSA. I got a pretty good wage. The wife and I split up, and the bastards are trying to screw me for a fortune. I wouldn't mind, but I give the missus a good few bob a month, which she is happy with, but they are still after me for more,' Winnie explained.

'You've got kids, then?' Jack asked.

'Yeah, I've got two lovely kids. They're not the issue. But those CSA people are after blood.'

'How are you fixed for money?' Jack asked.

'I've got a few pounds, and my partner, Millie, works for the NHS and she has money. Living on the canal is quite cheap, so we are alright. I only have to dodge the Waterways people every now and then. They don't like you moored up in the same spot for too long.'

'Do you see your kids?' Jack asked.

'Yes, fairly often. My ex is good like that. They come down to the boat, I take them for a ride, we have dinner and then she picks them up later. Everything is now fine between us. She has another guy in tow, which is okay, and he is good with the kids. I have Millie. Everything is sweet,' Winnie explained.

'Do you miss your previous married life, your home, job etc?'

'I do and I don't,' Winnie said. 'The job was perfect. I had trained hard to get all my qualifications, and the airline I worked for was brilliant; the money was great. Everything after the court case just collapsed around me, and I just thought, bugger them, bugger everybody, and I came and lived on here. I do miss my kids, though.'

'I miss my lovely daughter. Funnily enough, I miss my wife

as well, even after everything she's done to me, but I just have to accept it, and move on,' Jack said.

'That's it, mate, we move on, to dwell in the past is fatal.'

The next day, Jack got up late, and after some breakfast, settled down with his laptop.

It was about half eleven when there was a loud, frantic, knocking on the roof of Ingrid and he could hear Winnie's voice.

'Jack? Jack! Quick, there are two coppers on the opposite towpath and they're heading our way.'

Jack unlocked the doors, and let Winnie in.

'Bloody hell, they are probably trying to find those responsible for the motorbike fiasco,' Jack surmised.

'They are probably looking for a black man. We are as rare as rocking-horse shit round these parts,' Winnie added.

'Are they in uniform?'

'No, plain clothes,' Winnie muttered, looking out of one of Ingrid's small portholes.

'How do you know they are coppers?'

'You can smell them a mile off. Oh, sorry Jack, nothing personal.' Winnie was genuinely apologetic.

Could be the bloody Russians, as well, thought Jack.

'Look, I've got to hide. If they find me — a black man with a broken hand — they will arrest me, as a dead-cert.' Winnie sounded panicky.

'Get in my shower and lock the door. If they insist on searching, I will tell them my wife is in the bath.' Jack encouraged Winnie to hide.

Sure enough, about five minutes later, the two men knocked on the door and introduced themselves as police officers, showing Jack their warrant cards. They were very polite and told him that they were investigating an act of serious criminal damage to motorcycles at the White Friar's Mill pub the night before. No mention of a fight.

They suspected, from information that they had received, that a West Indian male and a white male were involved. They then went into the normal list of relevant questions. Have you seen a black male? Have you been moored here long? Were you in the pub last night? Did you witness any fight?

The answer to most of the questions was a resounding no.

'No, I haven't seen a black man.'

'No, I wasn't in the pub last night. I'm moored too far away.'

'No, I saw no fight.'

'Don't know anything about motorbikes.'

'Only been moored here since yesterday.'

'Do you want to look around?' Jack asked the police.

'No, thank you, Sir, it won't be necessary.'

Lazy bastards, Jack thought. The first rule of any good copper is to take advantage to seek and look, especially when invited to do so without a warrant.

'Who owns the boat in front of yours?' the officer asked Jack.

'No idea. I've only been here two days, and I've not seen anybody.'

The second police officer, who, until now, had been silent, said, 'Your face looks familiar. May I ask your name, Sir?'

Jack hesitated, and then remembered. 'William Harris.'

'What do you do, Mr Harris?' he asked.

'I am a writer; I write magazine articles. I like the peace and quiet that the canals give me.'

'Well, thank you for your help, Sir.' The police officers said goodbye and left.

Jack watched them. They looked over Winnie's boat from

the outside. Found nothing, and then walked away. After about another five minutes, Jack let Winnie out of the shower room.

'That was close,' he said. 'I'm sure that bastard recognised me.'

'Thanks again, Jack, for covering for me. Let's chill out now. My Millie will be here this afternoon, and I'll get her to cook us a good West Indian curry.'

Jack went out onto the towpath and watched the two police officers walking away in the distance.

There were no more similar incidents for the rest of the day, but both Jack and Winnie kept a good lookout for strangers.

Millie turned up in the early evening from her shift at the local hospital. She was a very pretty West Indian girl in her late twenties, only about five foot two to Winnie's six foot. Jack noticed she had lovely eyes. She looked great in her nurse's uniform.

Winnie told her how he and Jack had met, how Jack had helped him out in the pub, and the wonderful retribution of the drowned motorbikes. She listened and smiled, but Jack felt she took an instant dislike to him. Perhaps it was because he was an ex-copper. He knew that Winnie didn't like coppers, and maybe she didn't much like them either.

Nevertheless, she cooked a fabulous chicken curry for the three of them, the best that Jack had ever tasted, with rice and peas. She made it evident that she didn't trust Jack, though. The conversation was very stilted and just a little heavy going. For the next couple of days, Jack kept himself to himself, playing music, usually Country and Western, and writing articles that wouldn't be sent off.

It had been eight or nine days since the pub incident, and they were both still moored up in the disused lock.

Jack decided that it was about time that he rang Lily, to check in with her as she had instructed. He tried his best to get the phone on Ingrid to work, but either it had no signal or no battery. He went to ask Winnie if he could borrow his mobile.

'Sure. But if you want to make sure that the call can't be traced, why not borrow Millie's? Hers is Pay-As-You-Go.'

Jack took it, phoned Lily, and told her that he was fine. He didn't mention Winnie, the fight or the police. Lily told him that everything was alright her end, and that, in a couple of weeks' time, she would arrange for Ronny to pick him up, bring him home for a few days, and then take him to his first fairground site to work as a showman. Jack was happy with that.

When he returned the phone, Winnie confided that Millie was very worried about his hand. She had re-dressed it, but she insisted that it needed x-raying. Winnie didn't want to go near a hospital, but equally, he didn't want to antagonise Millie, so what should he do?

'Go and get it sorted out, mate. If it heals badly, you could be handicapped for life.'

After a long day, Winnie and Millie returned from the hospital. They banged on the roof of Jack's boat.

'What do you fucking make of that?' Millie shouted at Jack. She threw down a copy of a tabloid, opened at an inside page, where there was a large picture of Jack, and an appeal for the public to keep an eye out for him, as he was needed as a vital witness in an up-and-coming murder trial. *Report any sightings to your local police.*

The photograph was unmistakeable. It had obviously been taken many years ago — probably when he first joined the force — but was, nevertheless, pretty much how he looked now.

Winnie and Jack sat down and told Millie the full story of why Jack was on the canal hiding from the police and everybody As the tale unfolded, Millie grew very sympathetic to Jack's predicament, and warmed to him. But Jack was worried. He had been supposed to tell no-one, but this was now yet another person who knew who he was and where he was. Added to that, he didn't fully trust Millie. Winnie: yes. But Millie: no.

'You must grow a beard, Jack,' Winnie suggested.

'Yes, and wear some glasses,' Millie added.

'Don't you two worry about me,' said Jack. 'I'll be gone from here in a couple of days. Perhaps you are right, though. A new image wouldn't go amiss.'

'I could put a new colour in your hair. Your blond hair makes you very recognisable,' Millie offered.

Perhaps he could trust Millie after all, Jack thought.

Everyone in the country would have seen his picture. He knew he couldn't be seen too often in public from now on. He was, in fact, a prisoner again. Now, more than ever, he had to stay hidden.

Millie turned out to be very helpful. She did a lot of shopping for Jack and made sure that no-one on the canal became too inquisitive about the two boats moored in the disused lock.

Winnie and Jack would sit around listening to, and talking about, music, which Jack played on his laptop.

'Why do you keep listening to that Country and Western crap? Them sad songs make you depressed, Jack. Why not some brighter stuff like soul music? Rhythm and blues? Anything would be better than that, even Rock and Roll,' Winnie said.

'It's the words, Winnie. They mean a lot, they are well-written and played beautifully, not like your Reggae stuff, repeated strumming and drums. Can't relate to that at all. You must listen to the words, and follow the story that the song is telling,' Jack explained.

Winnie smiled. 'If you played all those Country and Western songs in reverse, the man would get his wife back, his horse wouldn't die and he would have all his lost money returned.'

They both laughed, enjoying each other's company.

Ten days later, Millie brought home another newspaper. There was an article referring to the government's handling of the relationships between Russia, America, their Diplomatic High Commissioners and the British Foreign Office. It mentioned the difficulties between them all: a lot of the troubles were a direct result of the murder of a Russian diplomat at the hands of an American diplomat. The main crux of the article was the new investigation into the murder.

'What's all this about Russians, Jack?' asked Millie. 'You never mentioned them.'

'Yes, it's a mess. It was best you didn't know too much, but you are both safe. Besides, I will be gone very soon,' Jack replied.

He couldn't tell them anything about the Russians because he himself had no information. He worried about it for three more days, and then decided that it was time to phone Lily again. He couldn't stay cooped up on a canal boat in a disused lock for ever.

'Lovely to hear from you, Jack. You've certainly hit the headlines, haven't you? Have you seen the papers? Good picture of you when you were younger. The write-up wasn't very good but it's obvious they are still after you.'

'Yes, I have the bloody papers, Lil. It's getting a bit difficult here now. I don't dare go out anywhere. I am becoming a bit of a recluse. I am surviving by the help of another boat-owner, but I think it's time I moved on.'

'No worries, son. It's a good job you rang. We're just about to start a two-week season at Weston-super-Mare. How would that be for you?'

'Sounds good, Lily, but —'

'No buts, Jack. I have arranged it all. My cousin, Harry — you remember Harry? — he is making a place for you.'

'What does Harry know about me, Lil?'

'Jack, you are one of us now. Showmen have a code. We are all cousins. Everyone is protected. You'll be safe with us,' Lily explained. 'How does tomorrow suit you? I could send Ronny up to collect you.'

'He'll never find me, Lil. I'm hidden in a disused lock. Tell him to meet me near White Friar's Mill. It's a pub. I had a bit of trouble there, so I'll moor up just south of the bridge, in case I'm spotted.'

'Yes, Jack, I know the place. It'll take Ronny about three hours by road. Meet him about eleven-ish? He'll have a bit of a surprise for you.'

'I'll be there. I can't wait to get out of here.'

'See you later, my love. You'll be alright. By the way, whose phone are you using? I don't recognise the number.'

'It belongs to the other boat-owner, the guy who has been helping me out. See you tomorrow.' Jack hung up.

Jack told Winnie and Millie that he was off in the morning. 'It's best you don't know where I'm going, but I promise I'll keep in touch.'

'Do you need anything?' Winnie asked.

'No, I'll pack up tonight and I'll be off first thing. How is your hand?'

'It's fine. Millie is keeping a good eye on it.'

'I'll not bother you in the morning, so I'll say goodbye now.'

Millie came to Jack and kissed him. 'I am so sorry I was a bitch to you when we first met, but I now know you are a good, regular guy. I like your little beard and I'm sorry I didn't get to dye your hair,' she laughed.

Winnie came over and gave Jack a hug. 'I'm going to miss you, brother. You're a good guy. Please keep in touch, either on my phone or on Millie's. I wish you all the luck, Jack. You deserve a decent break. We had some good times. Hate your taste in music but you are handy to have around when we have some motorbikes to get rid of.' Both Jack and Winnie began to laugh.

'Seriously, Jack, where are you heading now? What are you going to do?' Winnie asked.

'It's far better you don't know, Winnie. The less you know, the better, and, to be truthful, I don't really know what is going to happen next. Keep an eye on the papers — they seem to know more about my movements than I do.' Jack gave Winnie a final hug and left.

The next morning, after some breakfast, Jack steered out of the disused lock, turned left and made his way along the canal. The scenery was marvellous but Jack could not linger to enjoy it. He just wanted to get to White Friar's Mill to meet Ronny.

Chapter Twenty-One

IN THE MEANTIME

Gerry Forbes and Lee Wooding had arranged an urgent meeting. They had not heard from Jack for four weeks, and things were getting intense with regards to the police investigation.

Lee had been bombarded with calls from Cramer, who finally insisted on an actual meeting at the Yard. Lee reminded Cramer that he was only in contact with Jack over the phone, and that they had not actually met in person. Citing client confidentiality, he would not provide them with Jack's phone number. He didn't reveal that he, himself, had not spoken to Jack for over a month and had no idea where Jack was.

Jack's picture in the newspaper had brought in an avalanche of sightings from Lands' End to John o'Groats. It was causing a major headache for the police investigation.

Rice and Cramer sat Lee down and explained there was a real urgency to contact Trevor Frost, not least because he was needed in order to give evidence that Kim Brown was actually at the party. Frost's account would also be critical in putting Karen Dewhurst there, too.

It was obvious that DCI Chris Rice was under severe pressure when it came to the diplomatic angle of the inquiry. The Russian Embassy was not cooperating in any way, especially regarding the misuse of the diplomatic bags, and now the Americans were being unhelpful.

The investigating team, including the officers from Cambridgeshire Constabulary, had all come to the conclusion that the cover-up of the death of Popova was a conspiracy conceived by these women to hide their actions and to also mask their involvement in the lucrative business of drugs importation and supply. It seemed that Kim Brown was the dominant female, forcing or directing the others to assist her. That was a matter for her defence brief to sort out. She and Dewhurst had appointed the same solicitor, and it was believed that Dewhurst was still under Brown's influence.

There was one further matter that was being considered. Anna Smelt's solicitor was now suggesting that Popova was *not* dead before Kim Brown became involved and that it was Kim Brown who murdered the Russian girl — before, or as a result of, all the mutilations.

The pathologists could not confirm or deny this, as the body had been released to Popova's father for burial in Russia years ago, but they were searching their notes for any indication that Popova might not have been dead before Brown got involved. It would now be impossible for the body to be exhumed in Russia and re-examined.

Nonetheless, it was imperative to speak to Frost, and get his testimony recorded, before they put the case to the court.

Lee asked whether his client's original statement and interviews were not sufficient to be submitted to the court. DS Cramer pointed out that both his answers in interview and his statement had been recorded under different circumstances, and that his original interviews had been conducted by inexperienced officers who had asked all the wrong questions, meaning that

Frost's original answers, although truthful, were useless, because they bore no relation to the actual offences.

In the original interviews, there had been no questions regarding drug dealing. In the light of the statement from Anna Smelt, a different enquiry altogether was being conducted, which would assist the investigation of others that were present at the party. Trevor Frost was a vital link in their prosecution case.

Lee Wooding repeated the instructions from his client that he refused to speak to anyone until he was presented with the promised official free pardon, authorised and signed.

Aleksandr Popov was again called to the office of the High Commissioner at the Russian Embassy. The High Commissioner explained that he was very vexed by the extra pressure being brought upon the Embassy by the British Government seeking answers to numerous questions with respect to the actions of Popov's deceased daughter.

Investigations had been carried out in Moscow. Certain members of staff who were responsible for the diplomatic bags and their transportation had been identified and dealt with. It was discreetly, but firmly, pointed out that there now existed confirmation from those individuals that drugs and other items had been concealed in those bags, and that Popov's daughter ordered and received them.

It was impossible for Popov to deny the allegations that his daughter was dealing in drugs, imported from Russia. However, he would not entertain the fact that she was a lesbian, nor that she was sexually promiscuous.

When asked if his private investigations into the whereabouts of Trevor Frost were continuing, Popov had to acknowledge that they were, although, to date, Frost still had not been traced. He suggested that, as Frost had not been anywhere near his ex-wife or his family, he may have committed suicide. The High Commissioner advised Popov that if his actions, or any results of those actions, were reported to be connected with Russian Legation, not only would the Embassy not back him in any way, but they would also deny all knowledge.

CIA agents working in the UK alongside the English police had been very helpful in trying to locate Anna Smelt's friends and contacts. FBI agents in the US had been very busy tracing the suppliers of the drugs to Smelt and those who concealed them in the diplomatic bags.

Arrests had been made and investigations were continuing, which involved more diplomatic staff in Washington. Quite a lot now rested on the testimony of Anna Smelt, and if Smelt's attorney's allegation — that it was, in fact, Kim Brown who had murdered the Russian girl — was to be upheld, then the rest of her testimony would be brought into question.

Staff at the Foreign Office in London were out of their depth. They had no idea how to approach the problem of the misuse of the diplomatic bags. They had no idea how to placate the Russians, or indeed the Americans, or how to convince the Russians that Frost was innocent and Smelt was guilty. It was whispered that the Prime Minister might have to be called upon to intervene.

The Home Office and the Department of Justice were in conversation regarding the Free Pardon, but judges who sat in on the Department of Justice cases were yet to be convinced of Trevor Frost's total innocence of the murder or the assaults. Until the full trial had been heard in court, they were not willing to sign off.

To make up for their stupidity in losing Frost in the first place, Harvey and Clarke were tasked with trying to trace him.

They drew a blank with Jack's sister, who intimated that Jack had killed himself. When they asked why she thought that, her husband, Peter, ordered them to leave and not come back. Both were still very upset and hurt and wanted nothing more to do with the officials from the Home Office.

Harvey and Clarke also tried to find Valerie, but her house remained empty. When they called at her parent's house, Ted told them that no-one had seen Jack since his trial, other than at the visitation rights hearing. He very nearly said that Jack had not attended any of the visitation days but, as he still wasn't sure of these two men — they could be the ones that followed him and Valerie from the Family Court that day — he stayed silent. So, the Home Office were none-the-wiser as to Jack's whereabouts.

Gerry was baffled by Jack's disappearance. Something was very wrong. Both he and Lee were well aware of the current situation, and that Jack was being sought all over the country, with his picture plastered over the national papers and tv news programmes. He couldn't understand why Jack hadn't been in contact, especially after all the media coverage.

Lee confirmed that none of the money in the William Harris bank account had been touched, and that the regular payments for the magazine articles Jack had written had also stopped.

The owner of the second-hand car business phoned Lee and told him that the police had identified him as the last registered owner of the car that Jack had bought. The car had been found, totally burnt out, in Hertfordshire, and they wanted to know why. The dealer told them he had sold it to a man for cash, and that was it. He showed the police the receipt for the car, which bore the name of William Harris in a badly written scrawl.

Nevertheless, neither Gerry nor Lee could accept that Jack had taken his own life, in spite of the evidence of the burnt-out car. His body hadn't been found anywhere, after all.

'The only thing we can do is to contact Valerie's solicitor. He may have information on how the visitations with Emma are going,' said Gerry. 'If we knew where the meetings were taking place, we could go and meet Jack there.'

'Jack won't thank you if you interfere with him seeing Emma. You know what he's like where his relationship with his daughter is concerned.'

'We have no choice, Lee. We must try and find Jack now at all costs,' Gerry said.

As anticipated, Valerie's solicitor couldn't, or wouldn't, help in any way. Gerry suggested they arrange a meeting with Valerie, in the presence of her solicitor, for a face-to-face, admitting that they had lost contact with Jack and that they needed to speak to him urgently. The meeting was organised, and Valerie attended, along with her father.

Valerie appeared very drawn and sad. Gerry thought she had lost some weight. She didn't look good at all. He thanked her for her cooperation in attending the meeting, and then carefully explained that, although they were representing Jack, they had not been in touch with him recently, and that, as things were progressing in the police investigation, it was imperative that they contact Jack to receive instructions. Might she, perhaps, be able to get a message to him via Bridget O'Connor?

Valerie was quiet for a few moments, and then started to sob.

'I don't mean to upset you, Mrs Frost, but can you tell me how the visitations between Jack and Emma are going?' Gerry tactfully asked.

Valerie continued to cry.

'They are not going at all,' Ted butted in. 'It's been over a month now, and Emma has not seen her father.'

Ted then went on to explain what had happened: how the visits between Jack and Emma had been going so successfully that Valerie decided to meet Jack face-to-face.

'That was categorically prohibited in the court agreement,' Valerie's solicitor protested. Gerry and Lee glared at him.

'I loved him,' Valerie blurted out, whilst continuing to cry.

'Then Jack came to Valerie's birthday party,' Ted said.

'It was my idea, not Jack's,' Valerie hastened to explain. 'He didn't want to do it, in case he got arrested for contempt of court or something. I wanted him to come for Emma's sake. They were getting on so well together, and we also got on well together in that first meeting. I really wanted him back in our lives.' Valerie started to speak more clearly through her crying. 'Jack came to my party, and I had a good time, although I didn't give much attention to him, which was my fault. Jack spent all his time with Emma. After putting her to bed, he left early. I wanted him to stay but he insisted on going. We arranged to take Emma for a family day out the following morning. As a nice surprise for Jack, I had booked an interview with the Family Court to retract all my objections and have the court orders lifted —'

'You never informed me of this, Mrs Frost,' Valerie's solicitor butted in.

Gerry, Lee and Ted all turned and glared at him. They really wanted to tell him to shut the fuck up.

'The next day, I went early to the Family Court and signed a statement, and it was to be submitted to the bench at the next hearing date. I then went on to the nursery to meet Jack and Emma, but when I got there, Jack had left and Emma was in tears. Bridget explained that Emma had told Jack about the police arriving after he had left the party. Jack thought that I had arranged for the police to attend to arrest him, but I hadn't, of course. Some bloody neighbour had complained about the loud music in the garden; that's why they were there.' Valerie was calming down a bit by now.

'Tell them about John, Valerie,' Ted prompted.

'Yes, I was dancing a lot of the night with an old friend of mine from my last job. There was nothing in it. John's gay, in fact. Anyway, he got a bit drunk, and we allowed him to sleep on the sofa. Emma told Jack that morning that 'Uncle John' had stayed the night, and Jack must have added two and two and made five! It wasn't Emma's fault. It was mine.' Valerie took a moment to compose herself before continuing.

'Bridget told me that Jack was crushed. He cried a lot and then told Emma that he couldn't see her again, and kissed her goodbye. Jack told Bridget that nobody was going to see him again. He thought that because I wasn't there on time, I was arranging for the police to come and arrest him, but I wasn't; I was at the court making a statement.' Valerie began to cry again.

'And you haven't seen or heard from him since?' Gerry asked.

'No, not a word. I went everywhere to see if I could find him. He was not at our old house, nor any of his other haunts. I did go and see his sister, but she was too upset to speak to me. Her husband threw me out, blaming me for Jack's actions.'

'What do you mean?' Lee asked.

Valerie was crying again. 'Jack must have gone straight to their house from the nursery and told them about John, the police and everything. He said his goodbyes, and apologised for all the trauma he had brought upon them. Peter and Jean were of the opinion that he was going to kill himself. I didn't want any of this. It was all a big mistake. I want him back.' Valerie was sobbing uncontrollably. 'Do you think he's dead?'

Gerry sat quietly, trying to piece the whole scenario together.

'So, what you have told us is this. You and Jack were back on good terms, and you were happy for Jack to see Emma whenever he wanted to. You were actually speaking to him?'

'Yes,' Valerie blubbed.

'You invited him to your birthday party?'

'That was my idea, not Valerie's or Jack's,' Ted interrupted.

'He put Emma to bed and then left, earlier than expected, without saying goodbye to you?' Gerry asked Valerie.

'I ran after him and begged him to stay but he wouldn't,' said Valerie.

'What was this about the police turning up shortly after Jack left?' Lee asked.

'Some bloody neighbour, who couldn't mind their own business, phoned the police and said the music in the garden was too loud. The police looked around, asked us to turn it down, which we did, and they left. They were only there about ten minutes,' Ted told them.

Gerry then asked quickly, 'It wasn't one of the "friends" at the party who phoned the police was it? Not this John? Could he have phoned to get Jack out of the way?'

'No, I am sure it wasn't. At least, I think I'm sure. The officers just said they had received a complaint about the noise. I offered them a drink but they refused,' Ted said.

'You said, Valerie, that the next day you went to the Family Court and made a statement asking for all the restrictions that had been put on Jack to be lifted, and after that you went to the nursery?' Gerry asked.

'Yes, I went to the court early. I was there at nine o'clock.

They asked me to write a statement of retraction, and then I had to swear an oath that I had not been influenced in any way by any person to retract my objections, and sign it. I then went straight to the nursery to tell Jack the good news.'

'What time were you to meet Jack at the nursery?'

'At ten, but the court procedure took a bit longer than I'd expected and, in the end, I got there at about eleven thirty. Bridget told me what Emma had told Jack, which she said had immediately crushed him.'

'My God, Lee, this is now very serious. He has been accused of something he hasn't done. Lost his wife, his family, his home, his job, his friends, and when he at last thinks things are going to work out fine for him, he finds his wife is having an affair and conspiring to have him nicked and put away for good,' said Gerry.

'I was not having an affair,' Valerie screamed. 'I love Jack. I should have trusted him years ago when he swore he was innocent. I wasn't trying to get him arrested. I love Jack, and now it's too late.' She was shaking uncontrollably.

Gerry was very sympathetic. 'Valerie, I am so sorry; I didn't mean to upset you. I was just trying to piece together events as Jack might have seen them. Now, as you know, it's imperative that we find him. What about any of his friends? Have you tried any of them?'

'We've tried all his friends. Most of them dropped him after his arrest. Those at the party were there for Valerie, not for Jack. We are as desperate as you,' Ted said.

'Can I suggest,' Lee said, 'that all of us, from now on, keep in touch, and communicate with each other without all the officialdom? Any ideas on how to find Jack, let's share. I for one do not believe Jack would have done anything so drastic, but wherever he is, he will need our help.'

Everyone agreed, with the exception of Valerie's solicitor, who said, 'Well, this is most irregular!'

They all swapped details. Valerie included the address of the safe house where she was staying with Emma.

Although no further forward than when they had started, now Gerry and Lee knew why Jack had gone missing, at least. They agreed that they were not going to share this new information with the police; at least, not yet.

Chapter Twenty-Two

DEEP MUSIC

Jack faithfully steered Ingrid towards White Friar's Mill. He was both apprehensive and happy to be starting a new life. He moored the boat just before the bridge. The bikes were all gone now, but the memory of them being dragged into the canal still brought a smile to his face.

He waited for about an hour, until finally Ronny came on to the boat. Jack was glad to see him, a face that he knew he could trust. But Ronny had some bad news.

'Jack, it's great to see you. I didn't recognise you with your beard and long hair — a big change from the photos in the papers,' Ronny began.

'It's good to see you, too, Ronny, and it will be good to see Lily and Dotty again. Seems like I've been cooped up in here for ages, just like prison, but with better food and fresh air.'

'There's been a change of plan, Jack. You won't be seeing Lily just yet. She's alright but she has changed things up a bit. Here are the keys to a motorhome she's bought for you. It's not new, but it is in great condition and I've cleaned it throughout. It's a Mercedes Benz; I think you'll like it. It is registered in her name.'

'Another mobile home?' Jack asked. 'I'm getting used to the caravanning life.'

'Now here's the plan. You're going to go straight to Weston-super-Mare. Lil had a bit of a scare about a week ago. She saw some men hanging around the yard at home and she didn't know if they were police or what, so she sent me to buy the motorhome, register it, and get it cleaned up. You'll be living in it. I've stocked it out for you, and it's full of diesel. She sent me up here to deliver it and I'm to take the boat back to the marina. Here's Dotty's mobile for you to use. They won't be able to trace you on that one.' Ronny passed over the phone and the van keys.

'Who were those men?' Jack asked.

'We don't know; we didn't find out. They didn't come into the yard, not with our dogs anyway, but Lil didn't want to take any chances.'

Jack was a bit concerned about the men turning up at Lil's yard. Could they turn up at Valerie's or her dad's as well?

'Lil sent you some money.' Ronny handed Jack an envelope. 'Now, this is the important bit. Here is the address in Weston where you'll find Harry, her cousin, who is expecting you. I've put all the details into the sat nav and set it up for you.'

'Sat nav? Very modern. I've not used one of those.'

'Just follow the directions and you won't get lost. You can't miss Harry. He has pitched the fairground near the seafront. He'll put you to work and look after you.' Ronny stood. 'You'd better be off, Jack. I've got to get to the marina. Charlie is going to meet me there. Let's get your gear into the van.'

Jack didn't really want to go; he was enjoying Ronny's company. They carried his cases and personal stuff to the motorhome. Thanks to Millie's shopping trips, Jack had accumulated a bit more property since he moved into the boat.

'Did you see these two men that Lily saw, Ronny?' Jack asked. 'You could smell a copper a mile off.'

'I didn't see them, Jack. Are they worrying you?' Ronny asked.

'A little bit, Ron, but we shall have to wait and see. Please keep a close eye on Lily and Dotty.'

'I always do, Jack. Don't worry about that,' Ronny replied.

Ronny untied the boat and they said their goodbyes. Jack pushed the boat away from the bank, waved a fond farewell, and walked back to the motorhome, jangling the keys in one hand.

The motorhome was a pleasant change from Ingrid, and more modern than the one that Jack had stayed in when he was first rescued. It had a permanent double bed in the rear bedroom, a shower and toilet, fridge freezer, microwave and television and, of course, the sat nav.

After stowing some of his possessions, Jack made himself familiar with all the controls. The sat nav was too complicated, but he had an instruction book handy. He placed the photograph of Valerie and Emma on the dashboard, to remind himself not to do anything dangerous whilst driving.

He decided to call the motorhome Betty; the registration letters were BET, so he thought it was apt. Before he set off, he checked the information that Ronny had fed into the sat nav. The postcode of the address that Ronny had given him to find Harry Grayling and the fairground in Weston-super-Mare checked out right.

It wasn't long before the sat nave had directed him to the motorway and Jack settled down to a comfortable journey. It was going to take about four hours, and he wasn't going to rush it. As well as having all mod cons, Betty also had a brilliant sound system, of which Jack took full advantage.

At first, the radio programme was all modern songs but it then turned into a Romantic Hour, where the DJ played every sad and romantic record he could find. Jack had always loved music of all kinds and found that sometimes the lyrics were written just for him in lots of different ways.

The songs that the DJ was playing certainly hit the spot. The first one to come on was *I'll See You in My Dreams* by Joe Brown, a song that went straight to his heart with its understanding of the pain experienced at the idea that happiness might now only be found in dreams. The words of this lovely song made Jack think immediately of Valerie, and how he would see her and Emma in his dreams, hold them in his dreams.

The next song was even more appropriate: *I Will Always Love You* by Dolly Parton. Jack found himself singing along. He was happy enough to join in, but his happiness was tinged with a bit of sadness when he related the meaning of the songs to his own situation. If he stayed, he would only be in Valerie's way — but his love for her would never die.

Next was Mike Berry's *The Sunshine of Your Smile*. Again, it was so personal. He sang along while looking at the photograph of Valerie and Emma on the dashboard, and their dear faces lit with smiles like sunshine. How he wished he had the right to love them as he wanted.

The motorway was not too busy and Jack was keeping to a steady sixty miles per hour. The motorhome was handling beautifully and, being on a motorway, there were no interruptions to the music from the lady on the sat nav.

Then the DJ picked out a great Country and Western singer and song: *Some Broken Hearts Never Mend*, sung by Don Williams. It was one of Jack's favourites. It was almost as if the selection had been hand-picked for his situation. As he let the music carry him along, he allowed some of his buried emotions to come to the surface. He truly did believe that some broken hearts never mend and some memories never end.

The next song reminded Jack of the night of Valerie's party, where he had carried the sleepy Emma in his arms and they had danced softly. It was *When the Girl in Your Arms is the Girl in Your Heart* by Cliff Richard. With Emma in his arms and in his heart, he had been holding a dream come true. Cliff Richard was given some beautiful songs to sing, he reflected.

Next up was *And I Love Her* by the Beatles. Nearly all the Beatles' songs were about love, and this was no exception. The song was beautifully composed and sung and Jack sang along with it until the last verse hit him hard. Yes, he thought, I know this love of mine will never die. I know that.

By now, Jack was getting quite melancholy and he was just about to turn the radio off, when *Tears* by Ken Dodd came on. He began to sing just as loudly as before and tears did start to roll down his face. Dodd was not only a brilliant comedian, but a brilliant singer as well, thought Jack. And what he sang was true: tears *can't* mend a broken heart.

Then came the classic by Clarence 'Frogman' Henry, *I Don't Know Why I Love You But I Do*. The words fitted Jack's mood totally. The last line in particular — I only know I'm lonely, and that I want you only — was nearly too much for him. Every word was hitting home. Once again, he was about to turn the radio off, when the DJ announced one last song for Romantic Hour.

It was *Make You Feel My Love*, sung by Adele. This song was the last straw for Jack. Adele's beautiful voice said it all. Jack had no idea that this was the very song that had set Valerie off crying that day in the nursery when she had been hiding from him.

Jack's tears were now in full flow and his concentration on driving was taking second place to his thoughts about Valerie and Emma. Finally, he did turn the radio off.

Fortunately, he soon saw the sign for a motorway service area, and decided to take a rest. He pulled into the car park, and switched off the engine. Emotionally drained, he wiped away all the tears and sat for a while, to pull himself together. Whilst enjoying a cup of tea, he played around with the mobile phone that belonged to Dotty, finding some timer settings, and a function for voice recording.

Suddenly, there was a knock on the side of the motorhome. Jack opened the top half of the stable door. Outside stood a man of about forty-five, in a dirty uniform and a high-vis jacket, which had seen better days. As well as his scruffy appearance, he had an attitude about him.

'There's no camping here. You'll have to move on,' the security guy said.

'I'm not camping. I am having a short rest,' Jack pointed out.

'You've been here fifteen minutes, and you've made yourself some tea. I've watched you. There's no camping here. Just move on,' the man said.

Not only was Jack was still upset, but he was also annoyed at this scruffy bastard's attitude.

'I am not fucking camping! I was just taking a short rest, like everyone else here. Now, why don't you piss off and leave me alone, you jobsworth arsehole?' Jack shut the door. He was in no mood for prats like him.

A short while later, there was another knock and when Jack opened the top half of the stable door again, he saw it was two uniformed police officers.

'Good evening. Security, here, tells me that you refuse to leave. There's no camping allowed, so I'm telling you to move on.'

This police officer was young, very stroppy and very stern. The second police officer said nothing.

'Officer, I told the security man that I had only stopped for a toilet break and a quick cup of tea. I've been driving for about two hours and I needed a break. I'm not camping. I'll be gone in a few minutes,' Jack explained.

'You gypsies are all the same. Where have you come from?' the stroppy cop asked.

Jack had to think quickly. 'I've come from Somerset on my way to London.' In fact, he was doing the opposite.

The police officer then got ruder. 'So, what drugs have you been selling in Somerset? Going back to London for more supplies, I suppose.'

Jack was amazed at the officer's attitude. 'That is rubbish, I'm going back to London to see my sister. I've been visiting friends in Minehead. Look inside if you want.'

Despite his lies, Jack kept calm; he knew there would be no drugs there. He trusted Ronny to have cleaned the motorhome thoroughly.

'I will, don't you worry. I don't trust you didicoys,' the officer said.

Jack opened the door fully, and the stroppy officer stepped in and began a cursory search. It wasn't a proper effort. Jack thought he was another lazy copper, who was just trying to annoy him by being rude and demeaning to him.

'So, what do you do for a living apart from thieving and tarmacking people's driveways?' the copper said, whilst glancing in some drawers.

Jack answered, calmly, 'I'm a writer.'

'What's your name?'

'William Harris.'

'Where do you live?' The police officer stopped his searching and began writing in a little notebook.'

'12B, Wilmslow Terrace, Hampstead,' Jack lied.

'Is this your camper van?' The copper continued.

Jack had to think quickly. Whose name did Ronny say Lily had registered Betty in?

'It belongs to my Uncle Harry. Harry Grayling. He lives in Flask Walk, Hampstead. Any more questions?'

'You gypsies have got uncles all over the place. Where are you going now?'

'I'm on my way home to London' He repeated the lie.

The police officer continued to look around the inside of the motorhome. The second officer remained just outside, by the back door.

Coming back from the rear bedroom, the surly copper went to the front.

'You've been told. Now, I am ordering you to pack up and get out of here, *now*,' the copper shouted.

'I've been driving for two hours and all I wanted was a break, to have a cup of tea and find a shit house. Seems I've found one in you,' Jack replied, sarcastically.

'Yes, you have found a shit house in me. Now get on your way.' The police officer was about to step out of the motorhome when he suddenly turned round and said, 'I recognise that woman in the photograph by your driver's seat. I recognise you now, beard or no beard. Your picture and her picture are all over the papers. You're that fucking deviant detective they're looking for! You're that dirty arsehole who murdered that girl and got yourself out of prison.' He grabbed Jack's arm as if he was about to arrest him.

Suddenly, the second officer, who, up until now, had said nothing, shouted, 'Leave him, Clive. The reports said it was only 'locate and trace', not arrest. Leave him be.'

The police officer let go of Jack. He turned and sneered at

him, 'I've got you, you dirty bastard. You gave us coppers a bad name. I'm going to call your location in.' He stepped out of the motorhome and walked to the police car.

The second police officer turned to Jack and said, 'I'm sorry about this, and his attitude. I know the full story about you, but he is a bit hot-headed.'

'Don't worry, Officer, by the time you get back to the nick, your Chief Constable will have the full transcript, because I've recorded it all on my phone and I've noted your shoulder numbers,' Jack said.

'I can only apologise again, Sir.' The officer walked away.

Jack thought about this 'locate and trace' report on him. To put the police off the scent, he drove off in the London direction, back the way he had come; at the next junction, he left the motorway and then rejoined it, making his way to Somerset again. He saw no further sign of the police.

When the second officer got back into the car, he said to Clive, 'You prick, he has recorded the whole incident and he's sent it into Headquarters. He has your number and mine. We are in the shit now.'

'Let's just call it in,' Clive said, sheepishly, 'and report that he's on his way back to London. I watched where he went.'

'Shall I also call it in that you were a rude and arrogant prick who overstepped the mark with the way you treated him? Don't you read anything? He was released from prison because he was not guilty of any murder. The bulletins that have been circulated only said, 'locate and trace', not abuse, take the piss out of and then arrest. You can fight this one on your own, buddy. You were totally out of order.' There followed a pregnant pause. 'Give me the details you recorded and I'll get them circulated.'

Clive handed over the notebook where he had recorded Jack's details.

'Where is the registration number of the camper van?' He was searching through the pages of the notebook. 'You were so busy running him down that you forgot to record the registration? You're unbelievable.'

He called their local police station control and reported they had seen a man that looked like the wanted ex-detective and that he was driving a Mercedes Benz motorhome, making off in the direction of London. He didn't elaborate any further.

Jack, of course, didn't in the details of the incident. The police would have wanted more information than he was willing to give, and would also trace the mobile phone. No, Jack thought, let the bastards sweat a little bit. Let them think I've reported their actions to their Headquarters.

His mood had changed, and he decided not to listen to his radio again. He drove in silence for another two hours, following the instructions from the sat nav.

Chapter Twenty-Three

APPRENTICE SHOWMAN

It was about half eight in the evening when Jack arrived in Weston and found himself driving along the seafront, where, on a wide expanse of green, before the beach, he could see all the colourful lights of a funfair, with roundabouts and thrill rides and loud music. He pulled onto the site and parked up near the other caravans and fairground vehicles. The noise of the electric generator lorries, the music from the rides and the smell of the hot dog stands, the fried onions, the candy floss, all filled Jack's senses.

'You can't park there. This spot here is private,' said a voice from behind Jack. 'Only fairground vehicles can park here.'

Jack turned to see a swarthy-looking man of about thirty, dressed in a checked shirt, dirty jeans and Doc Martens.

'I'm here to see Mr Grayling. He is expecting me.'

'Ah, You must be Jack. Sorry about that. Yes, we've been told to keep an eye out for you. Mr G said you were on your way. My name's Jimmy. Nice to meet you.' Jimmy held out his grubby hand. They made their way through the fairground towards a very large caravan, much bigger than Lily's, with twelve wheels. It was about seventy-five feet long, and was surrounded by other smaller caravans, where all the fairground workers lived.

The noise and smells of the fair excited Jack, and he was agog at all the activity around him. People were milling around, enjoying the thrills and spills. Jimmy explained that they were not very busy at the moment, but that they expected more punters, come the weekend.

They knocked on the door of the large caravan, which was opened by a mountain of a man.

'Hello, boss. I found your Jack, roaming around the car park,' Jimmy said.

'Jack, it's great to see you, come on in. Ivy, Jack's here,' Harry Grayling shouted to his wife. Harry was tall, muscular, with large hands. He had a ruddy complexion and a cheerful smile.

Ivy came running from the other end of the caravan. 'Jack, oh, Jack, it's wonderful to see you.' She grabbed hold of him and hugged him. Ivy Grayling was smaller than her husband. Rotund, warm, she also had a warm smile of welcome on her face.

They were definitely pleased to see him, which made him very happy and relaxed, especially after his confrontation with the police.

'Now, sit down and have a cup of tea,' Ivy said. 'Lily has told us everything, so it's down to us to make a showman out of you.'

'Yes, you're with us now. Tell me, how are Valerie and the little one?' Harry asked. 'Haven't seen a lot of you since the wedding.'

'Harry!' Ivy scolded her husband. 'You know what Valerie did to Jack. Don't be so daft.'

Harry apologised for his stupidity. Jack went on to tell them the full story, right up to the afternoon's encounter with the police. He declared that he was looking forward to his new career, and that he was willing to take on anything, and was going to try and put all the past behind him.

'We'll make a good showman out of you, don't you worry.

After tea, I'll show you around and introduce you to everyone. We'll move your motorhome, and hide it amongst the others, in case them bloody coppers come sniffing around,' Harry said.

'I'm not too worried about them yet, they think I'm back in London at the moment,' Jack giggled. After about an hour of catch-up conversation, Harry took Jack out into the fairground, introducing him to the men and women who ran the stalls and rides.

Everyone was very pleased to meet him. They were all very friendly and it seemed the word had been put around that he was Lily Grayling's godson and was joining 'The Firm'.

It was a large fair with Dodgems, The Whip, a Ghost Train, Galloping Horses, and other rides and roundabouts for the kiddies. The stalls were also varied, with darts and hoop-la and so on, and various candy floss stands and burger bars. Harry explained that the whole fair was run on two large generator lorries parked at the rear of the site. The generators also ran the electrics to the caravans.

'We'll get you hooked up as soon as we can,' said Harry.

Jack was absolutely loving it: the noise, the smells, and the enthusiasm of the punters who were all there to enjoy themselves. Everyone was happy and smiling — something that he hadn't seen for a long time. After all the weeks cooped up on his own, in motorhomes and the boat, not to mention his years in prison, it was great to see so many people walking around free. It was a bit before ten when the fair started to quieten down, and Harry took Jack over the closing-down procedure.

'The generator that controls the rides is switched off first,' he explained, 'and then all the rides are disconnected separately. All the seating is covered up against the weather and secured from theft and tampering. Then the side stalls are curtained up with all the prizes packed away. The very last job is to ensure that the diesel tanks to the generators are full. It's the last job because if you spill any of the fuel, you can wash it off you before the morning. The last thing you want to do is walk around all day smelling of diesel,' Harry laughed.

'What happens after close-down?' Jack asked.

'We all go back to our vans, have a shower and perhaps something to eat, and then some of the lads go to the nearest pub, if there is time. You've already met Jimmy, so, for the time being, I'll pair you up with him and he'll show you the ropes. Don't worry, Jack, you'll be fine.'

Jack watched the close-down procedure, concentrating on who did what. Surprisingly, it didn't take long, and soon the fairground was transformed from a loud, colourful and bustling site to a quiet and dark area.

It was Jimmy's turn to be night security and therefore it was his job to walk around with two of the dogs, to ensure that no-one tried to steal or damage any of the stalls or rides.

Jack was knackered, so soon he returned to his motorhome. After a quick wash, he went straight to bed, still excited and, if not exactly happy, then content. He said goodnight to the photo of Valerie and Emma and went to sleep straight away.

The life of a showman was governed by numerous rules and the first rule was that every showman must start his day with a full breakfast, just in case something happened on the fairground that meant a break for food wasn't possible. With a good breakfast inside him, he would be able to work on. Probably the most important rule was checking every thrill ride for safety. Every nut and bolt had to be checked, including the grease points. There were many more rules and each one was important in its own right. Jack made sure to learn them thoroughly.

The best time of all was when the fair opened to the public: the loud music from the rides; the smells from the hot dog stalls, the doughnut fryer and the candy floss mixer; and all the young children with smiles on their faces, enjoying themselves.

Jack reflected how Emma would love it. Yes, she would be absolutely delighted by it — the roundabouts and the sideshows — but, as always, thoughts of Emma and Valerie dragged his mood down.

Jimmy was a great help and Jack learned a lot from him, including how to load the lorries and vans in the correct order, with all the floorings, timber works and canvases, making it easy to unload at the next venue. Jimmy had been a showman since birth. Both his parents had been showmen all their lives and he had the fairground in his blood. Now, aged thirty, he lived alone in his small two-berth caravan and was sweet on Jenny, who lived with her mum and dad. Jenny's dad ran the Dodgems along with Jimmy, whilst her mother had her own Hoopla side stall.

At the end of the fair, Harry and Ivy called all the workers together and told them how much money they had taken. The next site was Minehead, a couple of hours away, where they would stay for another two weeks. After packing up, the big lorries and heavy vans moved off first, travelling through the night, so as not to cause any traffic problems.

After a very early breakfast, Jack and some of the others left for Minehead. Jack had Jenny and her mother in his motorhome, for company. It was a very pleasant journey. They arrived at about half eight and immediately began to unload and set up the rides in the positions that Harry had marked out. Jack was helping to erect the Galloping Horses ride when Jimmy came running up to him.

'Jack, read this.' Jimmy was holding a daily newspaper.

MURDER TRIAL TO GO AHEAD

At long last, the date has been set for the trial of the American diplomat accused of murdering her Russian counterpart. The main witness, ex-detective Mr Trevor Frost, missing for nearly a year, still hasn't been traced. Frost was convicted in February 2002 of the murder of Ms Natasha Popova, a diplomat within the Russian Embassy.

An unofficial sighting by Berkshire Police stated that a man answering the description of the missing detective was seen at a motorway service station on the M4, heading towards London. There have been further sightings in the UK and abroad, but none has been authenticated.

This newspaper is offering a £10,000 reward for anyone with information on the whereabouts of Trevor Frost.

There was a number to ring with any information ,and also an old photograph of Jack.

'What will you do?'

This was a real body-blow. Jack couldn't answer for a moment.

'Nobody would recognise you from that photo, Jack, not with your beard and long hair. You'll be alright.'

Jack let out a long breath. 'I'll talk to Harry, later. Meanwhile, we have a fair to erect. I'm told the safety man comes in three hours, and we must be ready for him.'

'True showman attitude. Well done, Jack. You're safe with us,' Jimmy said, and went back to work. Jack read through the article again. It brought his mood back down to rock bottom.

As soon as the safety checks on the rides were signed off by the inspector, Jack knew that Harry would be free to talk, so he showed him the article.

'We'll keep you away from the public, at least until this trial is over. You can do night security and background maintenance.

You'll just not be out there where you can be identified.'

Jack was quiet for a few minutes, then he burst out, 'Fuck them. I'm not going to hide away anymore. I'm fed up with constantly looking over my shoulder. If they want me, let them fucking find me.'

'That's my boy! Alright, Jack, we'll protect you as best we can, but we must be careful — there is £10,000 on your head.'

'Ten grand? Is that all I'm worth? Fuck them! When this is all over, I'll be suing someone for a lot more than that.' Jack was livid. 'I've got nothing to hide from, Harry. They know I'm not guilty of anything and they've fucked my whole life up. Fuck the Russians as well.'

'You may be able to mess with the police, Jack, but you can't trust those Russians, let's be a bit more careful.'

'No, Harry. I've had it up to here with being careful. I've had years in custody, no contact with anyone, now getting on for a year hiding in anonymous flats, motorhomes and a canal boat, always on my own, constantly worried about what move I am to make next. I have a new job which I am doing as best as I can, new friends and I am beginning to enjoy myself. From now on, I am going to try and live my life properly again.'

'I agree, Jack. You are doing well after what you've been through. Everyone on site likes you and is happy that you are staying with us. Look, after we've set up, the gang is going out for a drink tonight, ready for a busy fortnight. Why don't you go with them? You deserve a break and to have a bit of fun.'

Jack finished off his day with gusto. All the rides had been constructed and tested; all the sideshows were built and ready to go; the rubbish bins had been put out and even the last-minute small jobs had been completed. At last, he could return to Betty, where he washed and made himself some dinner.

At about half past eight, he had just finished drafting a new article, grateful for the rest from his physical labours, when there was a knock on his door. It was Jenny, looking very pretty in a pale-pink top, and striped mini skirt.

'Are you coming out with us?'

Jack was a bit apprehensive. 'Am I dressed alright?'

'You look great, and you smell good as well,' complimented Jenny, taking Jack by the arm. 'Come on, let's enjoy ourselves.'

'Be careful, Jen. Jimmy won't like you playing up to me.'

'I'm not worried about him; I don't belong to him. He has no call on me.'

'I thought you two were boyfriend and girlfriend?'

'No. Jimmy likes to think so, but we're not, really.'

They met up with about six others and walked into Minehead town. They were joined by a dozen more, including Harry, Ivy and Jimmy, who didn't look too pleased when he saw Jenny holding onto Jack's arm, although he said nothing.

They went into a pub where a DJ was playing some good, loud music. Everyone was drinking, but Jack only drank lager shandy. He loved watching everyone enjoying themselves. Jimmy and Jenny were dancing and seemed to be happy, as were the other fairground showmen. Jack was tempted to ask some other very pretty girls there to dance, but he decided that he just couldn't. When it was his turn, he got up to buy a round. The barman looked at him with a questioning look on his face. Jack wondered if he had been recognised, but the barman said nothing.

Although enjoying himself, Jack thought he had better leave after his second pint of shandy, but Jenny and the others talked him into staying. After his third pint, he was pulled onto the dance floor by Jenny. Before he took to the floor, Jack ran up and spoke to the DJ.

A crowd got together and they danced in a large circle. It was the first time in years that Jack had danced, other than with Emma at Val's party, and he was going to enjoy it. The next record the DJ played was the one he had requested, and it seemed to set him alive.

It was *Dance the Night Away* by The Mavericks. Jack began to dance wildly. He sang the words that he knew by heart, feeling his happiness returning with the beat of the song.

Harry and Ivy smiled. Jack was now dancing on his own, watched by a happy crowd of dancers as he sang at the top of his voice. Somehow, as he danced, the future did feel brighter to him, even if he did have to say no to Valerie, his own true señorita.

Harry turned to Ivy. 'Look at him,' he said. 'He's only had three pints of shandy. He sure can pick his songs.'

'Just listen, Harry, this is what he wants to say. He wants to dance the night away — good luck to him — but we must keep an eye on him, just the same,' Ivy added.

Jack was happier than he had felt in years. He walked home, still singing 'Tomorrow's looking bright...' with Jenny on one arm and Ivy on the other. Observed by Jimmy, Jack gave both Jenny and Ivy a friendly peck on the cheek to say goodnight.

Then he went to bed and slept like a baby.

Chapter Twenty-Four

MEANWHILE

It was seven weeks since either Gerry or Lee had heard from Jack. They had had many meetings with Valerie to discuss how to trace him, but each attempt drew a blank. Valerie looked worse every time they saw her. She had lost a lot more weight and her eyes were red and puffy from continuous crying.

Jean was also very upset by his disappearance.

'He actually said goodbye to me as if it was for good,' she cried.

Valerie had been hoping that once Jack had found out he had got the wrong end of the stick, he would come back, if not for her, then, at least, for Emma's sake. Emma had become quiet, and depressed. She blamed herself for her daddy's disappearance, and Val could not convince her otherwise.

Gerry and Lee called another meeting with Valerie, her mum and dad, and Jean and Peter. Valerie explained that she had contacted nearly everyone she could think of, but none of them claimed to have seen or heard from Jack.

Gerry told them that Jack was thought to have been seen on the M4 motorway services, heading for London and that they believed that Jack was back in London. Lee said that he had made enquiries with the Prison Service to ascertain if Jack had made friends with any other prisoners, who might have been recently discharged but they informed him that Jack had made no friends in prison. He had kept himself to himself.

Ted suggested that some of Jack's relatives may have lied to protect him but Jean corrected him, saying that she was the only relative Jack had got, and that she and Peter were just as upset about Jack's disappearance as anyone.

Lee informed them that if Jack was not found, or if he was found but refused to cooperate and the trial returned a verdict of Not Guilty, there would be no free pardon forthcoming. Jack could be rearrested and a retrial called.

Ted asked about the Russians. Gerry acknowledged that this was still an issue and that his contact in the Foreign Office had informed him that Popov and his agent contacts were still actively searching for Jack.

They were all desperate to know what to do next.

Valerie offered to give her side of the story to the newspaper that had posted the reward money with a plea for Jack to come forward. Gerry agreed that this could be a good idea, but he also thought that Jack might simply see it as another trick to get him arrested. Ted put forward the suggestion that a request to the Commissioner of Police for a televised appeal to Jack to come forward might reap results, but Gerry pointed out that the prosecuting body could not be seen to pre-empt the innocence of the witness.

The time-frame for finding Jack had been severely shortened by the accused females' defence counsels issuing a demand that a trial date be set sooner rather than later.

Things were not looking good for Jack, whether he was dead or alive.

Chapter Twenty-Five

SHOWDOWN AT THE FAIR

Jack was feeling great. Everything was behind him and he had started to live again. The dance had been great. He had enjoyed Jenny's company very much. She was friendly and lots of fun. Jimmy hadn't looked too impressed, but Jack had been careful not to be over-familiar. She was pleasant to be with, but his heart still belonged to Val.

The fair opened to the public the next day, and Jack and all the other workers were very busy. After the fair closed, Jenny came round to Jack's with some dinner she had cooked for him. She stayed for a while, and they chatted and listened to music. Jack suggested that on the thrill rides, where music was played all the time, it should be louder and more upbeat, to get the crowds moving and enjoying the experience more. Jenny agreed, and they started to pick out tracks they thought would get the punters going. They decided to make a playlist.

The next evening, when the crowds built up, Jack was maintaining the machinery and ensuring that all was well, when Harry Grayling decided to put him on the Waltzer. It was a very popular ride and there were always queues waiting to get on.

'He deserves a bit of fun now, Ivy. Let him loose on the public. I think he will do just fine,' Harry said.

Jack was on the Waltzer when Jenny came over and suggested that he put on their compilation. When the music started, things began to hot up. Jack stood on the edge of the platform and began to dance, facing the waiting crowd of customers.

The track was *Burning Bridges* by Status Quo. The distinctive heavy beat began and Jack started to hop in time — and so did the audience. He waved his arms and swung his hips — and so did the audience. As Jack spun around, so did the audience. His head was spinning with the words that once again seemed to describe his emotional situation. He felt that, at last, he could walk away from his old life; he could burn his bridges and call it a day.

Everyone was loving it, including Jack. Everyone was dancing and happy. Harry and Ivy wandered over to see what was going on. They couldn't believe their eyes.

'Is he drunk?' Ivy asked, as Jack spun around on the edge of the ride.

'No, he's just enjoying himself, and it looks like the punters are loving it,' Harry replied.

As soon as the track was finished, on came *Rockin' All Over the World*. The punters' dancing never stopped. When the ride finished, they clambered onto the Waltzer to fill up the ten cars. Jack tried, as quickly as he could, to get their fare money before the operator started up the ride again.

Just before it started, Jenny came running over and joined Jack. They hugged each other, happy that the ride was full and their idea of loud, rocking music had done the trick. This time, Jenny joined in the dancing. On the undulating platform of the ride, Jenny and Jack were jiving together and, in the showground, so was everyone else, all obviously enjoying the music. That night, the Waltzer made the most money of all the rides.

'You've done very well tonight, Jack — you're a true showman.

Lily knew you had it in you,' Harry said.

'It wasn't me, Harry, it was the terrific music, but it proves that if the punters see the showman dancing and enjoying himself, then it must be alright for them to let their hair down and enjoy themselves,' Jack explained. Ivy agreed.

Later, in Jack's caravan, he and Jenny were again talking music and drinking coffee when Jimmy knocked on the door.

'What's going on? What are you two up to?'

'Nothing, Jimmy. We are just getting some more music together for the other rides, like the Dodgems,' Jenny replied.

'What music do you like, Jim? You work the Dodgems — what would you like?' Jack asked.

'Don't need no fucking music. All this is a scam for you to get closer to Jenny,' Jimmy blurted.

'Don't talk like an idiot,' Jenny said.

'I've seen you. Dancing together, laughing together, spending time together. You're trying to steal my girlfriend,' Jimmy shouted. 'Well, fuck you! We'll see about this.'

Jimmy stormed out of the motorhome, slamming the door.

'I'll go and talk to him,' Jack said.

'No, leave him alone. I mean, it's not as if he owns me, like he thinks he does,' Jenny replied, holding on to Jack's arm.

'I've got to put him straight — he thinks I'm stealing his girlfriend,' Jack said, as he went to chase after Jimmy.

'Leave him, Jack,' Jenny pleaded. 'He thinks I'm his girlfriend, but I'm not. We were only having a bit of fun. We weren't doing anything wrong.'

'Maybe not, but I think we had better call it a night.'

Jenny tried to kiss him, but he turned away. 'Goodnight, Jenny.'

The next morning, Jack went looking for Jimmy. He was

worried about his attitude. Nobody had seen him, not even Jenny. Jack went and told Harry and Ivy what had happened and how Jenny was being a bit over-affectionate with him.

'Don't worry about Jimmy. He and Jenny have been friendly for years. He'll come round. Jenny is still a young girl and, if anything, she has a crush on you.'

The rest of the day was uneventful for Jack. He didn't see Jimmy, and the fair wasn't too busy. It was mainly mums and dads with their young children, so Jack took a long break in Betty, catching up on some writing.

At about seven o'clock, he was getting ready to return to the rides when one of the operators knocked on his door and told him that Harry wanted to see him in his caravan. Jack dutifully went straight over.

Immediately, a flash bulb went off in his face.

'What's all this?' Jack asked.

Suddenly, Jack recognised Valerie standing at the end of the caravan, next to the photographer.

'What's all this? This is a set-up. What's going on, Harry?' Jack began to tremble.

'This is none of my doing, Jack, believe me.'

Ivy came over to Jack and grabbed his arm. 'Someone grassed on you, Jack, someone from the fair here.'

'We are from *the Weston Gazette*,' the photographer said. 'Are you Trevor Frost?'

'Val, Val! What are you doing here?' Jack started to shake. 'Why, why? Why have you done this?'

'Jack, please listen. I'm so glad to see you, to see that you are okay. Please listen, Jack, you've got it all wrong,' Valerie pleaded.

'What's next, the local police? You bastards, what have I done to deserve this?'

'Mr Frost, we were contacted by a Mr James Finnegan who informed us that you were here and claimed the reward,' the photographer said.

'Where's that fucking Jimmy? I'll kill him,' Harry said.

'I don't understand all this, Val. Why? Why are you hounding me? I've done what you wanted. I've stayed out of your life; I've made every effort to leave you and Emma alone. What more do you want of me?' Jack was physically shaking and was beginning to speak faster, jumbling his words.

'I don't understand, Val. I didn't do all those things I was accused of. I love you, Val, I always have.' Jack was crying. 'I have loved you since the first time I met you. When you said you'd be my girlfriend, I was so happy. My love for you couldn't have been stronger. In front of all those people at our wedding, I promised before God that I would always love you. When you told me that you were pregnant, I couldn't have loved you more and then when Emma came along...' He almost choked on his distress. 'I have always loved you, I've never touched another woman, I promise.' Jack was crying now and he moved closer to the door of the caravan.

'Jack, please listen, please.' Val was also crying.

'No, I'm not listening to anyone. I've loved you all my life, Val, and that will never change. I've tried my best to understand why I deserved all this. I love you, Val, even now.' Jack paused and there was total silence except for the sound of Valerie weeping. He continued slowly, 'I love you, but I don't trust you anymore. You've done your best to finish me and you have succeeded. Without trust, Val, we have nothing. As much as it hurt, I was willing to give you everything: your freedom to live with whoever you wanted, money, everything, as long as I could see Emma occasionally, but you even took that away from me.' Jack was crying, shaking and could barely stand. 'I disappeared from your life once, I will now do it again, but permanently this time. I've hurt no-one, I've done nothing wrong, but I can't put up with this pain any longer, and prison isn't going to get me either. I would rather be dead.'

Jack turned to the Graylings. 'Harry, Ivy, thank you both for everything you've done. Give my love to Lily and Dotty.' He turned back to Valerie. 'Look after our lovely Emma. I know you will — you are a brilliant mother. Don't bother to look for me ever again, you won't find me.' He turned and opened the door.

'Jack, please!' screamed Valerie.

At the bottom of the steps was Jimmy. 'You arsehole! I thought you were my friend,' Jack said.

Jenny came running up.

'You are lower than a snake's belly. You dobbed me in, you shitbag, and for what?' Jack shouted at Jimmy.

'I'm sorry, Jack, but you were stealing Jenny away from me, and I needed the money from the reward so that Jenny and I can get married.'

'Get married?' Jenny screamed. 'I wouldn't marry you if you were the last man on earth.' She slapped his face hard.

Jack ran off into the darkness.

Valerie was uncontrollable, tears streaming down her face. Harry turned towards her. 'Well done, Val, you've finally broken the only man who has ever loved you. Why couldn't you have just left him alone? What a waste. You don't deserve a man like Jack.'

Valerie collapsed and was helped to a seat by Ivy. 'This is all a dreadful mistake,' she said, through her crying, 'Why wouldn't he listen? I didn't want him nicked. I love him. All the court injunctions have been cancelled, and I just want him back.' Ivy pulled Valerie into a comforting hug.

'At least we've found him,' said the photographer.

Harry stormed out of the caravan. 'If I get my hands on you,' he shouted at Jimmy, 'there will be another murder. Get all your things and get off this fairground. You are a grassing, two-faced, little shit, and I will make sure that you never ever work on a showman's fair again.'

'But Harry, he was after my Jenny, and I needed the money,' Jimmy started to explain.

'I was never *your* Jenny, you fuckwit. There was nothing serious with Jack — he's a married man — but he was fun. You just dragged me around like a dog.' Jenny slapped Jimmy's face again and stormed off.

'Fuck off and fuck off *now*! Get out of my sight, before I rip your brains out of your arse,' Harry shouted.

Inside the caravan, Valerie was explaining, through her sobs, how all the mistakes had come to pass. The divorce, the visits for Emma, the birthday party and the final misunderstanding the following day.

'Do you mean Jack has got everything arse-about-face?' Ivy asked.

'Yes. He's right, he's right. I should've trusted him, I should've believed him, I should've supported him in every way, but I didn't,' sobbed Valerie.

'Harry, Harry, we must find Jack and find him *now*,' screamed Ivy, opening the door onto the fairground.

The photographer was on the phone to his newspaper.

Chapter Twenty-Six

FINDING JACK

The *Weston Gazette* wasted no time in informing the police they had located Jack in Minehead. Cramer immediately contacted Rice, and they made arrangements to go down there at once. Knowing that the family were also frantic for information, Cramer also rang Ted to give him the basics, but he had already heard from Val, and he and May were making plans to travel to Somerset. Jack's solicitors were also informed, and they too made their plans to go directly to Minehead.

At the fairground, Valerie was devastated, and continued to cry uncontrollably. Ivy was comforting her. Harry was furious: swearing, and threatening to beat Jimmy to a pulp.

'I don't know where the fuck Jack's gone. His motorhome's empty and he's not on site. He's disappeared for good, now. Why wouldn't you just leave the poor bloke alone?' Harry said.

The photographer wanted to go in search of Jack, but Harry stopped him. 'You fucking leech. He's had enough, you've really done it this time. You've finished a decent man. You stay where you are.' Harry was enraged.

'Please find him, Harry,' Valerie pleaded. 'He's got it all wrong. I love him, Emma loves him. We need him back, tell him it's all over. There's no prison, no arrests, nothing.'

Harry said, 'I'll get a few of the boys and girls out there to search. Leave it to me. I'll close the fair tonight and get the crew out there. They'll find him. First, I'll make sure that fucking Jimmy gets out of here straight away and you'— he turned to the photographer, as though he was the scum of the earth — 'you make sure he doesn't get your fucking blood money.'

Jack had raced back to his caravan and grabbed the photograph of Valerie and Emma, his wallet, and his coat. He was crying and panicking. He wasn't thinking clearly. He didn't know what he was going to do, didn't know where to go. He ran and ran, until he physically couldn't run any further and he was out of sight of the town. He found himself at a bus shelter on the seafront, heaving to get his breath back. He put his head in his hands. He realised that there was only one answer, and he was scared.

An old man came into the shelter and sat down for a breather.

'Are you alright, lad?'

Jack didn't answer.

'You know there'll be no more buses today, lad? I hope you're wrapped up warm, if you're intending to stop in here all night.'

Jack lifted his head and looked around.

'Where is the pier?'

'You're a bit late for that, lad. The pier was demolished at the beginning of the Second World War to stop the Germans from using it as a landing stage. No, lad, Minehead has no pier.'

That put paid to Jack's idea of using the pier as an end to all his problems. He was going to have to think again. He edged along the seat and snuggled into the corner of the shelter, wrapping his coat around him, against the cold and wind.

'Are you alright, lad? You look a bit down. Is there anything I can do for you?' the man asked.

Jack lifted his head and looked out towards the sea.

'No, thank you, Sir. Nothing anyone can do now. It's all over,' Jack answered.

'Look, lad, nothing is as bad as it seems. Remember, for every problem there is a solution. You are young enough to find those solutions. There are many people in the world facing bigger problems than you.'

The man rose and, as he walked away, he looked back over his shoulder.

'Good luck, lad, whatever you decide. Hope you make the right decision for everyone. Goodbye.'

The old man was right, Jack thought. He must make the right decision for everyone concerned. He was physically exhausted. His muscles ached from running and crying. He stared at the sea for ages but his brain was not engaging. There was no way out, nowhere to go. He was so tired.

The wind coming off the sea was getting colder. He pulled his thin jacket over his head to shut out the world. As it grew darker and colder, Jack shifted himself to underneath the seat and curled up in a foetal position which gave him a bit more protection from the elements.

Over six hours had passed since Jack left the fairground site and it was now nearly two in the morning. The showmen reported back to Harry that they had searched every pub, café and restaurant in Minehead with no luck. By now the local police were on the scene at the fairground. They said all the right things but, in fact, they were as useless as a chocolate coffee pot.

Harry's large caravan was being used as a mini-information post. Valerie had been put into Harry and Ivy's bedroom to rest, and when her mum and dad turned up with little Emma, they joined her. Valerie was exhausted and couldn't talk much at all.

The police offered the services of a family liaison officer, but Ted blocked this idea. 'She's in no state to be asked daft bloody questions and to go over everything of the last few years with a stranger. No, thanks.'

The local police inspector pointed out that if they were to fill out a missing person report they would need more details. Gerry got angry and shouted at the inspector, 'Look, this guy has been arrested for something he didn't do. He was locked up for years, released from prison by the Home Office, and the Metropolitan Police now want him as a witness for a forthcoming murder trial. He believes he is wanted for breaking court injunctions by seeing his wife. He thinks the whole world is after him. Even the Russian Embassy is searching for him, and if they catch him before we do, he will be a goner. And now, his picture will be all over the papers by tomorrow morning. The man is *fucking suicidal* — we have got to find him before God Almighty meets him or the fucking Russians do. You can put that in your missing person report and leave us all alone, while we get on with the job of trying to find him.'

'I understand your mood, sir. But he couldn't have gone far, at least not out of Minehead, unless he got a taxi,' the police inspector said. 'There are no buses or trains. Do you know how much money he had with him?'

'Not a lot — I haven't paid him his wages yet,' Harry said.

'We shall check the cab firms — there only two or three — and we'll get back to you. Do you have a photograph of him?'

'Ask fucking David Bailey here. Apparently, he took one for his newspaper,' Gerry sarcastically piped up.

When Rice and Cramer arrived, they were more helpful. Gerry and Lee explained the full situation as to how Jack had got mixed messages on every move and had apparently decided to disappear and leave the world behind.

Chris Rice brought some good news. A Full Pardon had been issued (he had the certificate in his briefcase) and that should cheer Jack up when they found him. There was also paperwork to show that all injunctions issued by various family courts had been cancelled and — the most important piece of information — Aleksandr Popov had had his diplomatic status revoked, and had been subpoenaed to appear before a judge in the High Court, where he had been warned that if anything happened to Jack or his family, he would be held responsible under English law.

'How do we get all this good news to him if we can't find him?' Lee asked.

Gerry went into Harry's bedroom and spoke quietly to Valerie and showed her the Certificate of Full Pardon. Suddenly, little Emma grabbed hold of Gerry's sleeve. 'Please find my daddy, please.'

'I will do my very best, my lovely,' Gerry replied, and left the bedroom.

At about two thirty in the morning, the search was called off and everyone was told to get some rest. They would resume at seven.

All of Minehead's pubs, clubs, cafés and restaurants had been visited and had had a photograph of Jack issued to them. Even the massive holiday camp had been visited and their ten thousand guests had all been informed of the search for Jack.

Valerie, her mum and dad and Emma spent the remainder of the night in Jack's motorhome. It was immaculately clean: the way Jack always liked to keep it.

By dawn the next day, the world's media had turned up at the fairground. There were camera crews from most of the news networks from the UK and the USA and even reporters and camera crews from Europe. Three teams of eighteen policemen and women were being briefed by their inspector and being sent off to search Minehead.

It was by now about half past seven and the hope was that wherever Jack was, he would see or hear the news that he had been given a free pardon, and that he would show himself.

At about this same time, Frank Higgins, a bus driver on the H1 route around Minehead, stopped his single-decker at the shelter on the coast road. His bus was empty, as was usual at that time of the morning. As always, he got out, lit up a cigarette and walked round to the bus shelter to sit and look out to sea. As he approached, he noticed a large, huddled bundle under the seat. He bent down to look and realised it was a man's body. He tried to wake him. There was no movement. He tried again. There was no response.

Higgins had seen this before and he was sure the man was dead. He immediately phoned his supervisor.

'Hello, Frank Higgins here, route H1. I'm at Bus Stop 28, and I've found a dead body in the shelter. It's a man. It's cold and there is no response. Could you send an ambulance?'

'Right away, Frank. Don't touch anything. They'll be with you shortly,' the Supervisor replied.

After what seemed an hour, but was actually only ten minutes, the ambulance arrived. The paramedics examined the body. 'He's not dead! He's in a bad way, but he's not dead.'

They pulled Jack from under the shelter seat, covered him with a blanket and transferred him to the ambulance.

'Well done, Frank. We may have got to this one in time,' the paramedic congratulated him.

Jack was blue-lighted to Minehead Community Hospital,

about five minutes away, where he was immediately diagnosed and treated for acute hypothermia. His cold, wet clothes were removed and his body temperature, measured at 79 degrees, was slowly raised to a normal 95 degrees. He was still not conscious but did show signs of responding to the treatment.

As he was severely dehydrated, they set up a saline drip. A nurse sat with him, monitoring his vital signs, while a staff nurse began to look through his clothing and found his wallet. The name on the credit card was William Harris. He had a few pounds and nothing else, apart from a crumpled photograph of a woman and a child.

Back at the fairground, there was a frenzy of people all asking questions. Valerie was receiving help from a local doctor, and Ted and May had taken Emma to the beach and were looking for shells to keep her occupied.

Harry decided to open the fair. With only a skeleton staff, few of the rides could function, and there weren't many punters — mainly people from the Holiday Camp — but Harry thought it would be good for his showmen to work and keep their minds off the situation.

Gerry and Lee were beside themselves. Gerry was convinced that Jack was dead.

'Calm down, Gerry. Dead or alive, he must be somewhere. Minehead is not a large area,' Lee said. 'The thing is, the police here haven't got any idea how to search properly.'

'I know, Lee, you're right. They're doing the best they can. He must be somewhere.' Gerry was trying to be a bit more hopeful.

'I'm going out. I can't stand sitting around here waiting for news.'

'Where?'

'I don't know but I can't just sit here.' He got up to leave.

'Keep your phone on,' Gerry said.

Lee walked into Minehead. First, he tried the seafront and the fishermen's huts. He checked all the boats that had been pulled onto the beach. He then made his way into the town. There were three or four cafés and small shops. He checked two cab firms, but they had already been spoken to by the police and their drivers hadn't had a fare out of the town, certainly not a person looking like Jack.

Wherever he went, there were posters of Jack's face — fresh-faced PC Trevor Frost — when he joined the police force.

Lee found himself just on the edge of the town. He saw the local hospital and he thought he would give it a try.

Minehead Community Hospital was very clean and it smelled nice and sweet. He first spoke to a very helpful receptionist, who suggested he spoke to a sister on duty.

'She's not a sister really, only a staff nurse, but she is the senior nurse on duty. I'm sure she will help you in any way she can,' the receptionist said.

After a short while, a very pretty young staff nurse came through to speak to Lee.

'Hello, I'm Sue Russell. How can I help you?' she said with a lovely smile.

Lee guessed she was about twenty-five, and couldn't help but notice she was very attractive in her uniform, with her short blonde hair and lovely, round, smiling face.

Lee explained who he was and that he was searching for the missing Trevor Frost. 'Have you had any admissions in the last forty-eight hours?' he asked.

'Yes, but I shouldn't be telling you their names,' Sue said.

Lee looked at Sue and something clicked between them.

'Okay, but stay here,' Sue said reluctantly. When she came back, she was carrying a clipboard. 'Only three patients have been brought in, two men and a woman, but there is no Trevor Frost on this list.'

'What are the names, Sue?'

Again, their eyes met and there was a certain mutual sympathy between them.

'A Mr Warren, a Mr Harris and a Mrs Draper. That's it, that's all I can tell you, no more. I could get into serious trouble even for telling you that.'

'Thank you so much. You've been a great help. Perhaps after your shift I could take you to dinner?'

Sue smiled. 'I finish at five. How about we meet at half six, outside the hospital?'

'Here's my number.' He offered her his card. 'There is my mobile number as well.'

As Lee walked out of the hospital, he stopped dead, then ran back into the hospital and caught up with Sue in the corridor.

'Sue, the men — what were the full names?'

'I shouldn't say, but' — she lowered her voice — 'Christopher Warren and William Harris. Why?'

'You are an absolute darling, Sue. I think I love you! I will tell you all about it tonight; got to run.' He kissed Sue on the cheek and disappeared.

'Hello, Gerry. Now, it's important that you say absolutely nothing in case anyone is listening to this call and don't look excited, but I've found Jack!'

'What?!' Gerry exclaimed.

'I told you to be calm, just say yes and no. I've found Jack, but before we release the information, we must be careful. We don't want the police and the whole media circus descending upon us. This has got to be handled carefully and quietly. Phone me back when you are on your own.'

A few minutes later, Gerry phoned Lee. 'What's this all about? You've found Jack? Where is he? Is he alright?'

'He was admitted to the local Community Hospital. A lovely little place. He is an in-patient under the name of William Harris. I don't know anything more about the situation, but I have a friend on the inside and I hope she will be able to tell me more,' Lee explained. 'Give me half an hour and I'll get back to you, but it's important that you tell no-one, do you understand?'

'Where shall I meet you?' Gerry asked.

'Stay where you are. Don't come here, in case someone follows you. I'll find out what I can, and get back to you.'

Chapter Twenty-Seven

ALL IS REVEALED

Lee rushed back to the hospital and sought out Sue.

'I must speak to you, Sue, alone and in private.'

'My, my, you are keen. Can't you wait 'til tonight?' Sue said, with a smile.

'Sue, this is very important. Your Mr William Harris is in fact Trevor Frost, my client, the ex-policeman that everyone is looking for. What can you tell me about him? Is he alright? When was he admitted? How is he?' Lee was spitting out his questions at a rate of knots.

'Slow down, Lee. I have heard of the hunt for Trevor Frost. I shouldn't be telling you anything about William Harris, but —'

'If it gets out that he's been found, and he's in this hospital, your wards will be full of tv cameras and reporters from all over. It would be a nightmare.' Lee again explained the situation.

'Okay, William Harris was admitted with severe hypothermia and dehydration. He was in a bad way. He was found underneath a bus shelter bench exposed to the sea winds. He must have been there for hours. We got his name from a credit card in his wallet. He hasn't said much. We've kept him under sedation. He is responding well to the treatment.'

'Can I see him?'

'Not yet, he's still sleeping, but in about three hours, we'll wake him and try and get him to eat something.'

'Now, when he's awake and fit enough to receive visitors, I would like to bring his wife and daughter to see him. Would that be possible, Sue?'

'Yes, but only them.' Sue had to be strict.

'There will be no-one else except me and Gerry, another solicitor. Is there somewhere private that Valerie can see him without anyone else knowing?' Lee asked.

'He's in a side room, so yes, but I will have to tell the duty doctor that you are coming. Incidentally, from what I've read in the newspaper, isn't this the wife who divorced him and washed her hands of him? Do you think it's a good idea, Lee? It may be too much of a shock for him.'

'Trust me, he loves Val. Even though everything you've said about her is true, they were all dreadful mistakes. Can this private meeting be arranged?' Lee urged.

'Yes, it can, leave it to me. I'm sure the doctor will allow it.'

'You are a marvel, Sue. Thank you for everything.' Lee grinned and gave Sue another kiss on the cheek.

'This is going to cost you a large meal and a drink tonight, if you are still up for it,' Sue said, smiling.

'I sure am up for it — I can't wait. I want nothing more but to be with you. You've got my number. Ring me when you and the doc think it's okay for a visit,' Lee said.

'It won't be long now,' Sue said, moving a bit closer to Lee and holding his arm.

'One more question, Sue. Do you believe in love at first sight?'

'I guess I will have to after this,' Sue replied with a smile, and gave him a small peck on the cheek.

'Do you want me to speak to the doctor?'

'No. Leave him to me.' Sue moved forward and gave Lee a proper quick kiss on the lips.

'Sue, I thought I had better mention' — Lee paused — 'I think I like you very much. Is there anything I can do for you?'

'Yes,' Sue said, with a grin. 'You can shave that soppy thin moustache off your top lip. Makes you look like a resurrected Leslie Phillips.' She giggled.

'Will do,' Lee said, cheerfully, as he hurried out of the hospital.

'Hello, Gerry. No questions now, but meet me in the Atlas Café on the seafront and I will fill you in on all the information.' Lee's phone call to Gerry was short and sweet.

About fifteen minutes later, they were alone in the café. Lee told Gerry everything he knew. Gerry was astounded.

Lee explained, 'I have a very pretty friend inside the hospital and she will contact me when it's okay to see him. We must make sure that no-one else apart from you and me — and Valerie, of course — gets in to see him first, otherwise the hospital will be overrun with every Tom, Dick and Harry with a camera, microphone, notebook and a tape recorder. We don't want that.'

'Agreed. When your friend gives you the word, we must smuggle Valerie out of the fairground, and we don't want the rest of that crowd following us. Should we tell the police?'

'No. Definitely not. Just let him be for the time being. They will find out in due course, after we've composed a press release. If anyone asks, we'll tell them that Valerie is going back to London or something, so that they don't follow us.' Lee became very serious. 'Gerry, I don't believe this was a suicide bid. Jack was just exhausted and didn't know where to go or what to do.'

Gerry thought, then said, 'Let's put a game plan together and stick to it. I'm so bloody glad that Jack is okay and in safe hands.'

'He's in safe hands alright. My Sue will see to that,' Lee said.

'Your Sue?'

Lee explained as they made their way back to the fairground. There were still hordes of media hanging around waiting for any news on the search for Jack.

After about an hour, Lee got a phone call. 'Hi Lee, it's Sue. Your friend is sitting up in bed, and looks well. He's had something to eat, but is feeling very sorry for himself. He's not talking very much, and we are still calling him 'Mr Harris', of course. Duty doctor said he's fit enough for visits, so now might be a good time to come along.'

'Sue, you are a marvel. Where should we come? Don't want to be seen coming through the front door,' Lee said.

'No, you're right. Let me know when you are here. Walk round to the out-patient exit at the back of the hospital, and I will meet you there. It's not far from the ward.'

When Gerry opened the door to Harry's big caravan, Valerie was looking very forlorn and quiet. Emma was in the lounge area playing with her grandmother.

'Is there any news?' Valerie asked.

'No, afraid not. Why don't you and Emma come for a walk on the beach? We'll buy an ice-cream or something?'

'No, I don't feel like it, Gerry, honestly. I want to stay here, in case any news comes through.' Valerie sounded sad and tired.

'Please, Val, just you, Emma and Lee. We've both got phones and we'll be the first to know if anything turns up. Come on, a bit of sea air will do you good.'

Reluctantly, Valerie stood up.

'Where are you going?' asked May.

'I thought Val and Emma could do with some fresh sea air,' Gerry said.

'Good idea. I'll get my coat,' May said.

'No, it's alright, May. Let Val have a few moments on her own. We'll look after her.' Gerry said.

Val cast a curious glance at him, but dressed Emma in her coat and followed him out of the caravan.

They met Lee just outside the fairground, and walked along the beach towards the town.

'Would you like an ice-cream, Emma?' Lee asked. Emma nodded. Lee took her over the road to the shops.

Gerry turned to Valerie and said, 'Val, we have some really good news for you, but you must be careful how you react. We've found Jack.'

'Where? Where is he? Is he alright? Can I see him? Does he want to see me? Tell me, is he alright?' Valerie couldn't get the questions out quickly enough.

'Calm down, Val. You must be very careful not to let on that Jack has been found. Yes, he is well; yes, he is doing fine. He's currently here in the local Community Hospital.'

'What's happened to him? Is he alright? Is he injured?'

'Listen, Val, we must handle this very carefully. Lee and I will be taking you and Emma to see him very shortly, but we must keep this reunion under wraps. We don't want the world and its media army closing in on your privacy. He doesn't know you are coming in. This will be a great shock to him. Lee and I will see him first, and make sure that he fully understands that he is a free man, that there are no injunctions outstanding against him and that he won't be going back to prison, which is what he's been scared about. Now, just be calm — and don't tell Emma. Okay? Are you clear about what is going to happen?'

Valerie nodded and started to cry, more out of relief than anything else.

The four of them made their way towards the hospital. When they arrived, Sue led them to the side-ward.

'Wait here, please,' she instructed them. 'I'll take you and Gerry in first, Lee.'

'Mr Harris, you have a couple of visitors,' she announced.

Jack looked up, and when he saw Gerry and Lee, he placed his head in his hands. 'What are you two doing here? Why doesn't everybody just fucking leave me alone?'

'Nice to see you too, Jack,' Gerry said. 'Now, listen carefully. It's all over. I have in my possession your Certificate of Full Pardon for the murder, all signed and official. The injunctions have been rescinded and cancelled. There is no-one looking for you, and there is nothing to arrest you for. Do you understand?'

'How can I believe it?' Jack asked.

'Jack, Lee and I have been your true friends through this. We were certain you were innocent all along. We wouldn't lie to you now,' Gerry said.

'I don't know. How can I be sure? Is this just another trick?'

Sue butted in. 'Look, Mr Harris or Mr Frost, or whoever you are, listen to them. These guys are your faithful friends, and they care for you.'

'Listen to her, Jack. She is the beautiful angel who has saved your life and nursed you back to health,' Lee said, putting his arm around Sue's shoulders.

'There is someone else here who is keen to meet you, if you are up to it?' Gerry said.

'Who is it? The police?' Jack asked.

Lee went to the door of the side-ward and took Emma for a short walk, back along the corridor. Sue ushered Valerie in.

When she first saw Jack, she began to shake and cry. She ran to the bed and grabbed hold of him and hugged him close. Jack was totally taken aback. He hugged Valerie as hard as he could, and he began to cry too.

'Time we left,' Sue said, taking Gerry's arm. They too were in tears.

Jack's head was next to Valerie's head. Their tears met each other on their cheeks. Not a word was said. Jack could smell the lovely, sweet smell of Val's hair, what wonderful memories. He ran his hands through her hair, over her face, her neck and shoulders.

'Val, I love you so much.'

'Shush,' she whispered.

They kissed and that kiss lasted for so long. When the kiss ended, they looked each other in the eyes. Jack tried to speak but Val put her finger to Jack's lips to stay quiet and they kissed again. Jack just loved the feel of Val's body close to him: her lips; her hair; just to feel the bones in her spine. It was wonderful; neither of them wanted it to stop.

He could feel his heart pounding, or was it Val's heart that was pounding? They were so close, it was impossible to tell.

'Val, I want to say sorry,' Jack started.

Val interrupted him. 'Shush, Jack, there will be plenty of time for that later. Just hold me, and never ever let me go.'

She ran her fingers over Jack's face and beard, wiping away the tears on his cheeks. 'I'm never ever going to let you go again,' she said, smiling.

They kissed again, long and passionately.

'I have someone else who really wants to see you.'

Val went to the door of the ward and opened it. Emma was standing holding Lee's hand.

'Come on, Em. See who it is.'

Emma hesitated. She had never seen her father with a beard before.

'Is it...?'

As soon as Val nodded, Emma screamed, 'Daddy, Daddy, Daddy.' She ran and jumped on the bed and wrapped her arms around his neck. She stroked Jack's beard, tenderly.

'Are you poorly, Daddy?' Emma said.

'No, Peanut. I'm fine now.' Jack kissed Emma on the top of her head. 'Everything is going to be alright from now on.' Jack again gave Emma a hug.

'Why do you call me Peanut?' Emma asked

'Because when I first saw you in a photograph, when you were in Mummy's tummy, you looked like a peanut, so I called you Peanut. Do you remember that, Val?' Jack asked.

Val smiled and nodded.

They continued to cuddle each other, not talking. Jack noticed that Emma had closed her eyes. 'Is Emma alright?' he whispered.

'She's exhausted, Jack. She's been through so much just lately.'

'I'm so sorry, Val.'

'Shush, Jack. No apologies, no excuses, no recriminations. I love you so much. I just want you to hold us.' Valerie snuggled even closer.

After a few minutes, Valerie said, 'Jack, will you marry me?' Jack looked into her tear-filled eyes. 'Yes, please.'

Emma opened her eyes and looked up at them both and said, 'Are you two going to be married? I will have a mum and a dad?'

They nodded.

'Would you like to be our bridesmaid?' Val asked.

'Oh yes, oh yes.' Emma was so excited and kissed Jack and

Valerie at the same time. She jumped off the bed and ran to the door where, outside, Lee, Sue and Gerry were standing waiting.

'I'm going to be a bridesmaid; I'm going to be a bridesmaid,' Emma repeated excitedly.

Sue turned to Lee and said, 'You've shaved off your little 'tache. Was that for me?'

'Of course. If you didn't like it, it had to go,' smiled Lee.

'You are a sweetie. I'm liking you more each minute,' Sue said, and Lee pecked her on the cheek. Sue grabbed Lee and they kissed passionately, which knocked off Sue's nursing hat. They didn't notice that the duty doctor had arrived. 'How is our patient, Nurse?' the doctor asked.

'I'm sorry, Doctor,' Sue said, picking up her hat.

When the doctor entered the ward, Val and Jack were still kissing and cuddling.

'Well, it's clear that seeing your wife again is obviously the best medicine,' the doctor said, with a smile.

'I'm going to be a bridesmaid,' Emma said to the doctor.

'Well, I had better discharge you then, Mr Harris, so this wedding can go ahead,' the doctor said.

'If you can break yourself away from this young man, Staff Nurse Russell, we can complete the discharge papers. Congratulations, Mr Harris, and I think you are going to be a beautiful bridesmaid, young lady,' the doctor said to Emma, and he left the room.

Lee turned to Sue. 'I must speak to you, it's very important.'

'Not now, Lee. I have work to do.'

'No, this is very important, Sue.'

'So, now you've got your friend back, are you going to cancel that drink and dinner this evening?' Sue said with a smile.

'Sue, we only met this morning. You are the most fantastic person I have ever met, and all this in a few hours.'

'Could it be you are in love?' Sue paused and looked directly into his eyes. 'I feel the same way. I love you too. I knew it from the moment I saw you, and yes, I do believe in love at first sight.' She reached up and kissed him.

'I take it you aren't married?' she asked.

'No,' Lee replied. 'And I don't have a girlfriend either.'

'I don't have a boyfriend; no attachments,' Sue said. 'When we met – what? Ten hours ago — I saw a really nice man: smart, polite and caring. I thought what a great guy you were. I do admit that I was instantly attracted to you and wanted to know more about you but, in the meantime, you showed that you were also attracted to me and I was so glad. I feel the same way, wobbly legs, butterflies in the tummy, everything. Lee, we know we are in love; it can happen you know.'

Lee, with a big smile, took Sue in his arms and kissed her passionately.

From the other end of the corridor, the duty doctor spoke loudly, 'Nurse, the discharge papers if you would; otherwise, this poor man will be here for another night.'

Sue ran off to the nurses' station. Lee stood as if in a daze.

'If you feel up to it, Jack, we are going to try and get you out of here and back to the fairground unseen,' Gerry said.

'I feel up to it, Gerry. As long as Valerie and Emma are with me, I can do anything,' Jack said, smiling at Valerie. 'Why doesn't one of you get Betty and we can all go home together?'

'Who is Betty?' Valerie asked.

'Betty is the name of my motorhome,' Jack explained.

'Oh! We slept in her last night.'

'Good idea,' Gerry answered. 'If I can get some sense out of Lee, I will send him to fetch it. Where are the keys, Jack?'

'In the kitchen drawer. Do you have any idea where my clothes are? They've taken them away,' Jack answered.

'Don't worry about them. You must have a change of clothes in Betty,' Gerry said.

There was some uncertainty at the fairground about Lee taking the motorhome, but he managed to avoid answering questions directly.

All changed and ready to go, Jack said goodbye to the nursing staff and the duty doctor, and thanked them for all their help.

'Where's Sue?' Jack asked.

'Yes, where *is* Sue?' Lee echoed.

'That was the end of her shift. She should be back here in a minute,' the duty doctor said.

As they were leaving the hospital, Sue called, 'Can I come too?'

She was now out of uniform and was dressed in a stunning white tank-top and tight-fitting blue trousers. She ran straight into Lee's arms and pecked him on the cheek.

They all boarded Betty and made towards the fairground. Lee was driving, Sue by his side; Gerry was sitting at the small dining table and Jack, Val and little Emma were in the back bedroom.

Gerry suggested they stay hidden there until he had issued his press release. Then, when all the media, cameras, reporters etc, had left the fairground, they could reveal themselves. This would take some time, Gerry explained, but at least they wouldn't be pestered by everyone.

Jack wasn't worried; he was holding Valerie very close, and Emma was asleep between them.

In Harry and Ivy's large caravan, Gerry announced to everyone present that Jack had been found safe and well. He explained that for the time being, Jack and Val would stay hidden, until all the media circus had disappeared. Gerry then left and spoke privately to the local police inspector so that his officers could be stood down.

A press conference was hurriedly arranged, and, standing on the steps of Harry's caravan, Gerry made this announcement: 'Today, Mr Trevor Frost has been found safe and well and is currently on his way back to London to be reunited with his family. He would like to thank everyone for their concern and for their efforts in searching for him. He will be making a formal announcement shortly. Special thanks to the local police constabulary for all their contribution. Thank you.'

'That should satisfy them for a short while. Perhaps they will now all disappear,' Gerry said to Lee. He still hadn't told Harry, Ivy and the cops from London where Jack and Valerie were.

In Betty, Jack and Valerie began to talk quietly.

'Jack, I am sorry, so desperately sorry, that I didn't trust you, that I didn't believe you, but when it all happened, I went into shock, I didn't know what to think or do. I wasn't allowed to see you or communicate with you. The newspapers were saying horrible things about you, and then came the trial and what was revealed was horrific.'

'Val, I was also in shock. One minute, I was a happy father of a newborn baby girl, with a beautiful wife, lovely home and brilliant job, and the next minute, I was a beast and a murderer. I didn't know where I was, whom I could trust. It all happened so fast,' Jack stuttered. 'All of a sudden, my world collapsed. I told the truth in all my interviews, but no-one believed me. I had been totally drunk, and I was surrounded by so-called friends who kept giving me drinks. You know I don't drink much, Val. I am sure, now, that those drinks were spiked.'

'Oh, Jack, I'm so sorry. I should have known that you were not capable of all those things they were saying about you, and I should have trusted you, but I was in such a state of confusion, and when the police from the Murder Squad explained to me what evidence they had against you, I just couldn't believe it.' Valerie became tearful. 'All I had was Emma and my mum and dad.'

'Were you at the trial?' Jack asked.

'Yes,' Val whispered.

'I didn't see you. All I wanted was to see your face, but it seemed to be over so quickly.'

'I was hiding at the back. I couldn't bear to look you in the face, Jack, after hearing everything you had done.' Valerie bowed her head in shame. Jack kissed her head,

'But now you know it wasn't true.'

'Yes, Jack, now I know it wasn't true and I should have known that and supported you. I am so sorry that I divorced you.'

'I don't blame you for any of that,' Jack said. 'On hearing the evidence, it was probably the right thing to do. There were so many lies, it wasn't too hard for any jury to find me guilty, but what I can't forgive is the evidence that Kim Brown gave. I liked Kim. I trusted her, and I thought we were good friends. Karen Dewhurst was another one. The lies they told! All backed up by forensic evidence... Even I began to think I had done the things they said.' Jack fell silent for a short while. 'You know, they even controlled my legal team. I was recommended a female solicitor, who was useless. I was introduced to a female barrister, who was also useless and who didn't like me, and then there was a female judge, who had already made her mind up before the trial started. It all seemed a conspiracy against me, and for why? What had I done?'

'Were they gay as well, Jack, do you think?' Val asked.

'Who knows? There is nothing wrong with being gay, but it just seemed that every female was against me. I had done nothing wrong, except drink too much. There were six women on the jury, but when they heard the evidence as it was presented, a group of monkeys would have found me guilty.' Jack's eyes filled with tears. 'But worst of all was prison. I hated every minute of my time in there. I wrote you three letters, Val, but when I received no answer, I thought it was all over between us.'

'I wanted to reply but I didn't know what to say to a murderer who had betrayed me and our baby. I was advised by friends to cut you off totally. I am so sorry.' Val squeezed Jack's hand.

'I know, Val, no need for apologies, but it was then that I realised I would have to bear this on my own and, mentally, I switched off and kept everything to myself. I had no-one who would listen to me, no-one to turn to. The other prisoners turned on me, as they do when they know you were a copper. For six months they were shitting in my dinner and pissing in my tea, so I began to survive on chocolate bars and cans of drink from the tuck shop. I lost three stones in weight. I spoke to nobody except to say yes, Sir; no, Sir; and thank you, Sir.'

'It must have been awful for you.'

'It was, and the smells of the prison are still etched into my brain. It was helped a little by obtaining a jar of Vick's nasal jelly, and I placed a small smear up my nose every night which made it bearable. I learned that trick from a pathologist who carried out post-mortems.' Jack again kissed Val's head and cuddled her up closer. 'I still have nightmares about that place. I was determined not to be taken back there. I would have killed myself first.'

'How did you find Gerry? He's a lovely guy, very helpful and thinks the world of you.'

'I'd seen him briefly before my trial, but I didn't take him on. Afterwards, he actually found me. Six months into my sentence, he requested a visitation order. He explained that he wanted to start an appeal on my case. He was supportive from the start, but, in the end, we couldn't find any grounds to get an appeal going. It was shortly after that, that I received letters from your solicitor wanting to start the divorce proceedings.'

'Jack, I didn't want a divorce but I was still so confused and everyone told me it was for the best,' Val explained. 'I still loved you, but to have a murderer for a father to Emma… II couldn't bear it. I just took the easy way out.'

'No recriminations, Val, you did what you had to do for Emma. You are a fantastic mother and you have made her a beautiful girl; I am so proud of you for that. I am so sorry that I missed all her early years.'

They went through the whole story, filling each other in on everything they had mistaken and regretted and then, cuddling up to Emma, the three of them slept blissfully for another hour.

When they woke, Jack held Valerie by the shoulders and looked directly into her eyes.

'Val, did you mean what you said earlier on, that you want us to be married again?'

'Yes, Jack. I love you so much. From now on I am not going to let you out of my sight.'

Chapter Twenty-Eight

FINALE

Gerry had taken Emma out to give Jack and Valerie a bit of time on their own. Suddenly, the door to the bedroom burst open.

'Okay, Jack, you can get out of that bed. You're a showman now, not a hairy-arsed copper — there's work to do.' It was Lily, with a big smile on her face.

Jack and Val jumped out of bed to lots of kisses and cuddles from all.

'This fairground has got be broken down and on its way to Torquay by tomorrow,' Lily said. 'By the way, I love you both, and I'm so glad to see that there is a happy ending.'

The trial of Anna Smelt for the murder of Natasha Popova began in Court Two of the Central Criminal Court, Old Bailey. Her co-defendants, Kim Brown, Karen Dewhurst, Jennifer Wilson, Barbara Hancock and Patrizia Rossi, all stood in the dock. They each had their own defence team. The charges ranged from murder, desecration of a body, GBH, falsifying evidence, perjury, through to drugs importation and drugs supplying. The press box was full, as was the public gallery.

Fortunately for the judge and the courts, all the defendants had submitted previous pleas of Guilty. The judge stated that, in sentencing, he would take this into consideration, as the Guilty plea had saved putting witnesses through the trauma of giving evidence, and had also avoided a lengthy trial. Jack was called to enter the witness box and give an Impact Statement, to tell the court how the crimes of these six defendants had affected his life. He explained the extent to which the false imprisonment had had a lasting and profound change in his personality and how he was having to make considerable effort to build up his reputation and confidence again.

The statement had a great effect on the judge and the jury.

Smelt stood up. She was dressed in prison fatigues

'You, Anna Smelt, a United States diplomat, are accused of having used your position as a person with immunity to import drugs into the UK and to supply the drugs market for your own gain, of having conspired with others to conceal the death of Natasha Popova, and of having engineered the evidence to place the blame onto another. Your Guilty plea has been noted.'

Smelt's counsel rose to his feet and reminded the judge that his client had admitted the offence to the authorities, and that she also was facing further charges in the USA of drug exportation and offences under the diplomatic privileges system. She had received absolution from her religious leaders; she was very ashamed and had total remorse for her crimes.

The judge was quiet and then looked Smelt straight in the eyes. 'You have pleaded Guilty to a most horrific crime and, with others, covered up your actions. As we have heard, you totally ruined the life of a serving police officer. I sentence you to prison for eighteen years.'

Smelt began to sob.

The judge continued, 'I will give leave to your solicitors to apply for you to serve your sentence in your native country, where I am informed you will be facing other legal proceedings to do with the misuse of your diplomatic privileges. Take her down, officers.'

Smelt was led away by two female prison officers to the cells below the court.

Kim Brown stood up, but looked down at her feet. She looked ashamed and could not meet anyone's eye. Her counsel gave a brief, and not too convincing, résumé of the reasons why a very successful detective sergeant with a list of commendations from High Court judges for excellent detective work against all sorts of serious crime, went down the criminal road of sex, drugs, for the sake of monetary gain.

The judge addressed her. 'You were in a position of trust and were held in great esteem by your colleagues, most of all Detective Constable Frost. You and your friends engaged in a walk of life that, although not illegal, needed to be supported by money greater than your legal income.

'You decided to support your way of life by dealing in the distribution of drugs brought illegally into the country by the victim and Miss Smelt. You distributed the drugs to the community that you had sworn to serve, and who had trusted you. You betrayed that trust.

'Through your extensive knowledge of the system of forensic investigations, you, and you alone, devised a method of putting the blame for this unfortunate girl's death onto the shoulders of another. You, and you alone, saw a way out when a fight ensued between Popova and Smelt which resulted in the death of Popova. You, and you alone, placed the forensic blame onto an innocent man, who held you in great esteem as a friend and colleague.

'You, and you alone, influenced your like-minded friends to assist you in your devious plans.

'You, and you alone, desecrated the body of Popova and carried out the most horrific acts on that girl's body.

'You lied in interview, and committed perjury at the trial of DC Frost, to ensure that he was convicted of the crimes, knowing that he was totally innocent, in order to protect yourself and your way of life.

'Apart from pleading Guilty, you have shown no remorse. I conclude that it was you who was the instrument of this whole sordid affair, the author of the demise of this poor officer's career, and the cause of intolerable suffering. You will go to prison for twenty years. You will not be considered for parole until you have served those twenty years. Take her down, officers.'

Kim Brown mumbled something to the other four girls in the dock and was then escorted to the cells below the court.

Dewhurst and Wilson were each sentenced to eight years in prison, whilst Hancock and Rossi each received five years for their part in the affair.

Before rising, the judge addressed Jack directly. 'Mr Frost, I am sure that no amount of monetary compensation will restore the lost years you should have had with your wife and daughter, but I do hope that you regain that confidence and respect that you once had. Good luck to you, Sir.'

The judge rose and left the court.

Jack and Valerie did get married again, in a quiet little Register Office in St Albans. Gerry was best man, and Emma was their bridesmaid. In fact, it was a double wedding because Sue and Lee got married at the same time. Emma was bridesmaid for them, too. When members of the Showman's Guild put on a party, they do not hold back, and everyone had a wonderful time.

Jack was offered his job back by the Commissioner with a promotion to Detective Sergeant, but told him in no uncertain terms where to stick his offer. The showman's life seemed the best solution. It gave Jack and Val more time together with Emma. With the substantial amount of compensation money that came their way, they bought a large, luxury land-yacht which had everything inside it that a small family could want. Not cheap, but worth it.

Before the wedding, Jack had changed his name by deed poll to David Thomas. The change confused Emma at first, but she got used to it, and even became proud to call herself Emma Thomas, especially with friends from the private school which all Showman's Guild children attended.

This should be the end of the story, but there is still the Russian element to consider...

Mr Aleksandr Popov, an ex-KGB agent and oligarch, had amassed a fortune of millions of Russian roubles before being called to become a Diplomat with the Russian Consular team, working from the Embassy in Kensington Gardens. When his daughter was murdered, he became incensed. He would never accept that she was gay, although he did, later, have to concede that she had been importing drugs into the UK. She had been led astray, he asserted. Terrible morals in the west.

At an early stage, he attempted to arrange for Jack to be murdered whilst in prison. He redoubled his efforts when Jack was released. His actions to recruit some of his ex-KGB agents to find and eliminate Jack Frost were uncovered by MI5, and the Russians were watched very closely. It came to the notice of MI5 that the Russians had discovered that Jack had changed his name. Popov suggested to his thugs that, as David Thomas was a Welsh name, they should concentrate their investigations in Wales.

They never did track down Trevor 'Jack' Frost, nor David Thomas. Popov eventually returned to his homeland, a broken, and a poorer, man.

AUTHOR'S NOTE

The characters are not real... or are they?

The locations are not real... or are they?

The story is entirely a work of fiction... or is it?

ACKNOWLEDGEMENT

I am deeply grateful to Jill Glenn and Claire Steele
at By The Book. Without their professionalism and
expert guidance, this novel would not have been published.

BYTHEBOOK.PRESS